FEATURED AUTHORS

LAURAINE S BLAKE
RACHAEL BOUCKER
SAM FLETCHER
CAMERON SCOTT KIRK
JONATHON MAST
McKENZIE RICHARDSON
AUSTIN SHIREY

AN EERIE RIVER PUBLISHING ANTHOLOGY

WITH BONE AND IRON



Paperback ISBN: 978-1-990245-03-9
Hardcover ISBN: 978-1-990245-04-6
Digital ISBN: 978-1-7772750-7-5

Edited by Alanna Robertson-Webb
Cover design: Zoe Perdita @ Rainbow Danger Designs
Book Formatting by Michelle River

# ALSO AVAILABLE FROM
# EERIE RIVER PUBLISHING

## NOVELS

STORMING AREA 51

## HORROR ANTHOLOGIES

Don't Look: 12 Stories of Bite Sized Horror
It Calls From The Forest: Volume I
It Calls From The Forest: Volume II
It Calls From The Sky
Darkness Reclaimed
Midnight Shadow: Volume I

## DARK FANTASY ANTHOLOGIES

With Blood and Ash
With Bone and Iron

## DRABBLE COLLECTIONS

Forgotten Ones: Drabbles of Myth and Legend

## COMING SOON

It Calls From The Sea
It Calls From the Doors
It Calls From the Veil
Dark Magic: Drabbles of Fantasy and Horror
The Sentinel
In Solitude's Shadow
The Void
A Sword Named Sorrow

*This book is dedicated to our families and friends, to those who have stood by us, coffee in hand, and told us never to give up on our dreams.*

*In these strange times we would also like to dedicate this book to the front-line workers that fight to keep us all safe, to the parents that had to make the hard decision to stay home and the unseen and overlooked heros who make our lives possible. Thank you.*

# FOREWORD

We want to take a moment and thank you for purchasing this book, for supporting Eerie River Publishing and for experiencing the talented authors we've featured.

It's in our natures to seek comfort in words, and in a world of lockdowns and change, we hope these stories guide you on a written journey into worlds filled with magic and lore.

Inside this anthology of dark fantasy, you will read original stories filled with hope and delight, despair and ruin and everything in between.

*May you be forever entertained,*
Eerie River Publishing.

# Black Lake Tower

## Cameron Scott Kirk

Rain came down in sheets, driven sideways by the night wind. It created dancing, spasmodic water devils on the surface of the oily, opaque lake, and it pattered down upon the burden boards and center thwart of the small rowboat. Two hooded figures sat therein: one at the oars, the other huddled at the stern, both bearing the brunt of the storm that lashed Black Lake

Black Lake by name, Black Lake by nature.

In the middle of the water an obscene crag jutted, though this was no natural rock formation: here rose the thrice-cursed, sorcerous tower of Ashmith the Vile, known as Oberon the Dead-Dancer among those in the southern climes.

The two aboard the boat called him by a different name, for they hailed from the east. To them the old man in the jagged tower held the title Owl-Spoil, the Necromancer.

Tonight they would kill Owl-Spoil and take the Amulet of Ulfur.

Alvena stopped rowing and peered into the darkness scratched by glinting rainfall, elven eyes scanning the flecked lake.

Lia moved forward to join her at the oars, whispering, "What do you see?"

Alvena pointed. "Water golem. Get down."

There, at the edge of sight, the water golem stood. It was impossibly balanced on the surface of the lake, its massive frame seemingly made of glass, the pelting rain giving shape to the behemoth's presence.

"It's almost invisible," hissed Lia.

"That's why we cross in the rain. All the old man's traps and watchdogs will avail him naught. Be silent now; the current takes us past."

The two elven females crouched low as the rowboat drifted around the periphery of the unmoving water golem, the creature's square head tilted downwards as it stared soundlessly into the water.

When the boat had drifted to a distance deemed safe Alvena grabbed the oars once more.

"Let me row for a little," said Lia.

"No. You sit back, rest." Alvena pulled Lia's tawny cloak tighter around her body. "Just rest." Turning back to the oars Alvena began to gently row.

Lia coughed, and Alvena turned to look at her companion.

"I'm alright."

"I know." Alvena turned away, her vision blurred. She wiped dripping, auburn hair from her eyes and scanned the lake, the raindrops stabbing the surface of the water with such force that each drop sent up violent divots, like turf beneath a herd of raging wild horses.

But all the old man's tricks became visible in the downpour, and the sound of their approach was covered by the frantic hissing of water on water.

The plan was working perfectly, thus far.

Alvena did not like to put Lia through this, as the hardship of the rain exacerbated her condition, but they had to get to Owl-Spoil soon. Tonight, under cover of darkness and storm.

Lia coughed again, but Alvena could not turn to check on her welfare. Something moved beneath the water, something long, scaled and sharp-toothed. Alvena stopped rowing, raising a hand in silent warning. Lia muffled her next cough in the crook of her arm.

The thing beneath was hunting them.

Whatever it was it could not locate them in the downpour. It moved this way and that, chasing raindrops and rising above the water here and there to snap with a fanged maw.

But it had not pinpointed their location; once again the storm had worked in their favor.

The rocky outcrop on which the old man's deformed tower stood came closer. For a moment the hideous, scarred surface of the tower became illuminated in a flash of lightning, rocky skin pocked like that of a plague victim. After a few moments the rowboat crunched onto a small, stony inlet, and the two elves leapt nimbly to the shore.

They hauled the boat onto the pebbles, then Alvena retrieved her crossbow from the burden boards. She looked at Lia, "Your knife?"

Lia patted her hip beneath her brown robe.

Alvena nodded and the two crept towards the base of

the ungainly, obsidian tower a mere hundred yards away, each painfully aware how their footfall amongst the small pebbles sounded obscenely loud, even in the midst of a howling storm.

The base of the tower bore no door. Looking up the two elves measured the dark tower against the equally dark storm clouds, the structure seeming to warp and twist out over the lake. It threatened to collapse into the murky waters, like an old drunk slowly toppling.

Yet the dark tower stood, and the two females looked for a way to gain admittance.

"A glamour hides the entrance," whispered Lia. "I feel it."

"Can you locate it?"

Lia coughed and said, "The other side."

The stone base of the tower arced out of sight and, by following the uneven surface of the structure, they soon came to a point where the rain and wind seemed to disappear in a swirling vacuum.

"Here," said Lia. "The patter of raindrops is absorbed by the spell. This is the door."

Alvena smiled, her breath curling from her mouth to be punctured by the falling rain. "The old man's petty illusions have been revealed by the foul weather."

"We must both get inside. I feel the chill settling in my lungs."

Alvena's heart shivered with the icy touch of fear. "You must hold on."

Lia glanced at her companion and said, "Do not concern yourself. If we die tonight, it will not be the weather that undoes us." She closed her eyes and waved a slender, fine-boned hand through the air. A moment later a wooden door appeared, and Lia pushed a dripping palm against the lock.

The door to the necromancer's foul tower opened.

They entered, and the silence within echoed with the hissing of the rain outside. Both women stopped and listened in the darkness, the sound of rain droplets slipping from their tawny cloaks to the stone floor growing louder, amplified by the beating of their hearts.

"We come unseen," whispered Alvena. "The weather has been our ally thus far. Now, we climb. Are you up to it?"

Lia nodded, her elven eyes barely illuminating a set of stairs winding upwards into ill-lit blackness. She withdrew a long-bladed knife of elven make; the glowing, fine script on the blade an enumeration of her family's history for the past ten thousand years. The blade had tasted the blood of kings, wizards and walking corpses, but never before had it been drawn for the purpose of assassination.

"This is a mistake," Lia whispered.

Alvena stopped upon the first few steps and whirled about, hissing, "*This* is the only way. I know no other."

"It is dishonorable," said Lia, still musing on the curving, silver blade in her hand.

Alvena stifled her tears and anger. "We are here. It must be done. We cannot go back, we *cannot*. You know that! Too much rests upon this."

"My name will take its place on this blade," said Lia. "Promise me."

Alvena shook her head and approached Lia. "Not today. Not for a long time, if I have any say in the matter."

She removed Lia's hood from her head and gently brushed away the damp, caramel-colored hair clinging to her high-boned cheeks.

Alvena kissed Lia, then moved away. "Come."

Alvena began to ascend, and Lia, not wishing to be alone, followed her lover upwards.

◇━◆━◇━━◇━━◆━◇

The basalt wall of the tower sweated grime and moisture. Moss coated each tread upon the stairwell, creating precarious footing and giving even the light-toed elves reason for pause. Any step, if taken wrong, would lead to a lethal fall into darkness.

Lia said, "Why do wizards feel no need to install balustrades on their stairs?"

Alvena paused, leaning forward to inspect the stairwell, the pupils of her eyes swollen like those of a cat on the hunt in the darkness. "No wizard has come this way in some time. Nothing mortal has; I see no evidence of footfall." A moment later the taller of the two elves recoiled from where she examined the slippery steps and said, "Ugh, mold spores. Cover your mouth and nose, Lia. This is not a good place for you."

"Perhaps he is not here," said Lia, covering her mouth with the tunic beneath her robes.

Alvena looked up and swiftly notched an arrow to her crossbow. "He is here, I feel his malevolence. A heat comes from above, a warmth suffused with filth. Do you not sense it?"

Lia coughed. "I sense it."

"Watch your step. Let's move."

The two women came to a landing on which moisture congealed, pooling in dark liquid like blood. At the end of the landing the stairs continued upwards, while a corridor ran off to their right. The dark, echoing chasm that had grown in depth and darkness as they ascended ended there, the belly of the tower no longer empty. To their left several barred cells, vacant of all but decayed rotting straw, stood like iron, grilled mouths in skulls.

But one cell was not entirely empty: a small, white mouse was scuffling in the darkness amid the straw.

Lia knelt at the rusting bars and pursed her lips, blowing on her fingertips and extending her hand through the bars into the cell.

The mouse raised a curious, twitching nose, ran in a circle and then moved quickly across the cold floor. Lia placed a hand out, palm upwards, and the mouse stepped confidently into the flesh-cradle. The blond elf lifted the creature to the level of her eyes and smiled.

"We commune," said Lia. "I thank thee. We seek the master of the tower. Will you help us?"

The mouse squeaked.

"I am Lia. What is your name?"

The mouse squeaked again.

"Such a beautiful name."

The mouse squeaked in pleasure.

"Will you be my eyes?"

The mouse squeaked in affirmation.

Lia nodded and lowered her hand to the floor. The mouse leaped from her outstretched palm and ran across the landing, heading for the stairs leading ever upwards.

She stood, closed her eyes and slowed her breathing. Alvena returned her crossbow to her back and came close to Lia's side, who, eyes still closed, reached out a hand for Alvena to take. Together they began to follow the mouse as it adeptly leapt each step on the stairwell.

⟡━━⟡━━━⟡━━⟡

Lia Fadenheart was now blind, yet she saw. She saw through the eyes of In-the-Darkness-There-Is-Light, the white mouse now leading the two elves upstairs.

For his part, In-The-Darkness-There-Is-Light was eager to help the one called Lia. She was polite, respectful, and if there is one thing that mice respond to it is politeness and respect given. She also liked his name. In-The Darkness-There-Is-Light shivered with joy. He would hurry and lead her; he just hoped the visitation between the elven dames and the master of the tower proved a happy occasion.

⟡━━⟡━━━⟡━━⟡

Alvena watched Lia's face as they ascended, her eyes closed, head slightly tilted backwards, and the taller elf marveled at the beauty of her companion. It was a beauty that had not waned even after two-hundred years, despite the shadows beginning to darken the soft skin under the fair-headed elf's eyes. Alvena had to forcibly tear her eyes away to make sure neither of them stumbled as they climbed higher within the tower, following the surprisingly swift rodent.

Neither of them spoke. Alvena knew that the opportune meeting with the small creature favored them in their quest, but also that Lia's tether to the mouse was fragile, a bond easily disrupted. Yet luck favored the brave that night: as the weather outside had given them an advantage over Owl-Spoil's outer defenses, so too would the mouse prove an invaluable ally on the inside.

Alvena could not help but glance again at the fair, gentle creature at her side. *Gods*, she thought, *Lia is so beautiful.*

As language must be translated so must vision, as colors, shapes and luminescence are all perceived differently by each creature.

At first Lia struggled to grasp what it was that In-The-Darkness-There-Is-Light saw. A series of grey waves rushing at the edges of her field of vision overwhelmed objects nearer the center, warping them and pulling them apart. Gradually the grey waves slowed, allowing objects to take shape and assemble into recognized patterns, then color began to seep in.

The mouse turned right at another landing and began to head down a low-ceiling hallway, but then stopped and raised quivering whiskers in the air. Backtracking along the paved floor he returned to Lia and squeaked.

"What does it say?" asked Alvena.

"A trap, pressure plates within the floor that lead to acid-filled pools below."

In-The-Darkness-There-Is-Light moved softly forwards and sat upright on a rectangular stone set in the floor.

"Follow the mouse," whispered Lia. "Step only where he indicates."

"Perhaps you should open your eyes for this," whispered Alvena.

Lia shook her head. "The bond between us, once broken, cannot be established again this night. I believe our guide has more to show us."

Without a word Alvena knelt and allowed her companion to climb onto her back. Grunting, the taller elf regained her feet and carefully stepped only on those stones specified by the small mouse. At regular intervals he would turn and sit upright, seeming to say, *This one, walk here.*

In this way the two elves navigated their way over the death pits. When the white mouse suggested the danger had passed Alvena gently lowered Lia to the stone floor.

In-The-Darkness-There-Is-Light squeaked in a low pitch.

Lia said, "He tells us to wait here while he scouts ahead. He says there may be one more obstacle before we reach our goal; quiet while I see through his eyes."

The two females waited as In-The-Darkness-There-Is-Light moved on ahead, turning left down another corridor and up a short flight of steps.

Lia, eyes still closed, saw alongside the little white mouse as he approached a door. Crumpled in front of the door sat a figure, sunken head on chest. It was a corpse, cobwebbed sword still in hand, rotted tatters of leather armor falling away from the shoulders and chest.

*This one,* thought In-The-Darkness-There-Is-Light, *still lives.*

*It is undead*, thought Lia in response.

*Undead. Yes, I understand.*

*Can you bring it to us?*

*You wish to make acquaintance with the undead?*

*We wish to remove it from the door, and deal with the thing on our terms.*

*You will surprise it?*

*Just so.*

*I will attempt to wake the undead*, thought the mouse. With that he sprang up, crawling onto the exposed thigh bone before moving upwards to the slack jaw resting on its rotted chest.

In-The-Darkness-There-Is-Light bit the undead on the nose, taking a small flint of cartilage out of the slumbering corpse's face.

The mouse jumped to the floor as the undead warrior flinched and sat bolt upright: a sleeper awakened from dreams of the dead. The skeletal remains of the once-mortal gained unsteady feet, beginning to follow the mouse. The undead moved with alarming alacrity, belying its clacking, unsteady walk.

*Hurry, little one*, thought Lia. *Do not let it catch you.* She turned to Alvena and opened her eyes, almost collapsing to the cold, stone floor.

Alvena lunged and caught Lia, a look of concern on her face. "Are you alright?"

Lia steadied herself. "Our little friend brings the undead. Be ready."

The once-mortal soldier rounded a corner in the labyrinthine halls of Black Lake Tower and saw the small white mouse sitting at the far end of a corridor.

The undead raised its rusting sword and lumbered forward, eager for retribution for the unprovoked attack on its person while it slept.

The mouse, seemingly unafraid, simply cocked its impertinent head and began to clean its whiskers, almost tauntingly.

The undead entertained visions of biting off the rodent's head as it closed the distance on the mouse.

Too late, the once-mortal realized something was amiss. It stopped and looked at its feet, skeletal toes poking out the end of well-worn leather boots. Underfoot the floor comprised slick, mossy tiles. This was not the corridor where the death pits lay beneath false stones, yet caution crept at the back of its scalp all the same, like maggots once had before they had buzzed away, gifting him the remainder of his dried flesh.

Flesh that now crawled anew, crawled with suspicion.

The once-mortal turned and started at the sight of a tall, auburn-haired elf female, crossbow braced against a powerful shoulder.

The creature gave a gurgling laugh. *No mortal weapon can harm me*, it thought, but Alvena Thallan possessed no mere crossbow.

The bolt entered the undead warrior's chest, exploding into blue light that filled the creatures eye sockets, and other cavities.

A moment later the creature dissolved; nothing but

rotted armor, smoking boots and yellowed teeth remaining.

In-The-Darkness-There-Is-Light gave a squeak of delight at its first glimpse of magic.

Lia crept from the shadows and knelt near the mouse, using the last remnants of the fading bond between them. She thought, *We must go on alone now, little friend, for our encounter with the wizard of this tower will be dangerous. I have no desire to see you embrace harm, but you have assisted us beyond measure, so for that I thank thee.*

*You are welcome, elven dame.*

*A parting gift for you.* She bid the mouse come closer, gently blowing a perfumed breath upon the small rodent.

Alvena returned her crossbow to her back. "We must go. We are close now."

In-The-Darkness-There-Is-Light marveled at the gift Lia had given him. *I will not forget you,* he thought. *My children shall know you passed this way, and their children.*

Lia smiled, and In-The-Darkness-There-Is-Light wondered if he were the first of his kind to fall in love with an elf.

The tall, lithe ones left him, and the small white mouse scurried off the other way, into darkness, still wondering.

◇━◦━◇━◦━━◦━◦◆━◇

The door, now unobstructed by the undead warrior, happened to be unlocked.

Alvena and Lia, magical crossbow and dagger in hand, glanced at each other as they pushed the door back. They both knew that they had one chance at taking Owl-Spoil, for they must kill him before the words of a spell left his ancient lips.

The door opened onto a dimly-lit antechamber: a small, round carpet of plush material supported a circular, oak table without chairs in the center of the room. Upon the table, on a silver pedestal, sat a crystal orb. An ornamented window in the opposite wall peered out onto Black Lake below, lightning flashing across the rain-streaked pane.

The two elven women moved forward. A light source from an adjoining room dusted a set of three marble stairs, leading to a passageway off to the left, and Alvena nodded towards the steps. Before she could set foot on the first one Lia laid a hand on her shoulder and pointed to the orb on the table. The two females approached and peered at the scene pictured within the orb: there were two figures climbing a wooded hill, one blonde the other auburn-haired, pointed ears betraying unmistakably elven origin. One carried a crossbow, the other a dagger.

Lia opened her mouth, fear scrunching her brows, and looked at Alvena. "He knows."

A man's voice, deep and resonant, filtered through from the next room. It said but one word, "Come."

Lia cast Alvena a pleading look and pointed back out of the antechamber.

The taller elf shook her head. *Too late to run.*

Taking the three steps swiftly Alvena and Lia entered the passage to the adjoining room, scanning ahead for any sign of the old wizard, crossbow and dagger raised and ready.

They found him in a library, a black-robed man taking a book from the shelf in front of him.

He had his back to them, so Alvena took the shot.

The magical bolt entered the nape of the man's neck, and disappeared.

Owl-Spoil the Necromancer turned around, one thick eyebrow raised on a wrinkled forehead set below a receding hairline.

Yet he was not old, perhaps fifty years as measured by mortal man.

His voice was deep and lilting. "Now, that was uncalled for. Let's start over." He clapped the book shut and smiled, though his smile faded a moment later as he glanced around the small library. Stroking his black-grey mustache with his free hand, he said, "I'm sorry, I don't appear to have any seating arrangements for guests. It's been some time since I had any, you see."

Alvena notched another bolt with shocking fluidity and let it fly.

This bolt hit Owl-Spoil over his heart, but, like the last, vanished.

Owl-Spoil scowled. "Will you please stop doing that?"

"Throw your blade!"

Lia stared at her knife, and then at Owl-Spoil, who clasped the book across his abdomen, looking very much like a stern schoolmaster. He said, "Please don't waste your time. You seem like the rational one, so just put your blade away."

Lia hesitated. Alvena threw aside her crossbow and

leapt towards Owl-Spoil, a war-cry on her lips.

He waved a hand and Alvena twisted through the air, crashing into a bookshelf on the other side of the room.

"I mean you no harm," said Owl-Spoil, "though clearly the same could not be said for either of you. Especially you," he said, looking at Alvena who was unsteadily regaining her feet. "Now, if this idiocy continues, I will have no choice but to hurt one or both of you."

Alvena lowered her shoulders, ready for another headlong charge.

"Stop!"

Alvena stared at Lia.

"Just stop," said Lia. "It's over."

"No," said Alvena.

Lia shook her head and dropped her blade.

Alvena held out her hand. "No, please."

Lia coughed, tasting blood on her lips.

Then the floor twisted to become the wall and Lia fell against its cool surface, the darkness taking her.

⬦━━◦━━━◦━━⬦

Lia awoke in a bed of soft down, under light, warm blankets. On the bedside table was a steaming cup of tea, or thin soup; Lia could not be sure. The room was lit by several candles.

Alvena stood at a bay window staring out at the thunderstorm raging over the lake, hands on her hips and face lit by flashes of sharp lightning. She turned at the subtle stirring of the blankets as Lia rose to a sitting position.

"How do you feel?" Alvena came to sit with Lia on the bed.

"I am well. Where is Owl-Spoil?"

Alvena nodded to the door. "In his library."

Lia looked around. "Our weapons?"

A shake of the head. "He has taken them."

"Are we prisoners then?"

Alvena shrugged. "The door is not locked."

"We are free to go?"

"We came for the Amulet of Ulfur."

"You cannot still hope for that. He is too powerful. We have failed, so let's simply leave with our lives."

Alvena took Lia's hand and looked imploringly into the other's eyes. "We have no life together without the amulet, not for long."

"Then let's just make the most of what we have left." Lia's robe lay across the foot of the bed; it was dry, and she slipped it on over her tunic. "I would speak with the wizard."

Together the two silently padded to the door and out into a thinly-carpeted corridor.

They found Owl-Spoil once more in his library, a library that now possessed several comfortable-looking chairs in stark contrast to the bare first appearance of the room.

Owl-Spoil turned at their entrance. "Ah, Lia, you are awake. I am delighted this time to be able to offer you both a seat." He waved an arm around the room.

The two elven females sat on a plush divan of ruby satin, the wizard sitting opposite them in a cushioned wicker chair, clasping his hands and resting them on his knees. Owl-Spoil seemed genuinely pleased to have guests.

"Wonderful, neither of you seek to attack me. Tea?"

Alvena shook her head, Lia nodded.

The necromancer disappeared into a shadowed alcove and returned a minute later carrying a tray containing three cups of steaming tea. He placed the tray on a small stool between them, and, glancing at the red-headed elf, said, "A third cup in case you change your mind, Alvena."

"Is it poisoned?"

The man paused a moment, then smiled as he sat. "My dear, if I'd wanted you done away with you wouldn't be sitting on my chairs enjoying my company." He looked from one elf to the other. "You're here for something. I hope you don't find me presumptuous for asking what it is." Owl-Spoil sat forward and picked up his cup.

Alvena remained silent, so Lia decided to take the lead. "The Amulet of Ulfur."

The necromancer raised an eyebrow, his eyes shining. "Ah. *That*." The man seemed lost in thought for a moment, then he sighed. "That doesn't exist," he said. "It's a fairytale."

Alvena spat, "And we just take your word?"

Owl-spoil shrugged and spilled a little tea on his wrist. He winced and dried it with the sleeve of his black robes, this being carefully noted by Alvena.

*He can be hurt*, she thought.

Owl-Spoil went on, "Take my word, or don't. The stories speak of an amulet that gives eternal life, now that should already raise one's suspicions. Eternal life does not exist, not for man nor elf." A thought seemed to play across the man's brows. "Why would two elves be seeking such an artifact? If there is one creature in this world that is practically immortal it is the elf."

Neither of the elven females answered.

The man went on, "Two thousand years is not enough for you? You seek more? One might call elf-kind a little selfish."

Again neither female spoke, but Owl-Spoil noted Alvena turning to look at Lia, sadness playing beneath the surface of her proud face.

And then he knew.

Owl-Spoil turned to Lia. "You are sick. You are dying."

Lia nodded.

Owl-Spoil nodded in turn. "You think this amulet can heal you?"

"We know it can," said Alvena.

Owl-Spoil sat back in his chair. "And rumor has led you to believe that the Amulet of Ulfur is here?"

"Yes."

He sighed. "A wizard in an ominous tower in the middle of a dark, stormy lake. Of course it's here, of course. Where else?"

Alvena's brow sharpened. "I do not understand."

"I have heard elves aren't good with irony, nor its palsied cousin called sarcasm." He looked at both females. "It's not here, if it even exists, which I doubt."

Lia nodded. "We are sorry to have disturbed you then."

Raised brows. "*Disturbed* me? Attempted murder hardly qualifies as mere disturbance. However, I am willing to overlook your enthusiasm for fairy tales, as I enjoy them myself. How old are you, Lia?"

"I am two hundred years by the lunar cycle."

Owl-Spoil blew air from his cheeks. "Two hundred years is a good span of time for mortal man. It's older than I."

Alvena sat forward in her chair. "For man, yes. We are elven. Lia has been cheated. Our time together has just begun. This is not just. It is not fair."

Thunder rolled outside, wind driving rain against the windows as it threatened to splinter glass and give ingress to the storm.

"Fair?" Owl-Spoil breathed in deeply. "You come here seeking a means to redress that which is not *fair*?" He shook his head. "You are two hundred years old, the both of you, I assume. In your collective four hundred years wisdom, have you not yet learned the nature of fairness? It, like the amulet you seek, is merely a dream."

The wizard rose from the wicker chair and approached one of the bookshelves cocooning the library.

"If you do not have it, what are you guarding?" said Alvena.

"Guarding? I guard nothing. I do not encourage visitors, nor do I discourage them."

"You are a liar. What of the golem, and the fanged beast beneath the lake? The acid pits and undead guarding the interior?"

Owl-Spoil smirked. "Foolish child. You think I have set watchdogs to protect my person? I need no such protection. These things you speak of belong to the deranged persona who inhabited this tower before me. I have nothing to do with them."

Alvena sneered, "And what happened to the former owner of Black Lake Tower?"

Owl-Spoil whirled to glare at Alvena. "I am beginning to tire of your attitude. What do you think happened to him? Do you think I murdered him? I bought it from him. Paid good gold, simple as that. Rather mundane, isn't it? In fact, this whole escapade must be something of a disappointment to you, for there is no wicked wizard guarding an amulet of immortality at the top of a deadly, trap-laden tower. There is no battle of good versus evil, no stage for champions. There's only mistruths, misunderstandings and fantasy. I am sorry for the situation you find yourselves in, but you will find no answers nor resolution here tonight."

Lia reached out to put a hand on Alvena's arm. "We must go."

Alvena lowered her head. "You will be dead within days." She looked up, her sea-wall of arrogance breaking against a wave of pain. "Please, wizard, you must help us. You must help Lia!"

Owl-Spoil's face softened. He turned and approached the storm-lashed window, clasping his hands behind his back. "Do you know the lifespan of a white mouse?"

Lia looked up and stared at the man. "Two years," she whispered, thinking of In-The-Darkness-There-Is-Light.

"Yes, two years. In which space of time it lives a complete life, including having offspring, dreaming and loving." He paused. "You have had two *hundred* years."

Alvena stood, screaming. "She deserves two-*thousand*, like the rest of our people! Her illness is unheard of! She is too young to die! She is a beautiful soul! Even you who have known her this short time can see that; I know you can! I say again, this is unjust! Unfair!"

Owl-Spoil watched the rain cascade down the thin, fragile glass window. He whispered. "Two years. Two hundred. Two thousand. Would your grief be less? Would you feel less?"

Alvena seemed to collapse in on herself. Her voice softened. "Alright. I agree, I agree."

Lia looked up at Alvena. "Agree, agree to what?"

Owl-Spoil turned. "Once done, this cannot be changed."

Alvena nodded. "I understand. Please, you must do it quickly."

Lia stood and put an arm on Alvena's shoulder. "What are you speaking of? What has passed between you while I slept?"

Alvena looked away.

"Life," said Owl-Spoil. "Life."

Lia shook her head. "You said you could not extend life."

The mage's mouth turned down at the edges. "I cannot, but I can rebalance the scales. Make compensations and rearrange things, for a fee."

"You speak in riddles."

"Then let me speak plainly. I will transfer much of Alvena's life-force to you. She has approximately eighteen hundred years remaining to her. I will take three hundred of those and gift them to you."

"No."

Alvena shook her head. "It is the only way."

Lia turned back to Owl-Spoil. "And your fee?"

"One thousand years of her life-force. That way, you

are both left with three hundred years, and I live a little longer."

"No! You take too much!"

"That is the price. Pay it, or leave."

Alvena said, "We will do it."

Lia shook her head. "No, Alvena, he takes a thousand years of your life!"

"I gladly give them to have one more day with you!"

Owl-Spoil walked swiftly from the library, saying, "Then imagine the joy you can have together with three hundred more years of days. Find me when you are ready."

Alvena and Lia fought like the storm outside: lashing each other with tears, stinging each other's skin with cold and bitter reasons why the bargain must or must not be struck, deluging each other's spirits in a whirling torrent of screams.

Mid-argument Lia stopped and put her fingers to her lips. They came away with blood, and once again Lia Fadenheart felt Black Lake Tower dance and twist around her.

Alvena caught her lover in her strong embrace before Lia hit the floor.

"Owl-Spoil, now!!"

Somewhere in the darkness, up at the top of the necromancer's tower, Owl-Spoil the Necromancer smiled.

◇━◆━◇━━◆━◇

Alvena Thallan lay on a table in the wizard's laboratory. On another table, an arm's length away, Lia rested, eyes closed and breathing shallowly.

"Hurry, wizard. She is dying."

"One does not rush immortality, young woman." Owl-Spoil looked up from where he was pouring a purple liquid from a glowing beaker into a circular, stone bath of warm water. He laughed. "What am I saying? You are older than I. *Young woman*, indeed."

The laboratory pulsed with chemical color in arcane tubes of crystal and glass. Oranges and reds gave off strange smoke, the pungent odor of dark magic invading Alvena's nostrils. "Stop prattling, human, and transfer the years you have promised."

Owl-Spoil stiffened. "Your attitude makes it hard for one to sympathize with your plight. Fortunately for you, your partner is of a much more agreeable nature. I do this only to help *her*."

"Hah! You help yourself to a thousand years of elven life-force. Do not pretend any altruism."

The mage smiled from one side of his mouth. "Fair enough. Now take your clothes off and get into the bath."

Alvena rose from the table and removed her cloak and tunic. Nude, she stepped into the bath as Owl-Spoil turned an hourglass.

The mage said, "Thirteen minutes. Any more and you approach your own death."

"How will I know when the correct time has passed?"

"When the sands have run." The wizard noted the look of concern on the auburn-haired elf's face. "Do not be troubled. I have carefully measured the grains."

"Then my life is in the hands of your time-keeping," she said, slipping into the warm waters. "No need to be concerned at all."

Owl-Spoil grinned and approached Lia. He began to tug at her tunic.

"What are you doing?" asked Alvena.

"I am stripping your friend of her clothes. She must bathe in the same waters when the sands have run."

Alvena stood to exit the bath. "Then I shall do it."

"No! You cannot leave the bath once the waters have embalmed you. Stay, stay. Now is not the time for modesty on the part of your friend."

Alvena reluctantly submerged herself in the purple waters once more. The liquid was no more than lukewarm, yet she began to feel a tiredness overcome her limbs. "I grow weak, old man. What is this magic?"

"Your life-force is entering the water. You will, naturally, begin to feel rather delicate."

Alvena watched the man disrobe Lia. He did so gently, and Alvena allowed herself to relax for a moment. Her head began to spin as she looked at the sands tumbling in the hourglass. Not even half-fallen.

*Ashsmith the Vile is a liar.*

Alvena looked around the laboratory, puzzled. Who had spoken? Certainly not the necromancer, who seemed not to have noticed the small, but clear, male voice

The voice came again. *Oberon will kill you. You must get out of the water before it absorbs your spirit entirely.*

Alvena could not think clearly. *Ashsmith? Oberon? Who?*

*Owl-Spoil! He will kill you and Lia! Act now!*

Alvena turned, and there was the white mouse that had led them through the tower. He was sitting on the edge of the bath near her head, whiskers twitching.

*I do not have the gift of animal-speak*, thought Alvena. *This cannot be. We cannot commune.*

*Never mind about that now. I have watched you, and now see the truth. The mage intends to take your life-force for himself! All of it!*

Alvena knew, somehow, that to doubt the tiny rodent was to bathe in the pools of death; she stood from the purple water and stepped as silently as she could to the stone floor, a floor now threatening to spin out of control.

*I am too weak*, she thought. *Help me.*

Owl-Spoil turned at the sound of dripping water and frowned at the wet, naked elf trying to steady herself. "What are you doing? It is too soon!" Despite his ire the necromancer could not help but pause to admire her impressive musculature and sleek, sensual lines. This was the power of Alvena's bloodline, a power he now craved. "You have a beautiful body, elf, and strength undimmed within. That I see clearly."

Alvena raised an accusatory finger at Owl-Spoil. "You shall not have it. You shall not take my life, nor my spirit."

Anger bristled across the man's face as he stood to his full height. "We had an agreement." He gestured towards the still unconscious Lia on the laboratory table. "This is the only way to save your love."

Alvena felt her muscles begin to stop trembling, her strength returning too slowly. The mage, a vicious sneer on his face, crossed the laboratory floor towards her.

"I haven't dirtied my hands for some years," said Owl-Spoil, "but half of your vitality resides in the water. You are weaker than a newborn kitten. You shall reenter the bath, or I shall put you back there. Enough of your stubborn wilfulness!"

Alvena made a fist and punched the man in the jaw.

To her surprise, and very much to his, Owl-Spoil stumbled backwards and fell on his arse.

Getting to his feet the man wiped his mouth on the back of his hand, smiling as he looked at the blood there. The words of a spell began to dance on his rubied lips as he glared at Alvena.

The elf knew she must close the gap on the necromancer before he finished his spell, but her legs still seemed submerged in the waters of the bath.

Owl-Spoil suddenly shrieked in pain, the words of the spell lost. He screamed again and began to jump, and then In-The-Darkness-There-Is-Light scurried from the inside of Owl-Spoil's black robe. A kick from the necromancer caught him, sending him flying off into the shadows of the laboratory.

Alvena silently thanked the mouse for the extra moments as she aimed her own kick at the man's stomach. He doubled over with an explosive breath, and the elf followed the kick with another punch that loosened more of the necromancer's teeth.

Owl-Spoil attempted to execute another spell, his voice burbling. Red flecks flew from swollen lips, his tongue cut and teeth chipped. Alvena slammed her palm upwards under his jaw, causing the man to bite off the pink tip of his tongue, which fell between Alvena's breasts and to the floor. Owl-Spoil howled in rage and pain from between clenched teeth.

The strength that had temporarily returned to Alvena

began to fade. She must end the encounter soon, or tear the man's tongue fully from his mouth. She looked around for something, anything, to gouge him with. Her momentary distraction allowed Owl-Spoil to knee Alvena in her groin, then head-butt her. The elf saw stars as her feet slipped, legs collapsing while Owl-Spoil pushed her away. He moved quickly towards the bath and the purple waters.

*Do not let him enter the bath!*

In-The-Darkness-There-Is-Light scurried from the shadows and nipped at the necromancer's sandaled feet, forcing the man to jump and slide on the wet, slippery floor. In the next instant Alvena had him by the hood of his robe and pulled him backwards, his head hitting the stone and knocking him unconscious.

It only lasted for a moment; the necromancer immediately groaned, then began to come around.

Alvena looked around for a weapon. On a nearby table sat two glass containers, each holding a different chemical composition: one red, the other orange. The tall elf reached for the red liquid.

*The orange one*, thought In-The-Darkness-There-Is-Light.

Alvena took the orange liquid instead, forcing the mage's mouth open and placing the vial between the remainder of his teeth. She looked for a way to pour the liquid down the wizard's gullet, but the container was magically sealed. With the last of her strength she forced Owl-Spoil's jaws together, shattering the glass and spilling the contents down the man's throat.

Owl-Spoil screamed and spat bloodied glass into the air, orange smoke beginning to issue from his mouth and nose.

His eyes bulged, then the flesh melted from his face.

Alvena recoiled at the sight of the dying mage, but her attention soon turned to the unconscious Lia still lying on the table.

*Get her into the bath,* thought In-The-Darkness-There-Is-Light, *until your strength passes to her. Beware though, if you stay in the waters too long you shall fade from living memory.*

With reserves of energy she did not know she possessed Alvena lifted the blonde elf and staggered towards the bath past the corpse of Owl-Spoil, his fleshless skull smoking with acrid fumes.

Alvena collapsed into the bath, and as the purple waters rushed over her head she felt the cool charge of panic set blue fire to her nerves. An imprisoning sense of fear closed in over her, as surely as the water closed around her.

If she did not find the strength to get her head above the water then both she and Lia would drown, but this time the dark, magenta waters seemed to invigorate her where once they had enervated. She thrust her head upwards, breathing the arcane air lingering above the waters. She grabbed Lia and pulled her close against her chest, supporting Lia's head against her shoulder and checking for breath, one naked elf clasping the other in desperation.

Alvena prayed that the bath would do as Owl-Spoil had promised, and transfer life from one being to another.

Alvena noted the small, white mouse lying on its side on the laboratory floor near the bath, ribs stretching its skin and falling away again, breath coming hard to the rodent. The kick received from Owl-Spoil had landed, and the animal was clearly dying. On an impulse Alvena carefully cupped some water from the bath and reached towards In-The-Darkness-There-Is-Light, sprinkling the rodent in the water containing the life-energies of both herself and Lia.

A moment later the mouse flipped onto his feet and looked around, working at his whiskers with both front paws.

*Thank you, elven dame.*

Then    In-The-Darkness-There-Is-Light    scurried away.

Lia opened her eyes. She tried to exit the bath, but Alvena held her tightly as Lia twisted her head one way and then another, looking in consternation at the violet waters lapping at her breasts. "What is happening?"

"One more minute, my love."

Alvena kissed Lia on the temple, and from her hair inhaled the sweet scent of the woodlands of their home: cedar, white clove, mistletoe berries and juniper. As Lia's strength began to grow Alvena's diminished once more.

In a reversal of a few minutes earlier Lia hauled the now unconscious Alvena from the bath, and they both fell like new-born foals to the slippery stone floor.

"What have you done?" Lia put her lips to those of Alvena, gently touching the cold skin and listening for signs of life. "What have you done?"

Alvena opened her eyes, and Lia pulled her into a sitting position. The elves embraced as they shed tears.

◇━◯━◇ ━━ ◇━◯━◇

In-The-Darkness-There-Is-Light watched from a shadowed corner as the two elves dried themselves and dressed once more. They would spend the night and wait out the still-raging storm before leaving the accursed Black Lake Tower.

In-The-Darkness-There-Is-Light wondered if he, too, should turn his back on the tower; he could make a life for himself somewhere else. But where would he go? Besides, the tower had been his home for nigh on two years in his guise as a white mouse.

And for many years before that, in his other life.

Once he had been Rufael the Wicked, a powerful mage and the master of Black Lake Tower, before his trickster apprentice had betrayed him. That apprentice had thought it a great jest to turn Rufael into a rodent, and to have him eke out his days in the darkness and filth of the lower depths of the tower. No doubt it was the greatest ignominy that bastard Owl-Spoil could conceive of: to see his once-master sniffing at his own turds in the straw and muck.

But the elf, Lia, was possessed of a small well of magic, and with it she had gifted him memory, and the knowledge of a dormant power still buried somewhere deep within his being. It was he, In-The-Darkness-There-Is-Light, formerly Rufael the Wicked, that had denied Owl-Spoil his invisible defensive wall.

*A spell I taught that young, upstart prick.*

Yes, he had allowed the vicious one, Alvena, to have a chance against the necromancer, and she had taken it.

Oh yes, she had taken it.

In-The-Darkness-There-Is-Light laughed to himself as he watched the females walk arm-in-arm from the laboratory. Lia would live many more years; the illness within her body had been halted, for now. The other elf, Alvena, would live many *less* years, but if they were fortunate one would not outlive the other by many summers. And *that*, he thought, was what they mostly wanted.

And he, himself? He felt the power of both elven females surge through him. Alvena had been kind to offer a handful of the purple waters, which had saved his life.

Only fair, as In-The-Darkness-There-Is-Light had saved *both* of theirs.

The rodent scurried towards the bath and leapt onto the stone edge. The magenta waters below were cool now, but that did not matter.

Life still swirled in the waters, enough to fuel him for a multitude of rodent lives.

Or, if he was lucky, it would be enough to allow him to become human again. All he would need was a vessel, a shell, and it was a pity his apprentice was no longer a suitable selection. He would need something a lot prettier than that.

Something pretty, yes...

In-The-Darkness-There-Is-Light looked at the purple waters, smiled, and jumped back down to the floor. The vitality within could wait.

He began to follow the receding footfall of the elves.

He'd been a man, a mage, and he'd even been a rodent, but he'd never been an elf before.

Something pretty.

Yes, something pretty...

# CAMERON SCOTT KIRK

## ABOUT THE AUTHOR

Cameron Scott Kirk had a deficient childhood. He stayed in his room and read novels that filled his head with weird ideas. Due to his preoccupation with dragons, drunken damsels and dwarves in distress, he has very poor inter-personal skills.

He still prefers fantasy to reality because, after all, where do you get the opportunity to wield a sword against cave trolls in the real world?

Despite his shortcomings, Cameron has turned his hand to writing highly imaginative fantasy and you can find some of his work at the following links. If you want to. No pressure.

https://www.facebook.com/cameronscottkirkauthor
https://cameronscottkirk.wordpress.com/
https://www.amazon.com/~/e/B08W4R98SM
Twitter: @Cameron_S_Kirk

# Morgan's Story

## Sam Fletcher

The entire forest ignited the night Morgan died. His brother roared to the stars, noise hardly suffocated by the crackling smoke. This rage spread in flame for hundreds of miles, fresh rainfall providing no protection against the heat. Thriving evergreens caught instantly, endless acres of old growth thinned to ember.

Fauna, fleeing from their ravaged shelter, cried with him, but none of Kivati's followers left the scene until it was black as he felt.

The bonfire tonight was but a small echo of Kivati's rampage. None save a few scattered goblins joined, allowing him to sulk without chatter. Kivati looked deep into the flames, as if he were staring straight into the place they came from.

"Great Changer," Hoogdal interrupted this silence, breaking him from his trance. Kivati forced his stiff body to look at the kid. "My dad told me stories about Father Morgan from decades past, how he was the most feared man on Tatu. The quiet killer. The most expensive, too. A *thousand* links a head. Who knows what the council would have paid for his? They never would have gotten it though — that's how talented he was. The whole island knew his name, but they didn't know his secret."

The fire crackled; Kivati didn't say a word.

"Forgive me, sir," the young goblin continued. "I just don't understand. The most dangerous man on the island, the coldest, merciless executioner, gives his life… for *you* — his estranged brother." The others in the circle held their lips tight, resonating palpable nervousness toward Hoogdal's line of questioning. "I mean, if you were to believe the legends, you would think he was incapable of love at all."

The surrounding goblins flinched when Kivati straightened his spine, but the man didn't get angry. He simply remained still, arms folded, continuing to stare into the fire.

Then, he spoke. "He did love, once."

⟡━⟡━━⟡━⟡

Morgan held his stance, feet pressed into the thick grass he had used for whistles when he was younger. School had ended hours ago — the lawn remained empty and quiet. He rammed his arms out stiffly, palms spread and fingers tingling as he threw a wedge of dark energy across the yard.

With the first two fingers of her hands, Sela pulled it apart before impact.

"*Almost,*" she said, tying the strings of her burgundy, silk uniform. A gold pattern of a serpent and flame danced across the whole thing, the insignia of Morgan's family. "It just needs to be a bit more precise."

Morgan straightened out. He bent his knee over his toe, his back leg straight. He kept his legs just wider than his shoulders, creating a hollow space beneath his groin both front-to-back and side-to-side. Breathing deeply he drowned out all thoughts but condensing the air, of pulling the aether through it. He sent his palms at her once more, and once again she ripped the throw apart. The matter vanished.

Sela giggled at his frustrated groan. Her long, silky strands of black hair were but a few inches longer than his, her skin just a shade lighter. She was beautiful.

He repositioned once more, this time much quicker. He shoved his fists into the air with full intensity, muscles straining.

Sela's eyes widened as the thing launched toward her. It was more opaque than the others, and much larger. She screamed as she jumped beneath it, immediately pouncing up with two fingers in the air. A light, thin blackness surrounded each of Morgan's wrists and whipped him backward, pinning him to the willow trunk behind him.

She walked to him slowly, her swagger returned. With a swift motion his ankles were clamped as well; Morgan squirmed against the trunk. She leaned over, arms supporting her on either side of his head, as she kissed him with soft lips. "You're cute when you're angry," she said.

"Get me out of this," he said.

"You have to be more precise."

"I don't know what that means," he said. "Every one of those would have hit you."

"Well, yeah," she said. "That's because they were giant. It's impressive, really, that last one might have killed me. No one in class comes close to that."

"So you get it," he said. "What's your point?"

"My point is," she said, skipping away. "Let's see those blasts free you now."

Morgan shook himself against the tree, moving any way he could to get out.

Sela stopped in her place. "Give up?"

"Let me go," he said.

She lifted up with her fingers, and the bands dissipated. Morgan's body thumped the grass.

"I'm done for today," he said as she made her way back over. She sat down beside him, against the trunk. She rubbed his bicep.

"Why are you so mad?"

"I can't fail again," Morgan said through heavy breath.

"Because of Father?"

He pressed through his nose. "I'm the only one who makes sense calling him Father."

He closed his eyes, shaking his head. "Still, he doesn't care. I'm an embarrassment."

"You're not," she said, "he is. Why isn't he helping you?"

He exhaled through a narrow slit in his lips. "He doesn't even know where I am," he said.

Her head fell on his shoulder. "He's missing out." Their eyes met. "Smile," she said. "Today is beautiful."

His lips rose.

"There," she said. "I like that." The sun reached the point where it touched the horizon below the island, beneath the floating land they stood on. She nuzzled her head into his shoulder, and he lifted his arm up around her. They listened to the creek trickle behind them as the sky deepened to orange.

As the sun drooped farther so did Morgan's eyes. When the sky became cloaked in darkness he rustled himself alert.

"What is it?" Sela asked.

"I have to go," he said, tying the top of his uniform around his waist, revealing the cream shirt underneath.

"You're not meeting with those guys, are you?" she asked.

"I have to tonight. I almost forgot."

"You can't stay?"

"You know how much they need me." He hunched down to his knees and kissed her. "I love you."

"I love you too," she told him as he walked with haste off the lawn. "Be safe!" she shouted, but he was already by the dirt road at the bottom of the hill.

He met the goblins in the usual place, the damp, brick alley behind Squonk's Pub. Six of them perched about on the trash vessel, or leaned against the wall. They howled and clapped when he approached.

"Finally," Sedro croaked. "Get us something." He tilted his head to the back door of the pub, where raucous voices poured forth.

Morgan looked at the six of them, taking in gray skin, slender limbs and wrinkled faces. "You got cash?"

Scattered chatter. "You're a Bane," Sedro said. "Go."

Morgan nodded, moving around to the front of the pub. He couldn't argue with that logic. He entered the mass of big-bellied village folk yelling and throwing darts, and as he wedged his way to an opening at the bar he couldn't help but notice the occasional glance from the patrons. He thought at first they came from recognition, but there seemed to be an animus attached as if they smelled the stench of goblin on him.

He filled two growlers with berry cider and returned to the alleyway, where Sedro popped the cap to one of them and swigged.

"Why are you all hanging out here? Let's go somewhere," Morgan said.

"*Where*?" one of them snapped. "Your place?"

Morgan clenched the bottle when it came around. He took a sip.

"Exactly," the goblin said.

"What you wearing?" Sedro asked, eyeing Morgan up and down.

"My uniform," he said. Roaring cackles followed. The other six seemed to be wearing an informal uniform as well, all black and most of them hooded. They passed the bottles around the circle.

"You can't be seen with us, looking all pretty," said Cogg, with dark swells around his eyes and cuts across his arm.

"You look bigoted as your dad," came another.

"He's not a bigot," Morgan growled. The goblins turned silent. "He's developing a program right now to integrate your kind into the school."

"And what makes you think we'd want to go to your self-righteous school?" Sedro quipped.

"I didn't say you guys," Morgan said. "I meant goblins with potential." The cackles returned, and Morgan couldn't help but smile. "What happened to you, Cogg?" he asked across the huddle, eyeing the goblin's scrapes.

"Enforcer, what you think?" he asked. "Hardly escaped."

Morgan's teeth gritted. "It should be me! He can't keep doing this to you guys, you hardly have training."

A couple of howls grew. "Oh yeah, we should stay at home," Sedro mocked. "Hear that, guys? We have no training." The others laughed.

"It's not right that I don't get to be there," Morgan said. "I've done nothing but prove that I'm with you guys."

"Please," said Cogg. "You look more like an enforcer than half of them in armor."

"Your father schooled most of them," Sedro chimed in after a lengthy gulp.

"Am *I* him?" Morgan roared. "Do I act like him? Do I even talk to him?"

Silence choked the goblins.

"You don't want to be doing this," Cogg said, softer this time. "It's starting to feel personal."

"Beck didn't deserve it," Morgan said.

"Nine of us killed on sight this year," another goblin said. "Nine, all by the same guy. Don't they have anything else to worry about?"

"Some of us get caged," Cogg said. "But if you run into Graft — " he brushed his dark, serrated nails across his throat, " — you're not so lucky."

"Is it possible he's just the one put on those assignments?" Morgan cleared his throat. "Like, none of us were there. How much did they fight back?"

"Does it matter?" Sedro asked.

"I'm just saying that he might not be targeting anybody, right? He could have just been defending himself."

"*Nine*, Morgan. He's a speciesist, like all of them. Simple as that," Sedro said.

"We don't know that," Morgan said.

"*You* don't," said Cogg, "because he wouldn't do it to you."

"Wait a minute," Sedro said. "This isn't you talking, this is that girl." He looked around at the others. "What's the name again — Agoseris? She's been filling you with this shit."

"Sela is her name," Morgan said.

The six of them erupted in laughter.

"You want so bad to be a part of us, so bad to know what it feels like — and you're laying with the enforcers now!"

"She's not one of them," Morgan spat through gritted teeth.

"You're right," Sedro said. "She was just raised with their morals, supported by their income and molded by their techniques." Morgan balled his fists. "Now that I think about it, it's not so different from you and your — affluent ancestry."

"Enough, Sed," said Morgan.

Sedro came off the vessel, stumbling from the cider. "Oh, pshh — what ya gonna do, tell Dad?" He looked to the others for encouragement, but none came. They looked frightened. He returned his gaze to Morgan. "Just wait 'till Petrie hears you've been laying with Graft's daughter."

Black energy formed around Morgan's fists before he even fully processed the goblin's words. He raised them, primal emotions in full control.

"Morgan, relax," Cogg said. "He's just messing around."

"Am I?" Sedro asked. "What kinds of things are you saying to her, when we aren't around?" His gaze bounced across the others' faces. "Well? If it were up to her, we'd all be bloody as Cogg." Sedro listened to the crackling energy. "Go ahead, that's what they want anyway! Beat me like your bitch would."

Morgan shook, trying to restrain himself.

"Here, I'll help you," Sedro said, the last two words slurred together. He launched his palms outward, shooting a slab of darkness at Morgan.

Morgan punched, shoving matter twice as large, twice as thick, through Sedro's blow. The goblin took the blunt force of vibrating energy, which smacked him into the brick of the pub.

Blood trailed off as he slid down onto the hard ground.

The five others had wide eyes as they looked at Morgan, but they stayed put; a couple of them trembled.

Morgan looked at Sedro's mangled body, then across the others' faces. His pupils twitched as he thought. He couldn't pinpoint his feelings: not quite fear, not quite guilt, not quite anger, but some potion of them all.

Without a word he darted from the scene, through the alley toward home.

He ignored the bright beams of light coming through the enormous windows of the classroom the next day. As the professor droned about the theory behind group chants, Morgan wondering when he'd get to use them in practice, a sporadic tap interrupted this thought. Morgan once again glanced at the window. A crow had landed on the sill, pecking at the glass. Annoyed, Morgan thickened the air around the bird, vibrating it until it took off.

And then it returned.

*Tap, tap, tap.*

Morgan stared at the thing until he saw something below it. Sedro, with a braced arm and a bandaged head, stood alone on the grass.

Morgan stood up quickly. "I have to use the bathroom," he announced before throwing himself between the desks and scooting out of the room.

He joined Sedro out in the courtyard. "What are you doing here?" he asked.

"Petrie sent me. He wants to speak with you."

The words sliced into his ears, followed by a nervous pause. "What?"

"Petrie wants to speak with you. Do you know where he lives?"

"Look, whatever this is — we can work it out between the two of us."

"Should I tell him you refused, then?"

Morgan looked him up and down. "He'll kill me. He's going to kill me." Sedro looked at him blankly. "Go,

Sed. Get out of here before someone sees you."

"Fine, but go see him. It'll be a lot worse, you know, if he has to find *you*." Sedro left, Morgan lingering to look up at the classroom window, at the school, lost in thought. He went around back, to the narrow path through the trees leading to Petrie's cottage.

Nervousness panged him with each step. He'd never been this deep in the woods before — his father had warned him of the criminals who lived within, those fearing the public eye.

The thick evergreens almost fully eclipsed the sun, only allowing specks of light to poke through. They seemed to dull all sound as well, except the dull twitter of birds. Morgan listened to his heavy breath persist, his steps crunching the needles on the ground. This all made the trek much worse.

The trees eventually opened, revealing a small cottage on the other side where a stone chimney rose above a moss-covered roof. Morgan took slow steps before lifting the thick door knocker. After a moment the peep hatch slid, and out came Petrie's croak. "Morgan Bane, come in."

When the door opened Petrie stepped to the side to allow his guest to come through. Even with a slight hunch he stood a head taller than the boy, the tallest goblin Morgan had seen.

Petrie eyed his uniform. "I'm sorry to interrupt your studies."

Morgan entered slowly, both hands at his waist but ready to make a move.

"I was just rustling up some grub for myself," said the goblin. He sat down at the end of a thick oak table.

Wood scraps and sawdust laid around the place, enough to assume Petrie built it himself. Even his shirt, rough and patched, had an air of home-stitching to it. "Would you like anything to eat?"

Morgan glanced at the raw meat on the goblin's plate. The elder began to eat with his hands, wedging skin and fat between his sharp teeth.

"I'm okay," Morgan said. He couldn't take it anymore. "Listen, sir, if this is about the fight — "

"Please, Morgan. You needn't brag."

"Excuse me?"

"I knew you were strong before you threw Sedro into some bricks. Probably had it coming, huh?"

"What is this about, sir?"

"Ferver was murdered this morning. Do you know who that is?" Morgan shook his head. "Perhaps the greatest weapon manufacturer this island has ever seen. The most talented goblin one, at least." Petrie slammed a wooden device on the table with a loud thud, sliding it across to Morgan. "He crafted this sprig."

Morgan examined the thing. It looked like a wand but was thicker, with an orb on one end. "This tool is the simplest way to end a life," Petrie continued. "Quick, and pain-free. Takes a talented mind to run one properly, of course. With your power you wouldn't need to use one at all."

Morgan slid the sprig back.

"Ferver is an enormous loss in our community, you can imagine. This is several years' setback, and besides being an unjustified tragedy the monetary loss is incalculable."

"Was it Graft, sir?" Morgan asked.

Petrie cracked a wide, slow smile. "Indeed it was. Graft Agoseris." His grin faded promptly. "I've let this go on for too long. We need to send a message, need to let him know that we aren't as powerless as he may think."

Morgan's words were softer than usual. "What sort of message, sir?"

Petrie stood up and fetched a small chest off the ground. Out rang a piercing, metallic thud as he dropped it on the table. "His right hand — his *wand* hand — in here."

Morgan was tense. "I — I don't know. He's a top enforcer. I have no experience..."

"Oh, but you left my experienced killer bludgeoned," said Petrie. "It must be you. Rumor has it—you have the most insider information on his whereabouts."

"I don't know," said Morgan. "He'll recognize me."

"The others have doubts about you — say your allegiance is split," said Petrie. "I've vouched for you before. I feel your anger, your thirst for justice. Don't make me look like a liar, Morgan." He pulled a black key from his shirt pocket with a neck piece attached, sliding it across the table to the boy. "If you do this you're one of us."

Petrie didn't allow much time to calculate. Morgan closed his eyes for a beat, thinking of any new reason to decline, but upon opening them nothing came. He nodded. "It's the right thing to do, isn't it?"

Petrie nodded. "He's lucky we haven't retaliated much, *much* sooner." Morgan put the key around his neck. He stood and grabbed the chest on both ends. "By week's end, understood?"

"Yes, sir," Morgan said.

"*Petrie*," the goblin corrected him. "Good luck, boy."

It was a long morning. Morgan sat on the hard stool of the classroom, replaying Petrie's words in his mind. He couldn't distract himself from them; they repeated over and over, louder than the professor up front.

He thought of how he would do it. Day? Night? How would he isolate Graft? How could he not reveal himself? He thought of Sela, and what would happen if she found out. In the afternoon he did exercise training on the lawn with his classmates. It was the only class he had with her, so as soon as the class broke into groups he ran to her, pulling her by the wrist downhill to the creek.

They hid beneath the willow's long branches, and their lips meeting was the first time that day that Morgan had thought of nothing at all. She pinned him to the tree with aether, biting his lip.

He pulled back. "You love tying me to this."

"What?" She grinned. "You don't like it?" Her big, brown eyes reflected the sunlight.

"You just better learn some new tricks before they recruit you for enforcement."

Her brows rose. "And?"

"And what? You want to walk around with that ego?"

She slumped down to his side, showing an utter depletion of energy. Morgan rubbed his wrists as she dissolved the bands, and she wrapped her arms around her legs. "Not all of them are like that."

"Enough are. I don't understand — they act like the things they kill don't think and breathe like they do."

"Well, not just like they do," she said. "I'm assuming you're talking about Beck? He had sold assault weapons for years, you know that."

"Not just Beck," he said. "Another was killed yesterday."

"Yeah, the manufacturer? He's responsible for hundreds of deaths. What are you talking about?" She looked at him while he searched for words. "I'm just saying," she continued, "all of this stuff everyone's been saying, what's in the papers — there has to be some truth to it. Goblins are prone to crime, to violence."

"Not all of them," Morgan said. "There are other species in the Syndicate too."

"Okay, so most. Why do you think that is?"

"Because when Tatu rose, the human sorcerers were most powerful."

"So?"

"So, they formed institutions that only made that power gap wider. To this day there is nothing in place for them — "

"So?"

"So, of course they are going to be violent!"

"You always talk about how much they need you, but the more this type of stuff happens — the more they prove themselves to be dangerous, heartless — the more it seems like you need *them*."

Morgan paused. "Well," he said, still thinking, "Beck didn't deserve to be killed."

"Beck *was* a dealer though, wasn't he?"

"But he was just minding his own business, and — "

"His weapons killed dozens of people."

"*He* didn't deserve to be killed."

"*He* killed people, Morgan."

"So? He should be caged! It wasn't the decision of an enforcer."

"But it's the decision of a goblin? You have no idea what my dad faces every day. The goblins are brutal, vicious. Any wrong move, even a slight one, and an enforcer is dead. They show absolutely no mercy, but an enforcer should? The life of a criminal, a murderer, is more important? If he hadn't done it he would have been the one dead. You get that, right?" Morgan's eyes watered. As he felt the emotion build in her voice, his words choked. "What's wrong?" she asked.

"Nothing," he said, trying to restrain his nerves. "You're right. I'm sorry."

He couldn't get it off his mind. If he backed out the goblins would never trust him. Petrie might get violent, but if he did it, and Graft found out — he'd lose everything.

◈━◇━━━◇━◈

He walked past the door of his next class, up the stairs to his father's office. A man in a burgundy cloak stood in front of the door.

"Is my dad in there?" Morgan asked him. The man shook his head slowly. "Is he in the building?" Again, the man negated.

Morgan rushed back down the stone stairs. He raced to the lowest floor, dragging his fingers across the bricks. Eventually he found a divot and slid the wall back, revealing another stairway. He paced down it, the steps lit only by flaming torches.

At the bottom another cloaked figure stood. "Whoah, whoah," he said, arms out. "Students aren't allowed down here."

"Let me in, Crowe," Morgan commanded.

"Father didn't tell me to make exceptions."

"Let me see my dad, Crowe."

Crowe stepped to the side, unlatching the metal bars.

Morgan walked into the cold darkness of the basement, listening to the sound of dripping water that echoed against the stone walls. A torch lit the corner.

Morgan crept toward it, spying on his dad dancing about with a boy in exuberance. The two chanted together, some ancestral phrase, over and over again.

"Dad?" Morgan called.

Malachi turned, allowing light to shine on the long-haired boy behind him. The kid looked just a few years older than Morgan.

"Morgan," Malachi said. "What are you doing down here?"

Morgan squinted at the boy, his tan skin, and their matching robes. "This is what you're doing?" he asked.

Malachi cleared his throat. "Say hello to Kiva."

Morgan paused, refusing to look Kivati in the eyes. "He's — starting to look like…*me*."

"Well, he's your brother, isn't he?" Malachi asked.

"Is he?" Morgan returned, eyeing the specks of gray in his father's long goatee.

"Technically he looks like me," Malachi said. "People tend to imitate who they admire, yes? Perhaps you should try it."

"Will he ever attend school?" Morgan asked.

"No, no," Malachi said. "I see no reason for that. The school is obsolete for his potential. I'm very busy, Morgan, as I'm sure you can tell. What can I help you with?"

"I need to talk to you about something," he said. "I — don't know what to do."

Malachi's attention remained on Kivati behind him, dragging his thumb across his cheek.

"I'm scared," said Morgan.

At this Malachi turned again, examining his son's face.

"It's important, I think, this opportunity," Morgan continued, "but I don't know who I might hurt. And Sela — "

"This is about continually failing your defense exam?" Malachi asked. "Just do your homework. Train harder, and stop spending so much time with that girl. Please, Morgan. I have work to do."

"It's not that, exactly," Morgan said. "I — "

"MORGAN, ENOUGH!" Malachi erupted. "You have *everything*. Please stop whining so much. I'm busy."

"Okay, Dad," he said. "I'm sorry." He turned toward the entrance, and his father's attention had returned to the boy. They resumed their chant, and up the stairs Morgan could hear their harmonious laughter below.

⋄━◇━━━◇━◇

As night fell Morgan walked out the large, oak doors of his home. He looked up at the tower. The room was lit, but who knew if his father had come home, and his mother was probably in bed reading.

The thought of this made his jaw tense and his stomach ill; his hands were numb from vibration even before matter formed. He walked toward the village market in his normal street clothes, tying a mask over his head. It was an old potato sack tailored to the facial structure of a goblin. The sleeves for its long nose and sharp chin dangled off his face, empty. He didn't carry a weapon, just the chest with one hand.

As he approached he had to change course. A couple of trolls had arrived: giant, bloated, nude, sniffing around for scraps at the vacant vendors. He avoided them and headed up the north hill.

Atop the hill sat rows of modest homesteads, but they were sturdy enough. Bigger than the huts to the east, though smaller than any home he'd grown up in.

He gazed into a window of an olive-hued house. Through the pale blinds he saw Sela's outline, still and silent in her bed. His heart fluttered.

He circled to the other side of the home. The next window was several feet higher, on the second story, so Morgan sat the chest on the ground. He squatted and shoved his fists down, sending energy into the earth below. He launched up and grabbed the edge of the roof with one arm, looking in.

Graft lay alone in his bed. Morgan raised his fist, absorbing black around it. Nausea filled his body as he looked at the hand dangling from the edge of the bed. He had one shot. No matter the outcome, Morgan felt guilty and weak.

He just hoped the feeling would vanish by the time it was over.

When he couldn't handle the energy's vibration Morgan released it full-force through the glass. The shards blasted in, the energy slicing into the bed. It collapsed the wooden frame on impact.

Morgan observed the damage, but there was no body. No sign of Graft whatsoever.

"Who's there?" The voice came from behind him. He dropped down to the ground, where the enforcer had teleported.

Morgan stared for a moment, breathing heavily, before Graft drew his wand. Reflective, black armor appeared from smoke in the air, covering his sleeping garments.

Morgan stepped forward, launching slabs of matter Graft's way, but with a swish of Graft's wand they dissolved.

"Who put you up to this?" Graft asked.

Morgan tuned out the words, snarling in reply. He took another step; listening would only make it worse.

Graft lifted his wand, and rocks cemented Morgan's front foot to the ground. He lowered it in a flat line, and the earth collapsed below the boy.

Morgan fell into the hole to his chin. The wand bounced between Graft's knuckles in intricate patterns as the hard earth closed in around his neck.

Morgan killed all thoughts, letting his muscles take over. He shoved his energy through the closing earth and knocked it back, blasting himself out of the ground and landing just feet in front of the enforcer.

Graft sent the wand behind him, pulling a boulder from below the earth's surface. He launched it at the boy.

Morgan remained in a solid stance. He punched,

sending a hunk of matter through the rock. The shards exploded out, not slowing the dark energy a bit. It persisted to the enforcer, hitting his wand at full impact.

The blast ripped it from him, taking his hand and half of his forearm with it.

Graft's mouth dropped as he looked at his severed arm. Morgan held out his hand, covering the detached limb in darkness before pulling it through the air. The wand bloodied his palm as he removed it.

The boy moved in, watching the man's chin quiver. Graft fell to his knees, choked up. "I'll find out who you are," he said. Morgan used his free arm to squeeze his neck. "What — is this?" Graft asked with the last breath.

"Justice," Morgan said. He held until the man lost consciousness.

Morgan dropped him, arms covered in blood. The hand splattered into the chest when he plopped it in, and he locked it tight with the key from his necklace.

Clenching the chest to his hip he left Graft's body and the damaged earth. His thoughts returned, a deep sadness flooding him. He hobbled down the hill, still able to restrain his tears.

He paused, however, to let his vomit spill onto the long grass.

⟡⊷⊶⟡

Smoke wafted out of Petrie's chimney as Morgan approached, signaling that, even in such early hours of morning, the goblin was awake. Morgan clanked the door knocker.

"Morgan!" Petrie exclaimed. He opened the door wide, allowing him in. Several older goblins lounged in the living room, sipping dark liquid from jars.

Morgan handed him the chest and the key. Petrie clasped the thing and his eyes lit up, like a child about to open a gift. He undid the lock as quickly as he could and ripped the lid wide. He lifted the wand from Graft's palm and smelled it.

His wide grin turned to the others. "The boy did it." All of them stood and surrounded the chest, hollering and patting Morgan's back.

"You did what none of the others could do!" Petrie exclaimed. "So fast, too." He touched Morgan's cheeks with his fingertips. "Why do you look so pale?"

Morgan felt solemn and beat. He had no other expression to portray, so he shrugged. "It's over now," he said.

"I'm so proud of you."

"You — what?" Morgan asked.

"We will gather everyone to induct you officially. You'll be one of us."

One of the elders picked the hand up by the pinky, examined it. "Really clean work, child. You have skill."

A bit of life returned to Morgan's eyes. He slouched down in his chair. "No one else seems to think so," he said.

"Fools," Petrie roared. He stood and fetched a sack from a rickety drawer, tossing it to him.

Morgan undid the lace and looked within. "This is — hundreds. What is this?"

"You didn't think I wasn't going to reward you for your work, did you?" the goblin asked. "We need you, Morgan."

He clutched the sack and stowed it in his pocket. He nodded, making his way toward the door. "Goodnight, Petrie."

Sela didn't show to school the next day.

After a pitiful attempt to concentrate Morgan skipped class. He found her by the creek. She sat with her back to the willow, holding a part of a branch in one hand. With the other she used small slivers of black aether and whittled away at it. When a slice dissolved she'd form another, again and again until the wood took the shape of a man with long hair and a goatee, armor and a wand.

Morgan sat beside her. She turned to look at him, tears trickling from her eyes. He wiped them off and put an arm around her. "What happened?" he asked.

"The Syndicate attacked my dad last night," she said.

"What?" he asked. He squeezed tighter.

Her chin trembled. "I don't understand how they got away with it — none of them have any formal training."

"Maybe not like we have," Morgan said, "but they've been taught to kill."

She shook her head. "My dad, though — he was trained by the Academy. I don't understand. Why'd they do it?"

"I don't know," said Morgan.

"What an awful species, all of them."

"Maybe it wasn't a goblin."

"Only a goblin could do this! They're disgraceful, hateful creatures. They'll blindly follow what anyone tells them."

"And the enforcers don't?"

Sela's voice hardened. "What's that supposed to mean?"

Morgan looked out onto the trickling water, taking a breath. "Maybe — maybe if he had focused on something else, didn't target them so much, maybe they wouldn't be so hateful."

She looked up at him, eyes soaked.

"I don't know," Morgan continued. "My family's school is the only option for education. None of the Council's academies will accept them, right? What would you do?"

"I thought Father was going to let them enroll?"

Morgan shook his head. "Not until I graduate. Everyone thinks it'll take opportunities away from the people."

Sela buried her face into his shoulder. He squeezed her tighter. "Not today," she said with a muffled voice. "I don't need this today." Her voice fractured and weakened. "He hasn't left the medicine room yet. They left him for *dead*."

Morgan undid the tie in her hair, letting her locks fall freely, then wrapped it around his wrist. He touched his nostrils to her head, inhaling the familiar scent of wildflowers. "That's — a bit of an exaggeration," he said.

She lifted her head and looked at him. "What?" she asked. Morgan knew what he did. "You know who did it."

"What do you mean?" he asked.

"I know you know all of them. I know you've spoken with them."

"Not all of them."

"Morgan, I can tell when you're lying." Her eyes

were so wet, there was no way he could look like anything but a blob of color. "Don't do this to me today," she whispered.

Morgan looked back into her eyes, about to cry himself. "You'll never look at me the same," he said.

She wiped her tears, furrowed her brow, absorbed in thought. "I already don't," she said after a minute.

Morgan looked to the ground. "There's a lot going on — this is so much more complicated than it seems. This is centuries of injustice."

She brushed his cheek, working it down to his lower jaw. She squeezed tight. "Tell me," she said softly.

His tear hit her thumb.

Her chin quivered, her tears resuming their flooding. She looked up at him again, this time with a face so horrified he almost didn't recognize her. "*You*?" she asked.

Morgan cried, unable to hold it back anymore. "I had to," he said. "You know I had to." She stood up, but Morgan refused to look at her.

Eventually he did. She was staring at him, shaking, unable to speak. Both her hands boiling with black.

Morgan didn't say a word. She punched, the energy smacking him into the hard rocks of the creek bed. He looked up from the icy water, unable to breathe, as Sela's blurry figure sprinted into the distance.

❖━◇━━◇━❖

When night fell he met the others in the deep woods, where the goblins were scattered around a ring of hollowed trees. The place was of perfect size and discretion — they must have met there a million times.

Each of them wore their formal clothing. When Morgan arrived Petrie rushed to him and handed him a cloak, and he held a spear which pierced Graft's mangled hand.

"The man of the hour!" the goblin yelled. "The one who took Graft's wand right from his bloody hand!" He paused to cackle. "Morgan Bane!"

Few of the others cheered.

"Sit boy, sit," Petrie continued, gesturing Morgan onto a makeshift throne crafted from an enormous trunk. Morgan, moving with caution, did as he was told.

The goblin pulled out a wooden rod from the inner folds of his cloak, on the end of which sat a long, white fang with a black tip.

"You look scared, boy," he said.

"I'm not scared," Morgan returned.

"Uneasy, then?"

Morgan thought for a moment, but shook his head. He didn't know how he felt. It was new, all of this. He looked up at the goblin hunched over him, watched him look onto the crowd. Then he locked eyes with Sedro, who was still bruised and swollen.

Petrie handed the spear to the goblin left of him. He grabbed hold of Morgan's wrist, pulling the cloak sleeve up to his elbow. He pinned it to the armrest of the throne and held up the rod with his other hand.

"A hollow fang from the rarest serpent of the island, considered extinct by most records," Petrie said. "Ferver's creation, of course." He held Morgan's palm up, digging the tooth into his forearm.

Morgan winced from the pain.

The goblins watched as Petrie did this. He dug and

scraped into the boy for several minutes before straightening up and stowing the tool. He licked his thumb and wiped away the blood, revealing a sprig tattoo. A hollow branch of black ink was etched on Morgan's arm; small leaves stemmed off it, creating a simple design.

"The Sprig of Death," said Petrie, comparing it to the symbol on his own forearm. "For the growth of life."

Cheers came from the crowd.

"Welcome," said Petrie. "To — "

Sedro's scream interrupted him. He was pulled into the dark woods, disappearing immediately. The goblins all took a fighting stance, instantly alert.

Then Sedro's head rolled back to the middle of them.

Everyone wailed. "Graft?!" one of them yelled — they looked in all directions, seeing nothing.

Petrie pulled Graft's wand from his cloak and pointed it to where Sedro had been snatched. Then Cogg was yanked into the trees, and his head came flying back.

"The enforcers are here!" shouted one of them, barging up to the throne. Morgan stood up, fists at his side as he made his way to where the goblins were being shredded one by one.

The sight made Morgan queasy. Their brutalized corpses reaffirmed it for him: he had done the right thing. He looked at Sedro's head, thinking of their last interactions. His whole body started to tremble as he stood in the middle of the clearing, eyes panning in all directions as they waited for the next kill.

An enforcer walked up in full uniform, without a wand, and her armor was so big it nearly fell off of her. Morgan's shoulders softened. "Sela," he said, "you shouldn't have come here."

She held up her black, crackling fists.

"Come on," he said, hands out. "This isn't what you think it is."

Black matter formed around Morgan's neck, tightened. "I thought I knew you," she said.

"You do..." Morgan tried to get the words out. He fell to his knees. She came closer, holding her shoulders straight and chest out.

She looked disgusted.

Petrie stepped in front of Morgan, drawing the sprig from his cloak folds. At the sight of the weapon none of the goblins made a sound; they inched out of the way.

Petrie whipped his wrist. A dark-purple plume of smoke shot out of the sprig, and Sela was consumed whole.

As its energy depleted the smoke wafted down to the forest floor, Sela's lifeless body falling with it.

Morgan grabbed ahold of her. He stood, shaking, as Petrie's pupils twitched at the sight of the slaughter. "No more!" he wailed. "The next to die — is Graft!" He looked at Morgan, as if it were a command.

Morgan looked down at Sela's body in his arms, then up at Petrie. "Isn't this enough?" he asked. He kept examining the field of bodies, the forest floor painted burgundy.

"You already know the answer, don't you?" the goblin asked.

Morgan looked at the goblin's face, took in the horror in his eyes. He nodded and walked slowly away, carrying Sela's corpse home. The remaining goblins moved out of his way, not making even a breath of sound.

Malachi hadn't come home in the days that passed, but this was such a common occurrence that Morgan had learned to ignore it. He wandered into his father's study, surrounded by several stories of bookshelves. Much of their contents were his father's own journals.

Books fell to the rug as he climbed the shelves, uncapping boxes and searching tirelessly.

At last he revealed a thin case with a velvet interior — his father's wand.

He took it to the willow and sat next to the small mound where he had buried her, wildflowers growing at her head.

He sat with her as the water tricked down, carving into the earth and smoothening rocks. He was listening and breathing, but not thinking much at all.

He looked at the sprig etched into his arm, above Sela's hair tie. The scent of it drenched his nose, softening his heart and bringing tears to his eyes. He tapped the wand to his tattoo, thinning and stretching the color. At the top of the twig he dragged the ink around and around, layers and layers of thin petals forming until the top of the sprig led to a vibrant bloom: an agoseris.

The image of the forest floor bruised his thoughts, and Graft remained on the loose.

He touched the dirt with two fingers, eyes closed. He absorbed as much as he could of this moment, this calm, before tying the key around his neck; before night fell again.

As formidable waves crashed into the boulders below, Mavis slid the casket lid over her cousin's still body. It was the last time Kivati would see his brother's face.

Mavis had whittled the box herself with aether, turning it a brilliant, glossy black. After the crowd of goblins had said their final goodbyes they watched as dark energy consumed the casket. Mavis lowered it an inch over the ocean, and it floated farther and farther from the mansion.

Kivati watched as his brother drifted slowly away from him forever. He thought more about what the young goblin had asked him. Morgan's relationship to Kivati had never been warm, but rather full of jealousy and resentment. Hoogdal was right, there was little warmth to Morgan at all. He was the coldest killer Tatu had ever seen, and he wielded his magic with a strength few could comprehend. Not from fire, like Kivati, but from a darkness colder than ice: the lone substance filling the universe's vast emptiness.

And yet, he had given him his life.

When the casket became just a dot against the sliver of sun remaining, Mavis pressed a swift palm toward the tiles below her feet to send Morgan's cold body into the frozen depths forever.

Kivati could almost feel his brother hit the ocean floor. That's when he felt something else among the crippling cold. It had always been there, flickering and wishing to be freed.

It was present when Morgan sliced each victim to pieces, present when he fought for even the cruelest of goblins to receive an education, present when the village mob murdered his mother in defiance, present when a beast slayed his father, present when he filled the role of headmaster, present when Tatu itself crumbled by his own hand, present when he jumped in front of the blast that was meant for his brother.

It was present, too, when his corpse sank deep into the icy void for eternity — there was a fire within Morgan, hidden. One Kivati couldn't conjure in a dream.

# SAM FLETCHER

## ABOUT THE AUTHOR

Sam Fletcher wrote the first story that takes place on Tatu when he was ten. He is now a reporter in Washington's Columbia Basin, meaning he switches between the use of the Oxford comma several times throughout the day. His short fiction can be found in *Spark: A Creative Anthology*, *upstreet Literary Magazine*, Cloaked Press, and elsewhere. To get the best feel for his current projects, find him at fletcherstories.com or @fletcherstories on Instagram and Twitter.

# Dowser in a Dead Town

## Jonathan Mast

Vultures circled above the town. Adobe structures shimmered in the desert heat. "Probably not a good sign," Darren muttered to himself.

His horse didn't see fit to respond.

The man wore his long, dark coat and a wide-brimmed hat. His pistol sat in the holster at his side, spurs jingling as his horse plodded along the broken dirt road. Mountains rose to the east of the town, but otherwise an empty plain lay before him. Dry bushes tried to convince him that there was life here, but he knew better. This was a dead place, and that was a dead town. Now it was a dead town, anyway; Darren was probably too late to save anyone.

Again.

He rode down the silent main street, puffs of dust wafting up with each hoof-fall. Wind breathed against sun-bleached, adobe buildings that lined the street. Nearly-white light burned from the sky, so he and his horse cast a black, deep shadow. No one sat in front of the saloon, and no children complained from the quaint schoolhouse.

No sheriff watched from the office.

Darren directed his horse to the town well, situated on the right side of the street where a low, pale wall of brick surrounded what had once been a fountain. He dismounted, taking off his hat and waving it at his sweaty face. He stumbled into the wall, leaning over it, but whatever had fed the fountain was stuffed up with dust.

He sighed, putting the hat back on. Darren raised spread fingers over the fountain, closing his eyes and concentrating.

Something below the fountain rumbled ever so slightly as water started to flow. The interior of the fountain turned to mud, and then muddy water.

Darren plunged his hands into the liquid and lifted them to his face. He took it in, his horse joining him, and the man gasped after taking a long drink. He uncapped a canteen that was slung over his shoulder and filled it, and then did the same to another that hung from the saddle. After drinking again he finally turned and sat on the well's edge, looking around the town.

Nothing moved.

He shook his head and pressed his lips together. Taking a handful of water he splashed his face, then stood and made his way across the street to a building that was clearly a saloon. The horse elected to stay by the running water of the fountain.

Tables stood outside under a pergola, where chairs were tipped in the wind and half-buried in dust. Darren placed his hand on the grip of his pistol, ready to draw. He stepped through the door and into the darkness within.

Sand.

Sand everywhere. It was heaped in dunes against the bar, and against the far wall. He stepped around to see behind the bar.

Several men lay half-buried in the dust. Some clutched pistols, and one cradled a rifle, but none breathed.

Darren took off his hat and nodded. "Gents, sorry I got here late," he rumbled. "If it means anything to you I plan on making it right."

The corpses elected to keep any response to themselves.

He placed his hat back on. Some stairs on the other side of the room led to a second story, so he made his way up as his boots thudded on the wood. A hallway lined with doors led away from the top of the stairs; each door was closed. He opened the first to find a bedroom unoccupied, other than sand, and the second was the same. In the third he found two women covered in dust that dribbled from their mouths and eyes.

He removed his hat again. "Apologies, ladies." He knelt. "Any of you religious?" He reached a hand out toward the throat of one which bore a cross.

"Don't." A woman's voice whispered behind him.

He spun, his pistol drawn and ready.

A young woman leaned against the doorframe across the hallway. Her pale, blue dress was torn in many places, and her face looked like she'd been buried in dirt. Her long, dark hair had taken on a dusty color.

He reholstered his weapon. "Not many survive a dusting."

"Don't touch my mother," the young woman said.

"Wouldn't think of it! Just wanted to give a good

burial if that's what they'd want, plus it would help keep the varmints out." He stood a pace away as he inspected her dirty face. "I've unstopped the well."

She huffed a rough laugh. "How? Ain't no one can unbury a dusted well."

"Some of us can." He stepped around her and headed back down the hall.

The woman slowly made her way after him down the steps, and when she spied the gushing fountain she rushed across the street - thankfully the horse had the good sense to get out of her way and let her collapse against the wall. She buried her head in the water, drinking greedily.

When she finally returned to the surface for air, Darren asked, "You the only one make it through?"

She rolled herself over and sat on the ground, back to the pale bricks as she squinted in the piercing light. "Yeah. We deal with dusters all the time. They come in, make a fuss and then ask to be paid off. Sheriff's a rifleman, though. Usually one shot and he can take them out easy enough. This one, though..." She shook her head and swallowed, "just blew into town. Didn't make any demands, just whipped up the air and killed everyone he could find."

"He didn't kill you."

She waited a moment before answering. "He didn't find me."

Darren raised an eyebrow, but didn't ask.

The woman looked him up and down. "You law?"

Darren shook his head.

She gave a half-smile. "Well, that's good. Wouldn't be so good if some man came in here just to arrest me."

"And you are?"

She shrugged. "Laying low."

"Ah."

"You're a dowser, ain't you?"

Darren took a bandanna out of his coat pocket and dunked it in the water, tipping his hat off his head and wrapping the bandanna around his black hair. "Might say that."

She shook her head. "And you're chasing a duster?"

Darren shrugged.

"So you're insane."

He offered her a half-smile. "I've been called worse, ma'am." He crouched down to look her in the eyes. "But now, this duster, he say anything?"

"No."

"You see him before you went to ground?"

She shook her head. "Nah. I saw the cloud coming in and hid."

Darren nodded. "Well, how long ago?"

"Just yesterday."

"You were able to check everyone else in town? No other survivors, you're sure?"

"Look, mister, there ain't a lot of us here." She shrugged. "Easy enough to walk around. I was looking for water too, since you need a lot of it here to keep living. Had to take some canteens off the dead."

"And you dowere yelling at me for looting corpses."

"That was my Mama you were looking at."

"Ah, that's right. She's why you hang around a town where you're not appreciated?"

She looked away.

"Your mama don't appreciate you either, huh?"

She kept looking away.

"Well, I'm a dowser, yes. And yes, I'm after that duster that blew into town. He's trying to be headman of these plains, so he's been taking all the prettiest girls from towns to make sure certain other towns don't spring up." He offered a grim smile.

The woman frowned. "Why? Without towns it's just a bunch of dirt and rocks out here."

"Dusters love dirt and rocks. They also love being bully-boys, whipping up storms and shutting down towns til they get their way. Most towns, like yours here, are protected by their rifleman. Take a spark and grow it a thousand times? Anyone who can control flame can face down most dusters."

The woman nodded.

"But this guy, he's smart. He's not hitting just any town; he hit this town special."

The woman scoffed. "Ain't nothing special about it."

He raised an eyebrow and glanced at the well. "Your little well here – it's special. Not connected to a spring, so it's not just a trickle of water. There's an entire reservoir underground – I can feel it. Normally ain't nobody got time for us dowsers, not enough water out here for us to do anything worth doing, but here? With a little urging I bet I could make all that water come up. And then, well, your duster will have something big to deal with."

"And the duster, he knew there was water under the city?"

Darren shrugged. "He knew enough. He figured it was easier to take the town out than risk it, so it's my guess he's got a blacksmith in his employ. Might try breaking whatever stone is down there holding the water, but black-smiths don't fly on the wind like dusters. He's probably on his way out yet."

"So you're here now."

"Yup, and I'm going to wait for him."

"What about me?"

Darren shrugged. "If the town had still been here I figured I'd stay at the saloon and drink until the duster showed up, or if he'd already been here I'd bury the dead if I got the chance. You? You do what you want."

The woman looked away. "I hated this town."

Darren waited.

"They thought I wasn't worth anything, but it ain't like there's anything else I can do right now. No horses left in town, and I ain't gonna get far on foot, so I guess I'm staying."

Darren nodded. "Well then, I guess you are." He looked around, squinting. "But, if you're staying, I'll need to be calling you something."

"Bess." She tucked a smile into the corner of her mouth. "They call me Barrens Bess."

Darren nodded. "The 'thief with a heart of gold'. I've heard of you."

"And you? You got a name?"

"Darren."

"Just Darren?"

"Just Darren."

"Well, Darren, what's the next step?"

"Got any rain barrels around?"

They were able to gather six rain barrels. Six empty, dry rain barrels. Darren found stables behind the saloon and put his horse there with plenty of fodder, though it was dusty. He removed the saddle and let the horse do what it wanted.

Bess waited by the fountain with the gathered barrels. "So? What're we doing with these?"

"Filling them." Darren cracked his knuckles. "Let's see here...if I just think hard enough then maybe I can do this." He raised his hands toward the fountain, the water inside rippling and bending upwards as sweat stood out on Darren's forehead. Keeping one hand pointed at the bulging water he pointed the other toward a rain barrel. The water lifted itself in a clear arc and poured itself into the barrel, and once the barrel was filled Darren dropped his hands and fell to the ground.

Bess rushed over. "I ain't never seen anything like that!"

"Dowsers don't get the chance to show off much." He pointed. "Hand me the canteen?"

She brought it over to him. "What're the barrels for?"

"Insurance. I need some water close by, I think." He gulped from the canteen as he lay on the ground. "If I can control the water I might be able to hit the duster hard enough without using the water from below."

"You got winded picking up water and putting it in one barrel."

"Yeah, well, it's a long shot. God loves long shots. He told me that once."

"Liar."

"Sure I'm lying, but at least I make it sound good."

He was able to fill the rest of the barrels with brief breaks between each. Moving the barrels to either side of the street was a bit of a harder undertaking, but with much grunting, and some assistance from a dolly, they were able to do it.

"Now what?" Bess asked, panting.

"Well, we need to take care of the dead. Ain't no good if varmints get in here."

So they spent the rest of the afternoon digging. Bess made a guess to how many were dead, and they started hollowing out as many holes as they could. The sun took on a yellow tint as the day wore on, the sky eventually turning orange as evening settled in. The moon started rising.

Darren wiped the sweat from his face.

"If you're a dowser, why don't you just tell the sweat to stay out of your eyes?" Bess asked, panting. She wore a wide-brimmed straw hat to keep the sun off.

Darren shrugged. "Never thought about it."

She shook her head as she lifted another spadeful of dirt. "Sheriff Thompkins used his abilities every chance he got. He'd spark some flint and use it to light every lamp in town if you let him, and every duster I see just flies everywhere. They forget how to walk, I think. But you? You just sweat and act like any other man, besides filling up some rain barrels."

"Dowsing's pretty useless."

"And you think you're going to take down a duster?"

"Got some barrels now and got the reservoir below, don't I?" He huffed a laugh. "Ought to be good for something."

"Not if you're not already used to using that kind of power."

"Well, maybe I'll just die with the rest of your town then, won't I? Better dead than what he does with the towns he lets live. Serving a duster ain't exactly a good life." His eyes faded to a faraway place for a moment. "I don't intend that anyone has to serve this bastard much longer." He climbed out of the grave he'd been digging. "We should probably bury whoever we can while the sun's still in the sky."

Bess nodded and clambered out of her hole. "All right." She followed him back into town. It wasn't terribly far, maybe a hundred yards.

Darren gestured. "Where should we start?"

"They're all dead. Don't really matter, does it?"

"They're all dead, and that's why we show them respect."

"They never showed me any."

"And they never will. Dead people don't pay much mind to the living." Darren paced to the fountain and took a deep drink. "Well, I say we start with the women in the saloon. That acceptable to you?"

Bess paused for a drink herself and then nodded. "Go ahead, I'll get a cart. Your horse pull a cart?"

"Not unless you got some good food for him in return."

"Well, I guess it's you and me pulling then."

"So it is." Darren headed across the street and into the darkness of the saloon. He tipped his hat to the corpses behind the bar and made his way upstairs. Observing the women lying covered in dust on the floor of the room he knelt, taking off his hat. "Ladies, I'm going to move you now. I'm sorry, I don't know you or what you held about where you're at now. The graves ain't nothing special, but I figure you should be shown some respect."

Bess came up the stairs and leaned against the doorframe behind him, her arms crossed.

Darren paused. "Something wrong?"

"Just waiting," Bess answered.

He paused a moment, then refocused on the bodies. "Don't mind her any. I hear that maybe you didn't, anyway, but we can't have you sitting in here where you'll attract some nasty beasts. We need what's left of the town for the living. So, away we go." He put his hat back on and turned to Bess. "Right, let's get them moving." Darren bent to pick up a woman's shoulders.

"Not her, not yet."

Darren raised an eyebrow and moved to the other woman.

"Good." Bess took her feet. They hauled her down the stairs and placed her on the cart Bess had found in the stables. Back up the stairs to the one woman lying there.

"Can I have a moment?" Bess asked.

"Yes, ma'am." Darren stepped out and down the stairs. He put his hands in his pockets. Upstairs he heard shouting, then some crying and more shouting.

He turned to the bar. Nope. Of course the duster had made sure that all the drinks were gone, and if he took the drinks maybe he took other things too.

Maybe other people.

Darren whistled a tuneless song.

There was some more shouting from upstairs, then

Bess appeared. "I'm ready to move her now."

They hauled her down to the cart and piled her in. Darren tried to make sure they were both respectable. "Think there's room for a few more?" he asked.

"Depends how tall you want to stack them."

He grunted and headed back into the shadows. He took off his hat as he addressed the men behind the bar. "Gentlemen, I realize that at least one or two of you might have been respectable. You wouldn't want to be on top of women that you didn't vow to have and to hold. Well, we're trying to do right by you, so please pardon. I have no idea who you belonged with, if anyone."

"You could always ask me," Bess said.

"Yes. Well. If I knew, then I'd have to follow up on it." He shook his head. "Pardon the interruption, gents. We're going to get you buried." He replaced his hat. "Take this one's legs."

They were able to fit five corpses onto the cart, and before dragging the cart out to the grave sites they returned to the fountain. As she plunged her hands into the water Bess asked, "So why the show? If you're showing respect, shouldn't you show respect? And if it don't matter, why even talk to them like that?"

Darren shrugged. "Makes me feel better."

"But you don't want to do the work of actually showing respect."

"I'm showing more respect than robbing the dead."

Bess shook her head and chuckled. "Well, there is that."

"There is that." Darren took another drink. "Come on, we should get moving."

Grunting and straining they pulled the cart out to the graves, then hauled the bodies out of the cart and into each shallow hole. "You want to say anything before we cover them up?" he asked.

Bess smiled. "I think I got my last words in already."

"Suit yourself."

With their shovels they buried the dead, and they were able to haul out three more carts of bodies before the sky turned bruise-purple.

"We better take shelter," Darren said.

Bess nodded. "Varmints'll be out soon."

"They thick around here?"

"Not too bad, but you know how they get after the smell of death gets out. And without the people here in town to scare them off they'll come right up into the buildings."

"Hopefully they nose around out here and not in the town then." Darren scanned the dry plain. "With only two of us we won't be able to do much to protect ourselves."

Bess gazed back at the town. "I've got a place that should keep us safe."

"Hope it's big enough for my horse, or I'll have to spend the night with him here."

Darren whistled in appreciation.

Bess offered half a smile in the fading light. "I'm not always welcome in town. People are afraid of what I might steal next, so I always have this handy."

It was a cave, but one hidden by a small labyrinth of

ridges in the hills around a mountainous spur. The dirty, brown rocks surrounded them with cover, and even if someone was standing ten feet away they'd never spot the place. Darren could already feel the call of what made this particular cave so special: water flowed within.

Darren closed his eyes and savored the feel of a spring welling up from the reservoir below. "How'd you find it?"

"First time I stole I ran. My dad was going to kill me, I think."

"What'd you take that was so important?"

Bess turned away for a moment. "The combination to the bank's safe."

"Your dad was the banker?"

"The man in charge, yeah, and no one else had that combination. The crazy thing was I didn't even realize what I was doing. I was just a kid, you know? I looked at Dad, and all of a sudden these numbers dawned in my head. Stole them without ever meaning to." She huffed a laugh. "Well, I ran. Dad was in trouble, and I knew it was my fault. People were getting angry at him."

"Why didn't you just tell him the number?"

"Kids don't always use their smarts. Anyway, I ended up wandering to the ridge here. The sun rose, and of course I was idiot enough to not even take a canteen. I stumbled all over, and was walking right up there when I slipped and fell. Found myself at the entrance to the cave. Crawled in just to escape the sun, and found the spring inside. Drank, stayed out all night and wandered home the next day. That's when we figured out what I was."

"A thief?"

"Yep, a thief."

"You tell your dad the combination number then?"

Bess laughed again. "Yep."

"When did you start traveling?"

"Not long after. Once I was old enough that boys started noticing me, well, I'd steal little bits and pieces of them. Never on purpose, but when they're looking in your eyes it's hard not to take what they're offering. I felt real dirty, so I left to try and find a boy that maybe wasn't just trying to get my clothes off."

"You ever find any?"

"Yeah, surprisingly, but usually they were chasing after something else. Money. Power." She shrugged. "But then I started finding I could control what I took from people. Got to be real useful."

"Except back home, where they knew who you were."

"Except back home, where they knew who I was." She shook her head. "Mom never appreciated what I did, no matter how many mayors I was able to bring to their knees or how many people I protected." And then she turned toward Darren. "And now here I am, with you."

"Yes, ma'am."

"I've told you my story. Time to tell yours."

In the distance something large howled.

Darren's hand strayed toward his holster. "Maybe once we're safely in the cave."

"I'm not letting you in there unless I know who you are."

"You're going to steal from me?"

"Whatever I take, you don't have any more. You willing to risk that?"

Darren narrowed his eyes. His hand didn't move from his pistol. "I show respect to the dead, and I show respect to you. I'm not a man that'll force himself on you, if that's what you're afraid of. In fact, I suggest you stay here tomorrow when I go back to town. That duster should be back soon, I'd wager, and you don't need to be involved in that."

"Why are you trying to take out a duster? Why this one?"

Darren shrugged. "You seen how many people he's killed? That's reason enough."

"The dead bodies didn't scare you. You respected them, yes, but you weren't afraid to touch them or carry them. You've seen a lot of death already."

"I could say the same to you, ma'am."

They watched each other for a time. The sky grew darker. The thing howled in the distance again. Another howl answered it.

Bess shook her head. "You're lucky I've got a heart of gold."

"Luck is about all I've got going for me."

✧━◈━◇━━━◇━◈━✧

The cave was big enough for the horse too. Darren led him in and unsaddled him, rubbing him down and giving him some oats. The horse was quite pleased with this turn of events, even if a cave was a little unusual.

Bess pulled a boulder up against the mouth of the cave so nothing could get in, then they drank deeply from the water in the shallow pool within. Darren took out some jerky, which they chewed silently. Finally Darren turned his back on her, laid down and slept.

In the morning he woke sore and stiff, but ready for the day. Bess snored softly as she slept, and Darren drank from the pool before pushing the boulder away from the entrance of the cave. Orange light was seeping in: good. The piercing white of most of the day hadn't hit yet. He stepped out of the cave, then swore.

The dirt around the entrance to the cave showed pawprints, large pawprints. He counted at least three different sets. He'd hoped they'd be happy in the town, but the varmints had their scent.

Well now, it wouldn't matter whether or not the duster ended up winning their little fight, would it? They were all dead anyway.

He returned to the cave to check on the horse. It could stay at the cave; no use killing it in the fight. Darren grabbed the two canteens and filled them before stepping out of the hideout.

"Sneaking away?" Bess said.

"Not anymore."

Bess stretched on the ground and stood. "Let me get this straight: you're going to fight with a duster. You think you have a chance because of the reservoir under the town, but let's be honest - you're just going to wind up dead, ain't you?"

Darren nodded. "Could be."

"Well, this duster is a man. If he's been traveling by dust-storm a while he might be getting lonely, and a pretty lady might be able to get a mite closer to him than you could. I might get close enough to steal from him, even take his memory of how to use the air to whip up the storms."

Darren nodded again. "I suppose you could, ma'am, but you could have done that when he first came to town. You didn't."

Bess didn't answer.

"I've been thinking about that. You've fought against bullies most of your life; that's why people tend to hate you. Everyone's a bully, given the chance, and we all like shoving other folks around. Then this bully comes into town. He doesn't shove his weight around, he just wants to destroy the town. You went and hid, claimed he didn't find you, and yet every room of every building in town seems to be sandblasted. Every room. It's pretty clear you weren't out here when he attacked; ain't nobody been in that cave for a few years, near as I can tell. Something just ain't adding up, ma'am."

Bess pressed her lips together. She looked away, toward the sunrise where the orange of the sky had already begun to fade toward white. A light breeze stirred her disheveled hair. "I figured he was just another bully. Everyone saw him coming, of course, and our sheriff was a good rifleman. I was just going to let it all go, and even when he killed the sheriff, even when the dust swallowed up everything, I still thought it wasn't a big deal. He'd demand some money, some girls, whatever. The town deserved it, you know?"

Darren waited.

"So when he didn't make any demands, when the winds pounded at the town, when the sand killed more and more people, I hid. I didn't lie about that."

"So how'd you actually survive?"

"I did what I always do: I stole. The duster started searching the town, making sure there were no survivors, and I was by myself in my room above the saloon. When the door whipped open and his sand came in it tore into me, but I was able to steal what he saw from him. He forgot I was there, so he left."

"Why didn't you take more then?"

"I panicked." She turned her face to the town, to the few adobe buildings bleached in the sun.

"Seems to me a panicked person would just flail and take whatever she could. A person like that would just grab and run, not make a precise, calculated attack."

She glared at Darren. "Habit. I've been caught more times than I can count, cowboy, and you know what I've trained myself to do? To just take me out of their memory so there's no trail. If I stole more than that they'd know something was wrong. Someone gets up, visits a room and turns around to leave. They don't remember why they came. Easy enough thing to do, but here I got caught, so I did what I always do."

He chewed on that answer for a minute. "You can steal that fast?"

"I can steal what someone's thinking of, and if they're thinking of me I take it from them. And yeah, I'm that fast. I'm the best."

Darren gazed at the dead town. "Well, looks like I need your services."

They were silent on the walk back.

Large tracks surrounded the graves, and all the bodies had been dug up in the night. Darren took off his hat and stood over them for a moment.

"You ain't saying nothing," Bess said.

"No one to say words to." He replaced the hat. "So, here's the plan. The blacksmith comes into town, I'll take care of him fast. That should draw in the duster, and when he arrives I'll pull up all the water from the reservoir. I'll nearly drown him. I'll be able to hold him in the water. You need eye contact for your thieving?"

She nodded.

"Right. I'll keep him alive long enough, and once you've stolen what I want he's dead. Sound simple enough?"

"And all I do is keep out of the way until you've got him pinned?"

"That's the plan." Darren gave a smile. "Ain't often a dowser gets to show off, but today...well, town's gonna get a little wet."

As they came into town it appeared the varmints had also carried away the dead they'd been unable to bury.

"Hungry critters you got around here," Darren said.

Bess nodded. "There's a reason we didn't let kids play outdoors after dark; also a reason the cattlemen have to pay well to make sure their beefs are watched over."

"There a lot of outlying ranches?"

"Maybe used to be." Bess looked around at the horizon. "I'm guessing your duster took care of most of them."

Darren nodded.

They stopped at the fountain to drink up and fill their canteens – two for each of them.

"You been trying to figure out if there's anything worth stealing in my head?" Darren asked.

"I looked."

"What'd you find?"

"That you're someone I might steal from if I were on a job, since you got a lot of dark spots in there. Someone would probably pay for the kinds of things you know."

"Sure enough."

"But I'm not on a job. Right now I want to take care of this duster, and then maybe find a way back to civilization."

Darren smiled again. "I appreciate that, and now it's probably time for you to hide." He pointed.

On the horizon a smudge slowly grew: a dust cloud.

Bess wrinkled her nose. "He alone?"

"Should have that blacksmith with him."

"All right, I'll take cover. You better get the bastard."

"That's my plan, ma'am."

Bess looked at him, back toward the smudge, then back at Darren. She nodded and trotted toward the saloon.

Darren took a deep breath and another deep drink. The sun burned at him, bright-white now. He stepped out to the middle of the street as the dust cloud grew. It reached the top of the buildings from his perspective, then grew taller. It dwarfed the sky, a great thunderhead of dust.

The air had smelled of dirt before, but now the scent grew heavy. Darren pulled a bandanna over his nose and mouth, his hand resting on his pistol still in its holster. He lifted his chin to the cloud, watching as it grew over the buildings and surrounded them in massive billows. Static discharged within the cloud, sending lightning strikes arcing through the dust. In the distance varmints howled.

On the horizon a dark speck appeared, growing steadily larger. A chestnut horse trotted toward the town, a man upon it, and as he drew nearer Darren saw he wore heavy boots, heavy gloves and no hat. Dark goggles covered his eyes, and he drew the horse to a halt about fifty paces down the street before lifting the goggles from his face. He smiled. "Well, you're a dense one, ain't ya?"

"You the blacksmith?" Darren called.

"Yep. Been hired to seal up what's below."

"Can't let you do that. You go on your way, peaceable. I got no quarrel with you." Darren's hand still rested on his pistol.

The blacksmith crossed his hands over the pommel of the saddle. "Well now, that's too bad. I been paid too well to just go when someone who thinks he's someone tells me to."

Darren drew.

The blacksmith flicked a finger.

Before Darren could pull the trigger the barrel of his pistol sealed shut, and he tossed the useless weapon aside. "Well, now, that's inconvenient."

"Son, I'm good at what I do. Ain't a man can draw fast enough to threaten me." He tilted his head. "Now, I suggest you run and hide before you get yourself killed. You ain't got no quarrel with me? Well, ain't got no quarrel with you."

"I'm sorry to say I can't do that."

"Well, today's just not your day then."

The ground rumbled below Darren. He sprinted toward the blacksmith as the road began to shift. A slab of stone shot up beneath his feet, flinging him into the air, and as he flew he reached out toward a barrel.

It exploded, wood splinters flying in a sudden gush of water.

Darren skidded on his side along the street. The blacksmith jumped and turned toward the exploded barrel, even though the worst he got was wet, and maybe a few splinters. He turned back, eyebrow raised. "Well now, that's interesting. Ain't never fought a dowser before. If that's the worst you can do, though, this is gonna be brief."

Darren sat up, panting. "Oh, I got more." He flung a hand to another rain barrel. It burst, though this time he could concentrate. Not flying through the air can be helpful to a man. The water shot toward the blacksmith and his horse, the sudden torrent carrying slivers of wood and twisted metal. The white light gleamed in the rushing water as the mass struck the horse's flank. The creature reared, Darren taking the opportunity to stand.

The blacksmith clutched at his mount and sputtered. Behind him another barrel exploded, slivers striking the animal. After the third barrel the blacksmith fell off his horse, and thankfully the animal had the good sense to gallop away. Its hooves splattered the blacksmith with mud.

Another barrel exploded, the blacksmith throwing his arms over his head.

"You about ready to just head on out of here?" Darren asked.

The blacksmith rolled and flicked his fingers. Darren dodged as another shard of stone shot up from the street, but he couldn't avoid the second. He fell to the ground, the two men panting and staring at each other as they lay on the street.

The blacksmith grinned just before he flicked his fingers.

"Like Hell!" Darren grunted. The last barrel exploded as he twisted his arm to guide the water.

The packed earth of the road beneath him exploded. He gritted his teeth as he flung his hands down, water from the barrel arcing and shooting down from above. Wooden planks rode the waves as the blacksmith cried out. The wood impaled him, the earth beneath him turning red.

Darren stood from the heap of stones. He held his side. Probably a rib broken. Maybe more. "That was a lot harder than it should have been," he groaned, "but now it's time to face the main event."

The dust cloud had grown. It towered over the town, sending out tendrils to surround the buildings. Darren grunted as the wind struck him like a wall, his coat trying to drag him away. The fountain stopped flowing as the basin choked with mud. Thunder rumbled in the cloud. The sun turned red in the dust, the air growing chill.

Varmints appeared out of the dust. Dog-like things almost the size of horses, all claws, teeth, mangy fur and slobbery muzzles. Darren reached for more water under the town so he could use it to protect himself.

Nothing.

The blacksmith had finished the job; he was cut off from the reservoir. Darren had nothing. All the barrels were used, and the fountain was stopped. Even his pistol was useless, and now these hungry beasts were running right toward him.

He stood his ground, fists at his side. Breathing without pain took up most of his concentration.

The varmints dashed past him and disappeared into the haze of the dust storm, though one paused just long enough to pick up the blacksmith in its maw before running past.

"Storm must'a spooked them," Darren told himself.

Once more thunder rolled, and the sun turned nearly dark. Static lightning provided light as the dust cleared out. The storm raged around and over the town, but in the center calm reigned. A shadow appeared in the storm that resolved into a floating figure, the person stretching out his legs as he landed on the street.

"You have any idea how much it costs to hire a blacksmith?" The man sneered as he approached. The gaunt figure stood tall, wearing a long, dust-colored coat and a dark hat. His skin was very, very pale. "Let me see your face so I can kill you proper."

Darren pulled off the bandanna that had hidden him.

The duster's mouth stretched into a grin. "Darren! Well, it has been a while, hasn't it?" He cracked his knuckles. "You think you have any chance in taking me out? Really? You dowsers are good for tricks at the bar, sure, but against the fury of the wind? You're a nothing."

"I reckon so," Darren answered. He was awful thirsty with all this sand blowing around; too bad the fountain was stopped up. He grunted and pulled at the reservoir below. Could he pull any water through the rock wall? Sweat trickled down his face. "I reckon I don't stand a chance against you, not since your blacksmith did his job." He sighed, then grimaced in pain. "He did a number on me, too."

"You just rolling over? Dying for me? That might be the smartest thing you ever did."

"Let a man have a last drink." He groaned as he reached toward the canteen slung over his shoulder, letting the strap fall as he lifted the metal container. Sweat continued to pour down his face, his hands shaking. He unscrewed its cap and lifted the canteen to his lips, taking a swig.

"I'd think you'd want something stronger," the duster said.

Darren flung the canteen. It sped through the air, water exploding from the container and shattering the metal. Shards wrapped in water shot toward the duster, who dropped to the ground. The metal flew harmlessly over him.

Darren roared as he rushed toward the duster, and then his feet weren't on the ground anymore.

"Nice try, but I control the winds. I can pluck you off the earth as easily as I control the dust cloud." The duster shook his head. "You were always such a failure, weren't you?" He stepped close. "What do you think? Just let the dust run over your body? I've been learning how to carve people up, when I take my time. Polish them up just so."

A snake of dust whipped through the street.

"I think it could be fun to just take you apart, piece by piece. I could fling the dust and take off just a finger at a time, or maybe your hand. Start grinding against your stump, taking just a little at a time." The duster licked his lips. "For old times' sake."

"Put him down!"

The duster turned his head toward the saloon door. Bess stood across the street, her eyes blazing.

"What's this? Does Darren have a new friend?" The duster laughed.

"This is between you and me, Abel!" Blood dribbled from Darren's nose.

The duster flicked a finger. The winds pushed Darren, pinning him high against the wall of the bank. He strained against the air, his hands balled into fists. Veins stood out on his forehead. He couldn't move; the pressure was too great.

The duster huffed a laugh and turned toward Bess. He raised a pale eyebrow. "What do you want with a broken man like that? That nothing? No one wants him, not even his wife." He savored the words he spoke. He took a swaggering step toward Bess. "He's going to die today. You don't have to, of course."

As Abel approached Bess Darren struggled, grunting under the strain. He wasn't pushing against the winds, though.

The dust circled the town at dizzying speeds. Lightning arced above, striking the ground beyond the town, and something howled outside the walls of dust. Shadows moved in the storm.

The duster continued, "I'm guessing you didn't come here with him. You must be from this town, which means you're clever to have lived this long. I could use clever people. Come with me."

Bess met his stare, her eyes searching him. "Where do you keep the women?"

The duster smiled ever so briefly, and then a look of confusion came over his face.

Bess chuckled. "Now we can get all your treasures."

Her laughter was cut off. She turned red, her hands flying to her throat as dust wrapped around her.

"You know there's air inside a human body? Dusters usually focus on the big stuff, like making windstorms and all that, but I like looking at the little things too. And, right now, all the air's leaving your body. You're gonna suffocate, woman."

Bess fell to her knees, her face turning an ugly shade of purple. Her hands went to her throat, clawing and scratching at her own skin. Dust lashed against her face, tiny cuts oozing blood across all of her.

The duster laughed.

"Let her go!" Darren roared. He pushed harder.

Thunder rumbled, and something below the ground echoed.

The duster turned his laugh on Darren as he moved toward his captive. "Look at this. You had everything, even help," he waved a hand toward Bess, "but you're still nothing."

Her hands clawed at her neck, veins popping out around her eyes.

His boots splashed as he stepped into a puddle.

He stopped laughing.

The geyser shot him into the air.

"Yeah, I still got a trick or two," Darren said, still pressed against the wall. "And now I got the whole reservoir at my call." He groaned as he forced the water to his will.

Shadows took form out of the dust. Varmints raced along the street, trying to get away from the storm while froth dripped from their muzzles.

Blood dribbled from Darren's chin. "Your blacksmith didn't do a very good job. Water wears away rock, if it pounds hard enough." He let out a strained chuckle as he made a fist.

The water formed a ball around the duster, who hung in the water for only a moment.

The sphere burst. "You think you can just lock me up, Darren?" he spat. "I've got so much more control than you ever did."

The air rushed out of Darren. It pulled out of his lungs, out of his blood, out of all of him. Pain exploded inside him. Blackness wafting across his vision. The wind toppled the saloon, the schoolhouse and the sheriff's office.

The duster set himself down on the muddy ground. The geyser dying without Darren's control. Abel shook his head. "You're nothing. You've always been nothing. Even with all the help in the world, even with all the water below us, you can't out-muscle me."

Darren shook his head.

"You failed another woman now. You just ain't strong enough; you ain't clever enough neither. You never learned anything new, did you?" The duster shook his head. "Sure wish I could say you were a good fight, but you weren't even that."

The pressure increased, veins standing out on Darren's face. A knife of dust ran past his shoulder, slicing through his coat into his flesh.

"These plains are mine. The women, the gold and the cities. All of it. Ain't no one can stand up to me." He flicked a finger, and Bess would have screamed if she had any air left. Skin sheared off her arm.

Darren was nothing. He couldn't fight back; the duster was right. You'd think he would've at least learned a few more tricks, and now the air was being sucked from him. Sweat stung his eyes.

Sweat from his body.

Time to learn a new trick.

He choked out a few words. "Know what else is in the human body, Abel?" He gulped against the pressure pinning him against the wall. "Water."

The duster's eyes widened in surprise. He gasped, falling to his knees as he screamed.

Lightning arced as the dust picked up speed. The winds pushed faster and faster, howling down the town's street. Bess leaned into the wind, trying to suck air in.

The duster retched, sweat beading on his forehead. Tears leaked from his eyes, the wind carrying them away. Liquid dripped from his fingertips. He trembled, blood flowing from his ears and mouth. Abel's muscles seized. Finally, after moments that felt like years, he stiffened and fell over.

The wind circling the town ceased. Lightning arced, thunder rolled and Darren fell to the earth. Bess choked on the ground and coughed, dust showering them like a terrible rain.

Bess and Darren sucked in the hot air.

Done.

It was done.

And then they heard the varmints roar. They leaped onto the duster's body and tore it apart, then the pack turned its sight on Bess. They growled.

The woman turned her gaze on them, shaking her head in panic. "Nothing to steal," she panted.

Darren struggled to his feet and raised a hand toward the pack. He grunted, blood dripping from his nose. He hurt. Oh, he hurt so much.

"Bess, I can't pull water out of them! I got nothing left to give!" he wheezed.

Thunder rolled overhead.

"Bess, steal from the storm!"

The lead varmint stalked closer to her. Bess looked confused. She shifted her gaze upward, back to Darren and the varmints, and then to the sky.

White, white lightning arced from the sky. It struck the varmint, the sound of the energy splitting the sky. The explosion flung Darren back over the fountain, where he landed in the debris of fallen buildings.

When Darren could see again he stumbled to his feet. A dark crater marred the center of the street where the lead varmint had stood, and the four sizzling bodies of the rest of the pack lay scattered around the main street of the town.

He laughed. He cheered. He groaned in pain.

Bess rose from the other side of the street, blinking. "What the Hell did I do?"

"You stole."

"What do you mean?"

"Some people say that thoughts are just lightning in the brain." He shrugged. "I was desperate, and thought 'What the Hell, it's not like we got anything else to try'. My pistol was useless, and I couldn't douse anything."

Bess shook her head, confused.

"Dowsers control water, right? Dusters control air. And thieves?"

"I control lightning?"

Darren grinned and gestured to the street.

"I stole from the storm?"

Darren shrugged, then grimaced. "Ow."

She raced to him and embraced him.

Hours later they reclaimed the horse from the cave. "We got three canteens of water between us," Darren said. "Gonna be hard to get to the next town." His expression softened. "Thank you."

"For finding where he's been stashing all his new slaves?"

He nodded, eyes closed.

"Who's there?"

His eyes were distant. "My daughter, maybe. I hope."

"You ain't gonna be able to do much on your own." Bess mounted up. "You know, water and lightning make a good team."

"You want to ride with a nothing?"

"I like fighting bullies. For now, let's fight them together."

Darren nodded. "Sounds like a plan to me."

They rode into the evening together.

# Jonathan Mast

## About the Author

Jonathon Mast lives in Kentucky with his wife and an insanity of children. (A group of children is called an insanity. Trust me.) He's published in numerous anthologies and short story collections. His first novel, *The Keeper of Tales*, is currently available from Dark Owl Press.

Jonathon does NOT have too many books. He has too few shelves. Also not enough rooms to put the shelves in. His wife may be an enabler. Thankfully, so are his children.

You can find Jonathon at:
Website: https://jonathonmastauthor.com/
Amazon: https://www.amazon.com/Jonathon-Mast/e/B07NYTCVN2
Facebook: https://www.facebook.com/jonathon.mast.1

# Fury – A Wilder Light Tale

## Lauraine S. Blake

The lamps burned low. They flickered dark lines of omen over Evelyn as she threw her head back and arched. Inky shadows danced over bare skin and polished oak alike, conjuring illusions of the deepest fantasy as she took her pleasure. There was always something so powerful about the witching hour. So rousing, that deep pit of night bowed down to the base apex of day. It lent thrill to her purpose as she rolled over him to let silken skin meet sweat.

She breathed him in as if for the last time. His scent mingled, bittersweet, with candle smoke and the crisp, dry sage they stored his sheets with. The softest moan came to her, so she laid it upon the shell of his ear – it was the kind of primal utterance she knew drove him wild – and she yielded. Just as she had always yielded.

In the beginning there had been love and hot passion in their tangle of limbs and quickening of breath. Those fires had burned her whole; he'd been all she ever wanted, her heart's deepest desire. Yet recently those molten emotions had set, then broken, shattering to reveal the dark, smoking core of her hatred. After that the yielding had become calculated. It had a purpose to it that the night's deepest dark wrapped itself around and embraced.

She bit his neck when he moved over her and the shadows deepened. Darkness curled around them, powerful and ancient, summoned from the infernal depths of the world. He hissed as she drew blood, bowing back against the pleasure in that pain. She knew what she was doing – which buttons to press. His body was no mystery to her, just as hers was no mystery to him.

There was something hot in that blood. Something rich and powerful she wanted – deserved. He didn't notice as she murmured against his neck and slid her tongue along the wound. He was utterly distracted – utterly trusting. If she'd wanted to, she could have slipped a blade between his ribs. Yet why would she want that when there were punishments of a far higher caliber to be enjoyed?

A spell slipped from her lips. A spell, and something altogether darker. She was not disposable, and sooner or later he would realize exactly how indispensable she had been.

◇━◈━◇━━◇━◈◇

Kaeddrien smiled to himself and rolled over. His arms expected to find Evelyn, but the sheets beside him were already cold. The sense of missing her woke him fully and the smile faded. He rolled onto his back, limbs spread wide, to stare up at the thick, velvet drapes swathing his bed.

Some mornings he imagined his world was simply as

small as that canopy bed – velvet and smooth oak, silk and goose down. He would have liked to remain in that soft island of luxury, lapping up a dutiless eternity there, but only if Evelyn stayed too. Yet she never lingered past dawn, no matter how much he insisted that she could – *should*. No matter how much he wanted to repeat by daylight that which only existed for them long after dark.

"You're the king," she would protest. "It's not right for you to be with a Lowlander," she would add. "I'm not fit to be found in your bed." He would soothe her, correct her, then seduce her, but still she would be gone before dawn.

He heard the servants begin the morning bustle beyond his canopy's shores, and knew she was probably right. There would be talk if they found her with him, despite that her visits were a poorly kept secret. Her place was not there. When he'd been younger and more foolish – a prince and not a king – he'd offered her marriage. His father had stopped it, of course. Just as he would prevent his sons from marrying too lowly in their time. The message from his father had always been clear: *sleep where you like in your youth, Kaed, but marry well*. Have appropriate heirs.

So Kaeddrien would. He'd swallowed his desires and offered a marriage contract to Lady Sytalia D'Juline, the daughter of a man who owned the entire south coast of Basaine. Kaed had heard she was the most radiant beauty Juline could boast, and her father's power suited him. The date was set. All he had to do was let go of his love for a Lowlander. His closest friends had told him it would be easy enough, that a Lowland woman wouldn't keep his gaze once he took a Highland bride.

Even so, despite his upcoming wedding, despite that breakfast and duty awaited him, Kaed wished Evelyn had stayed. In his mind he'd have her share his bath, have her naked before him, dancing, as he took breakfast. Hers was not a Highland beauty, but it was the kind of beauty that spoke to him and whispered things to his soul.

He didn't fully remember how they'd met. He'd been drunk, most likely, scouring the taverns of Ilthyr, Basaine's sovereign city, after a blood-hunt as he and the lads took on a hunt of an entirely different nature. At sixteen she'd been the most beautiful thing he'd ever seen. That had been almost a decade ago, yet *still* he craved her, no matter that he'd been assured he wouldn't. Still, he missed her when she left before dawn. But that was Evelyn; she always had known her place.

They hadn't talked about his upcoming marriage; there never seemed to be time for such talk. Besides, it wasn't appropriate for him to discuss matters of court with her. Athough, by not speaking of it, he hadn't had the chance to say certain things – like that he wished she, Evelyn, was a Highlander, or that he'd far rather marry her.

He sighed and settled into his morning bath. The high shine of its golden surface gleamed where the sun caught it, spilling soft light across the bathing chamber. The water's lacework danced over the crisp, white walls, just as it always did. Everything looked completely normal. It smelt and sounded normal too. And yet, Kaed had a nagging sensation in his gut, needling him, telling him that something was different. Something was wrong. He pushed it away as he dipped his head beneath the water, then focused on the delicious fingers of the servant girl washing his hair. The soft pressure at the back of his head drew forth a shiver, which stole over him slowly.

Was it his imagination, or was the water far cooler than usual?

Ilthyr rose up around Evelyn, glistening golden in the early light as she hurried through its cobbled streets. The king's city was always the same, always pleased with itself and its indomitable pre-eminence. The capital of the Highlands didn't absorb the sunlight but reflected it – repelled it – with a radiance that it assumed as if by right. The same way that the Highlanders who dwelt within its walls assumed power by right.

A bristle swept through her, persistent and ever-growing as it had been for weeks. She, a Lowlander, was excluded by birth, by race. Power was not hers to claim, or seek, so she had taken it.

Ilthyr castle loomed behind her, imposing on her thoughts. Beckoning to her, asking her to confess her regrets, but she would not turn. She would not look at it, perhaps, ever again.

"I did it!" Evelyn was out of breath as she shut the splintered door and leaned against it. The loft she shared with her friend was a small space – ramshackle and not even vaguely watertight – but her heart clenched as she thought of leaving it. The apartment, with its sloping floor and creaking beams, represented her independence, her coming of age.

"Just like that?" Annie demanded, jumping up from where she'd been sewing on the floor. Annie the seamstress; always busy, always thimbled.

Evelyn smiled at her friend. "I can't believe how easy it was. He didn't even notice."

Annie's eyes widened. "Show me."

She did, holding out her hand and spinning a ball of fire onto her palm. The flames brought a grin of glee to Annie's face. It felt good – both the stolen fire she had dominion over and the approval.

"What now?"

"We should probably run, Annie. He'll notice at some point and piece it together."

Her friend nodded earnestly and glanced around their home with sad eyes. They'd known that was the price for stealing the king's magick: their old lives were forfeit.

Regardless, it was worth the cost – no matter what.

After all, Highlanders were like spoiled children as they ran around their castles and estates. Everything was chattel to them, just things to be used and then discarded. For years, Evelyn had believed Kaed to be different. Or, perhaps, she'd only profoundly wished he was. Either way, it had hurt badly – like a sharp blade between the ribs – when he'd proved her wrong.

For the longest time she'd truly thought he loved her, that his refusal to take a wife was for her. The old king had forbidden their union, so she'd hoped Kaed was only leaving a respectable mourning period before defying his father. She'd waited a year, then two, after Kaed's coronation. She'd never pressed him.

Her reward had been reading in the papers – *the papers* – that Kaeddrien was engaged to some trumped-up southern heiress. It had snapped something in her. Almost ten years of being lovers, and that was how they were to part? He hadn't even had the courtesy to tell her. To agonize a little…

Stealing his powers had been Annie's idea. She hadn't been serious, of course. They'd been talking the way jilted people always talk, imagining Kaed's head caught between the enormous jaws of some beast, or – his manhood mysteriously catching on fire. Or, better still, not working for anyone but Evelyn. The impotent king! They had laughed and enjoyed that one for a little while. Then Annie had said those fateful words, "What if he really did lose his power?" Even Evelyn had struggled to imagine him without a throne at his feet, but that wasn't his only power, was it? Nor was it the only thing of value to him.

In Basaine, kings always bore fire in their blood. It was how Kaed's father had kept order in the empire. Everyone feared that snippet of the Wilder Light – *magick* – and so it kept them at bay. Just as it, reportedly, kept the Darkness at bay – the vast, shadowy force that everyone uttered oaths of, prayed against, but no one understood.

Evelyn had long since decided that the Darkness didn't exist, that it was just another means by which the Highlands kept the Lowlands in line. It was how she'd justified tracking down and using the spell that stripped Kaed of his power, the means by which she took something precious from him as recompense for her broken heart. A power that now swam in her veins, hot, mighty and just a little intoxicating.

◇—◈◇◈—◇———◇—◈◇◈—◇

"Sire," Lord Commander Cavandish called to him as Kaeddrien strode towards the throne room. The parquet floor echoed sharply beneath his boots, announcing him. It was almost loud enough to drown out the Lord Commander's greeting. There was power in that. It was why he always descended the plain spiral stairs closest to his room, then walked the full length of the lower corridor to reach the forward spaces of the castle. His presence resonated before him – his people knew he was coming.

Cavandish drew nearer, dashing Kaed's hopes of ignoring him. "We have reports of a disturbance," he announced in clipped syllables. Theirs was not an easy relationship. Not since Kaed's father had died prematurely, transporting Kaeddrien into his kingship far sooner than Cavandish believed desirable. "It sounds like the Blyte."

Kaed paused, frowning. The last time the Blyte, or the dark creatures that came with it, had been a problem he'd been little more than a boy. "They are testing me, are they not?" he asked tiredly.

"As you say, Sire."

"Then have the servants ready my horse."

"Already done, Sire."

Kaed huffed and changed course. He wouldn't get anything done until he acquiesced to Cavandish's wishes and traipsed out to meet the Blyte. Some days it was not at all obvious who was king.

Evelyn and Annie caught a ride on a farmer's waggon as it trundled away from Ilthyr. The morning sun slid upwards as they bit into the countryside beyond the city limits. By late summer, every horizon in the Highlands had faded from green to golden. This year was no different. The land bustled in the distance as harvest entered full sway, but the Lowlanders working those fields – servants and slaves – avoided the King's Road entirely. Truthfully, only city dwellers used it, and even then, they did so sparingly.

The farmer couldn't take them far, but at least it was a start. Evelyn sighed happily as she watched the world go by. Perhaps she should have been anxious, or at least mournful, but instead she settled into the soft hay and felt herself slide towards sleep. The hay smelled sweet in her nose and crackled gently as her weight sank into it. It had been a dry month – perfect for making hay. In her sleepy haze Evelyn found herself wondering how well it would burn, and how sweet it would smell as it did.

Hay smoke didn't smell like wood smoke, nor did it quite smell like the wildfires that cut through living grass. It was something in between. She nestled into the sense of it as the waggon rolled rhythmically down the road while sunlight shifted patterns over her eyes.

She was ripped from sleep when Annie screamed, summoning her back to utter chaos. Fire. It was in her waking world just as it had been in her dreams, and somehow the waggon was ablaze. Fiery tongues, hot and hungry, rolled over the sheaves. Annie launched herself upright, tugging Evelyn from the cart and down onto the baked-earth of the road. They landed in a dramatic tangle of singed skirts and limbs.

Evelyn looked on in dismay as the farmer unharnessed his panicked horse then set about a frenetic dance, slapping his shirt against the flames. It was no good; the waggon and its cargo were long lost. "What the bloody hell did you do!?" he demanded.

"I was asleep!" Evelyn protested as she watched her favorite cloak burn. "I didn't *do* anything."

Annie shuffled beneath the farmer's gaze. "I was asleep too," she muttered and Evelyn knew she was lying. Annie always shifted like that when she lied.

The farmer snorted in disbelief. "Get out of my sight before I call the city guard on you," he growled. It was unlikely that he would; the city guard almost never helped Lowlanders. All the same, they didn't need telling a second time.

Evelyn grabbed Annie's hand and dashed with her, headlong, down the road. They stumbled over the ruts, focused only on putting distance between themselves, the farmer and, of course, Ilthyr.

Adrenaline burned out before they slowed and it was then Evelyn glanced back to confirm the cart, as well as its smoke, had been swallowed by the horizon. "Why did you lie?" she asked curiously. Her breath raced hotly through her lungs but the question felt urgent.

"Eve, it was you!" Annie was just as out of breath as she was.

"What was me?"

"You set the hay on fire. I saw you."

Evelyn blinked. "But I – I –"

"Have stolen the *Firesworn* powers of the king. You're going to have to be very careful."

Evelyn took a deep breath and nodded. "Come on," she muttered. She'd never imagined powers like Kaed's could be a burden. He'd always carried them with such entitlement – had always relished showing them off. Never had she imagined that they might have a mind of their own. It shook her, just as the fact that she'd enjoyed watching the haycart burn shook her. She knew she should have felt horrified by it, but she didn't. There was something powerful about destruction – something sweet.

⬦━◦◦━◦━━◦━◦◦━⬦

Kaed, and a small company of his closest guards, pounded down the road towards the Darkness. He was distracted by a strange feeling in his gut – a deep instinct that clamored at him and told him to stay home. It was the same feeling he'd had since waking. He shrugged it off even as sweat beaded his brow. He was young yet as king, and early in his reign. He couldn't afford to be seen as shying from power, or from threats.

They hadn't gone far when they came across a burning waggon and Kaed forced them to pause. "May I assist?" he called to the farmer.

The farmer, a Lowlander, bowed his head and shuffled. "My thanks, Sire. She is all but done."

Kaed eyed the fire. It was true; the embers were beginning to burn low, and the damage was completely irreversible. There was something strange about that fire, though. It didn't *feel* right. Or, to be precise, it didn't feel of anything at all. Kaed was used to being able to sense all fire, even the smallest flicker of a candle. His eyes roamed over it warily as he nudged his heels into his horse and moved on.

If he thought about it, that was the crux of what felt so wrong within him. He was empty in a way he'd never known before, which sent chills snaking over his skin. If he was sentimental, he'd say the feeling was reminiscent of all the times he'd acknowledged missing Evelyn. Although it was more than that – something deeper – like he was actually missing a part of himself. Still, that was absurd.

⬦─◦─◇─────◇─◦─⬦

"Horses!" Evelyn hissed and yanked Annie into the trees not a moment too soon. She caught sight of the banner – gold flames dancing amid red silk – and her stomach flipped. It was the King's Guard. Had he really worked it out so soon?

They cowered, wide-eyed and trembling, in the densest part of the thicket. Evelyn's heart thumped against her ribs, willing the Guard to pass them by.

Kaed didn't slow. Though, instead of relief, she felt the icy sink of rejection in her gut – once again. The bitter sting of his indifference. She took a deep breath and replaced the feeling with anger. Within moments the king appeared, his strong face fixed in concentration. Hollow, she watched him ride by. Kaeddrien Ilthyron was beautiful, he always would be, but no more would her heart bleed for him.

No more.

The first thing Kaed knew of the Blyte was the stench of it – it was like someone had smashed a barrel-load of rotten eggs. He gagged as he looked out over the ruined fields, where, for miles in all directions, the earth was cracked and seething as it rippled with a dark taint. The air tasted bitter and oily on his tongue. Somewhere deep within him, his power over the earth shifted and squirmed in revulsion, yet the flames in his blood didn't so much as flicker. That was odd; usually they roared through him long before he even sensed a threat.

"Well?" Cavandish asked.

Kaed had gone with his father a few times in his youth to burn back the Darkness. It wasn't difficult – any unskilled Magicai could do it, so long as they had the right mix of the Wilder Light: earth and fire. First you burned the blackness from the land, then you built the land anew. It wasn't hard, so why couldn't Kaed do it?

"Sire?" He could hear tension in the Lord Commander's voice.

"Scout the area. Report back," Kaed snapped at the guards. Their glances fluttered to Cavandish nervously, but they left as soon as he didn't counter the command. Kaed bristled; no one had ever second-guessed his father that way. He studied the Blyte bitterly as his men dissipated, then hissed, "It's not working," as soon as they were out of range. He felt like a child telling his nursemaid he'd just wet himself.

"What's not working, Sire?" Cavandish replied

even though Kaed was sure the man knew exactly what he meant. The bastard would make him say it anyway, it seemed.

"My magick."

✧━◈━ ━◈━ ━◈━◈━✧

Evelyn reached the edge of the Highlands and looked out in horror. The land was black and wretched, and it stank worse than anything she'd ever known.

"The Blyte," Annie muttered quietly at her side.

"What?" Evelyn's head whipped to her friend, but she could feel it in that place where the stolen fire roamed within her. It roared to be let out – to raze the shadows from the land. "But the Darkness isn't real!"

"Who said that?" Annie asked. "My ma saw it once. It scared her half to death – oh –" Annie fell silent.

Evelyn felt hot panic boil through her and the fire bucked. She had only the barest grip on it. "Move!" she shouted.

"What?"

"Move!" Evelyn screamed.

Annie dived out of the way just as a huge wall of fire erupted over the top of her. It arced up and out then plunged down, down into the depths of the world burning everything in its path. It was glorious. *More* it demanded, and *more* Evelyn gave it. "Yes," she said. "Yes."

It raced across the land, taking Blyte, farmhouse and animal alike. All were kindling to her awesome might – all must bow.

Distantly she heard her name, heard the word cried

in horror. It snagged in her, cooling her wrath just a little — enough to make her realize she had to stop. Enough to make her aware of what she'd just done.

The horizon was in ruins, though not from the Blyte – from her. She'd burned everything in sight. She'd burned *people*. It sickened her. Yet, even as she fell back to herself, even as the fire stopped and Annie grasped her wrist, she knew she wanted more. There was so much fire in her, so much *power*. She wanted to burn the whole damned sky, to tear it down to ashes.

"Eve!" A hard slap connected across her face and she snarled, tempted, just for an instant, to start with Annie. The thought stilled her.

"We have to go back," she muttered. "We have to go back to Ilthyr."

⬥━◦━━━◦━◦⬥

"What do you mean, your magick doesn't work?" Lord Gavernos asked wanly as Kaed closed his eyes. The repetition of his failure had been rattling around the council room, buffeted between the red tapestries of its walls, since they'd returned from the Darkness.

"Just that. It's not there. I can't access my *Firesworn* powers at all."

"But you're the king. The king *always* has fire – this is Basaine, the Fire Lands!"

Kaed felt a dull throb begin behind his eyes. He rubbed his neck in contemplation. *How?* That was the question they should be asking. After all, he'd lit his bedside candle without thought the day before, whereas now he couldn't even *feel* the roaring hearth the servants stoked to ward off the evening chill.

His thumb brushed a tender spot on his neck and he thought wistfully of Evelyn. She'd been a wild thing last night. It had been good; he liked her best when she was just a little violent. He shut out the room – the men standing amid dark oak and red fibres, all cast golden in the lamp-light – and replayed their liaison. It was his favorite thing to do when meetings soured him. She'd been whispering in his ear. That had been good too, had spurred him on…

The words, though: *Ill'na demisi nillai recommedi. Ill'na demisi illai meina. Ill'na demisi illai demisi.* They were such strange words, eerie words – almost like old magick. Almost like a spell.

He rose abruptly, suddenly hot with understanding, and marched from the room. "Sire?" he heard them call at his back. "Sire?"

He let their voices fall on deaf ears. He had a library to visit, and an awful, awful question to face – what the hell had Evelyn done to him?

◇━◦━◇━━━◇━◦━◇


It was the middle of the night when the bells of Ilthyr Castle clattered into life, wrenching Kaed from a restless sleep. "Daemoncai on the roof!" the cry went up beyond his bedchamber as boots rushed past his outer door. "Dae-moncai on the roof!"

Kaed surged from his bed, relieved that he'd not bothered to undress. The room was dark, shadowed wrong-ly without the lamps his powers usually kept burning even as he slept. The oak panels taunted him with their inky sheen, and his drapes jeered like foul-mouthed specters. He cursed bitterly as he buckled on his boots and sword.

"Sire, stay in your room!" Lord Cavandish barked at him as he joined the throng in the upper corridor. It made him feel like a chastened child, not the damned king of Basaine.

He would not.

"Arm the tar pit! Flame the arrows!" Cavandish bellowed towards the upper courtyard, which sat atop the enormous flat roof at the castle's rear, then he swung back to face Kaed. "My Lord Kaeddrien," he growled. "How do you propose to tell your people that you have no fire with which to defend them?"

They were near the huge doors to the courtyard, surrounded by men racing forward with swords in hand. Some wore chainmail, but most, like Kaed, only wore the clothes of court. "You want me to hide like a coward?" Kaed eyed the older man coldly as the night air, tinged with tar-smoke, caressed his skin.

"You have no heirs, Sire. No brothers." There was no respect on the Lord Commander's face – no compromise.

"I will not shy from battle, and I am your king, so you cannot make me," Kaed snarled. He could see the words *foolish* and *headstrong* marked out in the creases around Cavandish's eyes, but didn't care. Spinning on his heel, he left the man in the corridor then powered through the doors with his sword raised. He was sick of being treated like a child – a lesser – and he was terrified that, if he did not solidify his power despite what Evelyn had done, he'd be fixed forever as Basaine's weakest king. He could not let the Ilthyron line fall. It wasn't just fire that made

Ilthyrons superior, they *were* superior.

He dipped his blade into the tar pit and set it alight, even though it was physically painful to do so. Lighting his blade as a mortal would was the basest humiliation. Yet, to preserve his power, he would debase himself. The throne was, after all, the only thing he bowed to and proving Cavandish wrong was worth the sacrifice of dignity.

High above them he could see the Daemoncai – the Nightling – arching membranous, black wings before it shattered the air with an unearthly shriek. All around his subjects clustered, and urgent commands rang amongst them like the striking of a bell. He didn't let them get a good look at him, avoiding both scrutiny and questions as he set off, fiery sword in hand. His boots reverberated sharply against the stone as he dashed up the steps to the highest roof.

Flaming arrows overtook him. They lapped at the shadows around the beast, making it snarl, then cut off when Cavandish called a hurried ceasefire. At once, Kaed felt all eyes on him. *All* – including the Nightling's. Those eyes were beady-black and vicious-dark as it looked right into him, through him. It was as if the Daemoncai knew Basaine had lost its fire. That the hot edge of Kaed's power had been watered down and blunted. He hollered as he raced for the thing. It leapt up and backwards then lurched away from his burning blade.

Only yesterday he could have ploughed a stream of fire into the beast from far below and razed it from the sky; only yesterday he could have protected his people. The shame of it was considerable. "Faexing witch," he cursed under his breath. The anger gave him strength as he launched himself forwards, thrusting his blade into the air. It flew – by the sliver of earth-magick he still held – it flew. His blood spoke to the metal ore in it, commanded it, and so it obeyed.

Flames struck the Nightling across its underside. It howled, then crumpled, thudding onto the roof. Kaed's sword lay well over a man's length away – a useless streak of smoking steel – but he had his boot knife. He drew it and advanced on the foul creature. How *dare* it attack him when he was most vulnerable. How dare it!

He drew a sharp breath. Fetid smoke filled his lungs – a cruel reminder of all he'd lost – then, with the adrenaline of battle coursing through him, Kaed slashed the Daemon's throat. Black blood sprayed, thick, dark and stinking. It coated him, anointing him King of the Night as the Daemoncai vanished in a cloud of ebony smoke.

Vanquished – gone.

Kaed collected his sword, satisfied, then composed himself. He was not to shake; Ilthyrons did not shake. It took him a few more moments before he was ready to descend to the lower roof. By the time he did, the upper courtyard was completely full.

His court cringed from the sight of him – from the dreadful gore. Good. Cringing was good.

"Three cheers for our king," Cavandish took up the cheer with all the enthusiasm of a scolded child. "Hip hip hurrah, hip hip hurrah." It echoed three times as Kaed walked straight for him. The Lord Commander's eyes were tight – disapproving – as Kaed took some of the dark ichor coating him and smeared it across Cavandish's face.

"Hip hip hurrah, Cavandish," he simpered coldly,

then turned and walked away. In part because he badly needed a bath, and in part because his stomach was threatening to betray him and spill his guts in front of everyone.

Betrayal.

There was a lot of that going around. If he ever found Evelyn, it was very, very likely that his vengeance would be bloody.

⟡━◇━━━◇━⟡

"Run!" Evelyn yelled at Annie, but it was no good. The woman was just too slow. They clambered over a rise just as a swarm of great, dark beasts descended upon them. "You know I have to do it," she cried, indignant against Annie's certain disapproval. She didn't wait for a response as she unleashed the *Firesworn* might from her core and let it broil the very sky.

It tore out of her and pealed into the night, cutting through the beasts of Darkness like a hot blade through butter. She could have wept with joy for the reaping; the love she felt for those hot, sharp claws of flame. She scratched with them, scouring the earth and sky, hungry to devour every beast of night, but they were gone; it was over.

It wasn't enough.

She wanted more, so much more. Let the people burn – let the world! All at once she was acutely aware of something sharp and hard that sliced across the back of her head.

Then – darkness.

"Send riders in all directions. I want Evelyn Carter found," Kaed ordered just before dawn. He was standing by the window in his study watching the world below turn grey. Ilthyr city was no doubt already full of rushing people, already full of promise for the day ahead. Somewhere in all that chaos there had once been a young woman. She'd been beautiful, feisty and bold. She'd stolen the heart of the king of Basaine – then she'd ripped out his soul.

"Evelyn, Sire?" The name was the sharp toll of a prayer bell.

"Are you deaf, Jameson?" Kaed snapped. He'd not slept much, and the hollow ache in him was getting worse. The withdrawal from his magick felt like coming down off the drugs he'd enjoyed as a teen, only far worse. "Find Evelyn and bring her to me."

"Yes, Sire."

Kaed waited a moment before he crossed the room, annoyed by the plush carpet that muted his steps, and poured himself four fingers of amber liquor. He groaned softly as it burned in his throat. Gods did he miss the heat of his fire.

"May I suggest prudence, Sire?" Cavandish asked him from where he lurked by the door. The man was acting as if nothing at all had changed – as if Kaed hadn't proved him wrong only hours earlier.

"Can you get word to Sytalia that I'd like the wedding moved much sooner?"

"Any particular reason, Sire?"

Kaed cut him a foul look, but didn't answer. He had many reasons. Like, for example, that he needed sons with fire to bear as soon as possible. Like the fact that he didn't want Sytalia to hear of his change of circumstance – his impotency – and be repelled. He *would not* be Basaine's weakest king, and he *would not* break the Ilthyron line. However, he felt the need to explain precisely none of his reasons to Cavandish. The man was overstepping; again and again he stretched himself.

If he wasn't careful, he might find himself hanging right alongside Evelyn.

◈━◈━◇━━◇━◈━◈

Evelyn woke feeling woozy and weak. "What?" she muttered, opening her eyes only to shut them tightly against the light of day.

"I had to stop you, Eve. I'm sorry, I just had to." Annie's voice was sad and distant.

The world swayed around them as a rhythmic clinking made a chorus against the backdrop of creaking, rattling wheels. Evelyn groaned and tried to sit up. "Where are we?" she asked. Her blurred vision showed her some unsettling truths, including a prisoner carriage locked securely around them.

"I couldn't carry you," Annie sniffed. "I tried, but they were just too fast."

Evelyn sighed and gripped her friend's hand in her own. "It's not your fault," she murmured. Part of her didn't believe that, though. Part of her was angry that Annie had stopped her from lighting up the world. Annie: always sorry, always incompetent. Perhaps she *should* have burned her too. She squeezed once, then released Annie's hand – just in case. Unbidden, her eyes found High Ilthyr as it blurred into view, cruel and domineering as the Highlanders who dwelt there.

◇───◇──────◇───◇

Kaed paced. The carpet in his study, and the way it muffled his presence, was beginning to enrage him to the point that he fantasized about ripping it up and burning it. Had he his powers, he could have razed it to ash without removing it, and not a whisper of that flame would have touched the floor beneath. The fact of it left a thick fury in him, smouldering. What he had lost was more than anyone should ever have to lose.

He found himself alone, which was just as well because he wasn't good company. What would he say to Evelyn? How could he even face her after what she'd done? She was his first love, a woman he'd trusted absolutely, so why…

There was a knock on the door, and he sucked in a hurried breath. He supposed he was about to find out. "Come," he summoned and a guard appeared, tugging Evelyn beside him. She squirmed against the man's grip, looking far more dishevelled than Kaed had ever seen her. It jolted him, seeing her so unkempt. It revealed her for what she truly was – a Lowland whore, thief and beguiling serpent all at once. He planted his feet, hands behind his back, as he watched her. "Leave," he intoned.

The guard hesitated.

"Leave," he repeated sharply. The man flinched, then abandoned the room. Silence crowded thickly in his wake. Kaed snapped it by snarling, "Are you pleased with yourself?" His eyes somehow couldn't reconcile the filthy creature before him with the women he'd once envisioned wedding. "You've killed about a dozen people. Ruined property and animals alike. You *do* realize that?"

Nothing more than a soft hiss issued from her; there was no repentance in it.

"Or did you enjoy it? Are you so far fallen down into its power that already you're drunk on it, intoxicated? You're weak, Eve. Weak."

Her eyes were dark and cloudy as he approached her. She was still beautiful, he realized with a start. Even seeing the truth of her – the startling Lowland hunger and savage spite – she was still the most beautiful thing he'd ever seen. Her eyes softened a little, fading to a paler blue as if she'd read those thoughts on his face.

It snagged something in him. "Tell me what you did, and maybe we can undo it."

She shook her head almost violently. "Can't." Her voice was brittle glass. A broken, rasping thing that didn't really sound like hers. "You'll never get it back." Then she laughed. It was a cruel sound, so unlike her usual laughs of delight or the sultry caress of breath that had bubbled from her between his sheets.

He blinked – he felt it coming before it struck, not because any magick spoke to him, but because he knew her. After almost a decade he knew her every tell, her every motion. In a move faster than a whip-crack he looped his father's pendant around her neck. It was an ancient thing, steeped with a magick almost as old as time itself, magick that nullified the wearer's powers entirely. Essential when you raise infants with fire in their blood.

Evelyn howled. Or, at least, the *Firesworn* she-daemon she'd become did. "Let me go!" She struggled as he gripped her wrists.

"Are you going to give it back?" he asked coldly, but was answered only with the sound of cracked air as it scraped in her throat. It made him heavy to the core when he tugged her towards his table and took up the manacles resting on its glossy surface.

Somewhere deep within him he'd been hoping that it was all just some awful misunderstanding, that the loss of his fire had been accidental, not deliberate. "Why, Eve?" he asked her softly as he held her wrists firmly in one hand. Without the magick spurring her on, all her strength had failed and she was practically limp in his grip. He didn't loosen it.

"Because you were going to leave me," she murmured dully. "You were discarding me like day-old trash."

Her words froze him. "But I would never –"

"You're getting married, Kaed."

"I'm the king, of course I'm getting married. It doesn't mean I was going to throw you away."

"Then what? I was to be your Lowland whore? Your mistress? What, Kaed?"

"I don't know," he confessed. He'd avoided thinking about it, actually. "But this, Eve, this is too much. If you're angry with me, you lace my underwear with rosehip powder or ants. You don't rip out part of my soul. Not without at least talking to me first."

"You didn't talk to *me*. I learned of your engagement from the papers. *The papers*, Kaed."

He hung his head. "I'm sorry," he murmured and, perhaps, he felt it. At least a little bit. "Let's undo all of this. Give me back my magick, then let me make it up to you. Gods, Eve, I'll spend my whole life making it up to you."

Her eyes turned hard. "It's too late. You're only saying that because you want something I have. The moment I hand it over it'll be like I never existed."

He desperately wanted to step back and put distance between himself and the wintry-cold of distrust in her voice, but he still held her wrists. "You give me no choice," he intoned.

She turned her gaze away from him, glaring at the window with hot eyes.

"I still love you," he whispered on a broken breath as he replaced his grip with chains.

"Well then, maybe you should have told me that." Her voice cut through him like a wicked blade.

"You didn't give me the chance," he growled and crossed the room.

"No, that's right. Nine years never afforded you the opportunity," she snapped.

He sighed, pressing down on the sand in his eyes and the lump in his chest. It was irrelevant so he forced it from his mind as he knocked twice on the door to alert the guard that they were done. Evelyn gave a little toss of her head then offered him only a killing glare as the man entered to lead her away. She jerked back, halting as she drew level with him. "You should know, Kaed, that I didn't just take your magick. There are dark things here in Ilthyr, and they come to life in the witching hour. I borrowed from them and cursed your blood. Neither you, nor your sons, nor the sons of your sons shall regain Basaine's fire until at least a drop of Lowland blood is mixed in."

The horror of her words struck him deeply, like a knife blow to the heart. She had designed for him the ultimate daemon's choice. To have what he wanted he must pollute his line, must seed Highland heirs with a Lowlander. How could he mix his perfect blood with the imperfection of the Lowlands and cast the Ilthyron line down into nothingness – *common drudgery*? The ages would lament him as the king who broke the line, the king who weakened Ilthyron dominion over not just the Highlands, but the whole of Basaine. He felt himself draw up to his full height so he towered over her, then answered like a wounded lion. "It'll never happen, Evelyn. Highland blood *must* stay pure."

"And there it is! You think me low and dirty."

He looked her up and down rudely – a gesture he knew she hated. "I think you're the whore who stole my heart, then my magick. Well, it doesn't matter, *my love*, because henceforth I will banish magick. I'll reject it. If I cannot have it, then no one can. Henceforth, all who seek to master it shall burn at the stake. All who harbor it shall die for their sins. What say you to that?"

She gasped, at last seeming to reel back into herself. "But that's thousands – millions – of lives. You'll kill millions."

She watched his face in horror, barely recognizing that brutal king as the man she'd loved. "No, Evelyn," he replied. "*You* will kill millions. With no way to protect them from the Darkness, people will die. First famine, then drought, then plague. We will use the last of our powers to ward the Highlands against it, but, alas, I find I don't have enough power to ward the Lowlands too." His face had turned entirely cold – savage.

"You can't!" she rasped. The words stuck against the friction in her dry throat. "Kaed, you can't!"

He narrowed the blue-fire of his gaze at her. "I already have and *you*, Lowlander, will address me as 'your Highness.' I am your king, and I shall be treated as such." He nodded to the guard. "See that the pendant stays about her neck. She and the other Lowlander are to hang at dawn."

Evelyn pressed her eyes closed against the hot tears that threatened her. Poor Annie was hardly involved at all, but the king's furious face had turned from her and his door had slammed shut. There was nothing she could do but let herself be propelled down the hall, her feet skipping and bumping helplessly over the parquet floors.

Kaed felt himself settle heavily at his writing desk. There was so much to do – to decree – and so many of the council to face. They would blame him, he realized, for letting a bitter Lowlander steal that which was rightly his. Yet, Kaed had once before proved he was strong even without his power, so he'd prove it again. He'd be decisive with the law and his blade, then he'd teach his sons to do the same. At week's end he'd be married, and a new chapter could begin. Sytalia was already on her way; they'd summoned her through the whispering stones.

He sighed. Those too were magick. Could such a useful, daily enchantment be maintained, or would it have to go with everything else? He sighed again – more deeply. Where should he draw the line?

A knock sounded at the door, then Lord Cavandish let himself in.

"I'd thank you to wait until you're invited, Doren," he muttered acidly, using the man's first name to mark his disrespect.

"My apologies, Sire." Lord Cavandish bowed low, which was concerning. Kaed narrowed his eyes at him. "I don't suppose your powers are resurrected, by any chance?"

Kaed felt a dark dread draw in on him. "I have decided that, from now on, all magick shall be banned."

"I see," Cavandish replied. "Then, Sire, you will need that flaming sword."

Kaed closed his eyes and fought back against the throbbing tiredness he already felt. "Tell me."

"There's a Nightling hoard flying in from the North."

Kaed growled and rose to his feet. "So be it."

⸎

All around them Evelyn heard the screams and cries of people in the city. She sat in the dungeons chained to the wall opposite Annie, unable to reach or comfort her.

Ilthyr's dungeons were every bit as cold and unforgiving as its king. The walls were made of a thick, ashen stone, and the floor she sat on was a frigid type of filth she didn't like to think about. With the pendant on she felt better – freer – and more her old self. It caused regret to flood into her in huge, aching waves.

"What's happening?" she demanded of every person who ran by, but they all ignored her. She leaned her head back against the wall and felt the discordance of the fear and human clatter rattle in her bones.

It was well after midnight when Kaed appeared, smeared with dark muck and looking like he'd just stepped out of the very pit of hell. She jerked at the sight of him, struggling to stand. Kaed. Her Kaed – and *Gods* did he look fearsome. It chilled her. "You did this," he snarled. "You've doomed us all."

"What's happening?" Annie asked. Her voice was thick with tears.

Kaed's steely eyes didn't leave Evelyn's as he said, "The Darkness attacks. Ilthyr is falling."

Shame and dread crowded into her. It *was* her fault. "Let me help, Kaed. Let me stop them."

He snorted in disgust.

"She can do it," Annie said quietly. "I've seen her. You just have to stop her before she goes too far."

"I can help. Don't let Ilthyr fall because of your pride."

"My pride?" he snapped. "It's your treachery."

"Please, Kaed," she begged him. "Please." She remembered using those exact words with him in another circumstance. Then they'd summoned a seductive smile and blown his pupils wide with lust. Now there was nothing except fury in that beautiful gaze. Yet, whatever else Kaed was, he wasn't stupid. He growled, then called for a guard.

◇━◦━◇━━◦━━◇━◦━◇

The night stank of blood and sulfur. The sounds were of battle and dying things – both human and Daemoncai alike. Kaed tugged Evelyn roughly through the upper courtyard, forcing her towards the outer battlement. There was so much rage in him.

"You need to feel the difference between man and beast, then take only the beasts," he instructed. "Can you do that?" He knew it didn't change anything, even if she said no – or lied. Those men were dead either way, and more would follow. If he had to accept collateral damage, he didn't like it, but what choice did he have? It was that, or be the king who saw Ilthyr fall.

That was unacceptable.

"Yes, Kaed. Ouch! You're hurting me," she protested as he yanked her forward and pressed her up against a lookout.

"Try not to kill me," he muttered. The words were sour – ironic – as he flipped the pendant over her head and wrapped his arms around her tightly. The safest place when a poorly trained *Firesworn* worked was actually right next to them, unless you were the target – and even Evelyn wasn't that far gone. He hoped.

Immediately great, bright flames spilled forth and leapt out of her. They sliced through the sky and decimated the descending hoard. It was brilliant to behold – to *feel*. Because, that close, Kaed *could* feel it as it reverberated through her. The thin slip of earth-magick still resting in him shuddered at the raw, elemental power Evelyn had stolen as it enveloped them. He wept at the relief of the burning, at the relief of the *feeling*, at the relief of having Evelyn in his arms.

He didn't need to use the locket. She tucked the power away the moment the vanquishing was done, the moment the castle erupted in a victory cry.

She spun in his arms. "Oh, my love. Don't cry," she hushed him as she wiped away his tears with filthy sleeves.

"I never wanted anyone but you, Eve," he told her. His voice was weak and thready. Gods he wanted her. Even after everything, with her body pressed so close to his, he wanted to rip off her clothes and make her arch against the night. "But I *need* you to give it back. Give it back, and we'll talk. Give it back, and everything will be forgiven."

She turned cold in his grip. "No."

"No?"

"No. I can't. I don't know how. Surely, we can talk anyway? *I* can protect Ilthyr. We can marry, then I can pass the *Firesworn* powers to our children."

She was lying. He knew she was lying. And, even if she wasn't, how did she think he would ever be okay with what she proposed? To be rendered impotent by a Lowland woman who took his power, then threw it around as her own? How did she ever think he could love her like that? Accept that?

No.

It dredged such wild fury from his depths that it was

instinct which guided his hand to plunge a knife deep between her ribs. Shock lit her eyes as he covered her lips with his. "I will always love you, Eve, but if I cannot have my powers, then no one can." He tasted the copper tang of blood on his tongue, then drew back just in time to watch the light fade from her eyes. It was awful, holding her as she died.

Awful.

Yet, there were worse things. Being considered Basaine's weakest king was worse. Losing Ilthyr was worse. Being the last Ilthyron on the throne was worse. And, truly, being blackmailed by a Lowlander who'd leapt high above her station, was worse.

He took a breath and lowered her body, then cleaned the blade. "For you, I shall let the other Lowlander go," he added. There. That felt like kindness. Charity. Good kings gave both, didn't they?

He stood at the wall and looked out over Ilthyr as the city gathered itself, taking a collective breath. It wasn't long before Cavandish found him. "Sire," he said with a bow.

"Doren," Kaed replied.

"I don't think we'll need to worry about the Darkness again for a while. The last attack this severe was more than a century ago."

Kaed nodded; he'd sensed as much.

Cavandish took him in, his eyes lingering on the blood; both Daemoncai and Evelyn's. Black or red, they felt equally oily on his skin. "It will show strength, Sire, to declare magick too dangerous for others to use. We have already issued statements that the destruction on the fringes was not your doing, but the work of a rogue."

Kaed nodded again. "So it shall be," he muttered.

Cavandish bowed once more. "Very good, Sire." He glanced at Evelyn, though Kaed couldn't. He couldn't even *think* about her lying there. "I'll get someone to clear that up."

"Do you know what she said to me, Cavandish?" Kaed asked quietly. He didn't know why he'd chosen the Lord Commander to confide in. "She said *she* could be the one to protect our people in my stead."

"Absurd, Sire."

"She is a Lowlander!" he hissed. *Was* a Lowlander, he reminded himself.

"And a woman, Sire."

Kaed blinked. "Yes," he muttered. "That too." He hadn't thought of it, actually, that a woman might not protect Ilthyr as well as a man. It hadn't seemed relevant. Not in the same way that Evelyn being a tavern server while he was the king was relevant. That was relevant – wasn't it? He felt himself shudder, and shoved back against the tenuous idea that he might have just made an enormous mistake.

"Come, Sire," Cavandish bade him. "There is much to do."

Kaed glanced down over his kingdom once more as it picked itself up and put itself back together. He rolled his shoulders and reset the brittle steel at his core. He would regret nothing, for regret was the domain of the weak and lowly; the Evelyns of the world. Ilthyr was not weak, and neither was he. History would know the truth of that – he'd make sure of it.

# LAURAINE S. BLAKE

## ABOUT THE AUTHOR

Lauraine S Blake, author of 'The Wilder Light,' is an emerging British writer.  She loves to leave the real world and delve into the realms of fantasy — mostly dark fantasy and occasionally horror. In love with books from a young age, she decided to stare down dyslexia and just be a writer anyway. In her other life, she's an astrophysicist and tutor who delights in maths and science. Her up and coming work can be found in  Eerie River's 'Dark Magic drabble' anthology, Black Hare Press's '666' and 'Bones' anthologies as well as Dominion Press's 'Dark Towers,' 'Dark Magic' and 'Dark Servants' anthologies. To find out more about her work, please visit www.thewilderlight.com

# With Stunted Wings

## McKenzie Richardson

The girls raced along the palace grounds, unconcerned by the dirt that caught at the hems of their skirts. Nothing mattered but the sunshine, the fresh air and their time spent together. It hadn't always been that way. When they were young their parents had kept them apart, but once they'd discovered the other's existence there was no separating them.

They came upon the old well and stopped to catch their breath, their wings flittering excitedly. Leaning over the side Ond called down to its depths, her echoic voice ricocheting off the stone sides, which made Lätt erupt with laughter.

"Let's play hide and seek," Ond announced, turning to her twin.

Lätt nodded, always a willing participant in Ond's plans. She closed her eyes and began to count while Ond slipped away.

When she'd counted to twenty and opened her eyes, unsurprisingly Ond was nowhere in sight. What did surprise her was the sudden appearance of one of the stable boys. Lätt couldn't recall his name, but recognized the dull clothing and the scar that sliced through his right eyebrow. She didn't like the smirk he wore.

"Where's your misshapen friend, Princess?" he sneered. The scar crinkled as he sniggered.

Lätt glared, unresponsive.

"A perfect match, you two," he went on. "No one else would want to play with you. You're like a pair of broken toys."

Lätt's stubby wing twitched in recognition of his words. She was used to the half-hidden glances, to the whispers behind hands and eyes shifting away when she approached. Never had anyone spoken to her in such a way straight to her face. If Ond were here he wouldn't dare say such things.

"Poor thing, not even a real princess. Just a fake, a cripple."

Anger reared its head, along with something else. Deep down Lätt feared that, perhaps, he was right. Perhaps she wasn't meant to be a princess after all; she was a flaw, a mistake.

The fear won out, overtaking her senses.

The next thing she knew a wave erupted from the small well, pulling the boy into its shadowy prison. His screams echoed all the way down, ending with a sloppy splash. Horrified, Lätt stared at the well before finally coming to her senses.

Surprised by her actions she raced to the front of the palace, constantly screaming for help. Luckily the gardener came with time to spare and pulled the sodden boy out, none the worse for wear.

As he sulked back to the stables Lätt felt a reassuring hand on her shoulder.

"I didn't think you had it in you," her sister said, pride giving buoyancy to her tone. Both of them knew he wouldn't dare tease the young princess to her face after that.

⟡⟶⟶⟶⟵⟡

Lätt and Ond had entered the world under very different circumstances.

Anxious wings flittered as the best midwives in the kingdom rushed around the room, mopping the queen's forehead with cool cloths and bringing new sheets to soak up the blood. The ruler's first children were about to be born, all had to go just right.

The queen's pained screams pierced the air outside the castle window, where the full moon shone high in the sky.

As the moment approached the gleam of the moon faded, leaving the sky in utter darkness. One of the midwives peered out, shivering at the eerie blackness as the moon took on a charred appearance.

With one final, guttural push a new life was brought into the world, breathing its first breath of outside air, mismatched wings clinging wetly to its skin. There was no doubt in anyone's mind that the children born to the queen were the twins the prophecy foretold. All the signs pointed to it, except one detail was amiss.

The queen only bore one child that night.

As they wiped away the speckles and blood the tension in the room thickened, then curdled. They awaited the arrival of the other child, but nothing came. The womb had only held one.

On the other side of the castle, unattended by trained nurses, another child was brought into the world. A chambermaid gave birth to a girl, one who was fair and calm. Her arrival was otherwise unremarkable, except that she took her first breath at the height of the eclipse just as the young princess had. That, and she mirrored her uneven wings; one full, the other a limp nub.

It was impossible not to notice the children's other similarities, as they both shared the same gray eyes that perfectly matched the king's.

The girls lived very different lives. The child born to the fairy queen was named Lätt, for the moonlight that broke through the window after the eclipse. It had lit up her fair skin on the night of her birth, like a breath of fresh air; a new promise. The other, born to the chambermaid, was named Ond, for the darkness of the servants' quarters.

The announcement was made that the queen bore two children, confirming the prophecy, but gossip and rumors have a way of spreading like fire. They flicker, then consume all they touch.

◇━◇──◇━◇

Before a chance meeting in the labyrinth Ond had stayed with her birth mother in the servant's quarters, but they were drawn together like magnets.

Neither had seen another fairy with a stunted wing before, and they bonded over their shared frustration of being grounded. The world was not set up for flightless beings, and many places were out of reach to them on their own. They marveled at their similarities; the color and shape of their maturing wing, and the shade of their eyes like clouds just before a storm. Each felt less lonely after that.

Early on it was clear both girls had an affinity for magic, and the elements were strongly in tune with their emotions. Such connection was rare, and it was never seen so powerfully in ones so young. Once, when Ond's birth mother forbid her from venturing into the garden during a thunderstorm, Ond had accidentally sent a lightning bolt sparking through the window, igniting the wooden bed-frame. There were occasional landslides, spontaneous fires and brewing storms around the twins.

It was after the incident at the well that the queen finally relented to the king's pleas to allow the two to be taught together. She'd been hesitant before, partly out of bitterness for Ond's presence in the world, but also for the menacing tone of the prophecy regarding their future. She wanted her daughter to be well prepared to fight any evil that may come her way, but was concerned about teaching Ond the same skills.

During the day they were placed in the care of Tidsear, an aged wizard given the task of teaching the girls the art of elemental magic. Under the kind, wrinkled eyes of the old man Ond had never felt so loved, and she did all she could to please her teacher.

Eagerly the pupils learned to harness the burning rage in them to control fire. Tidsear taught them to channel their fear, using it to move water, and he showed them how to force their worry into the earth and crack its foundations.

Ond's face lit up, bright as the moon, as Tidsear handed her the stout bottle of rich, black soil.

"This is from Dorcha Coille, a forest whose trees block out the sun and cause perpetual darkness. It is the purest dirt known, and now that you have mastered earth magic you can use it to enhance your powers."

He handed another bottle to Lätt and her face shone. Tidsear had marked their mastery of each element with the gift of an elemental power source. Even masters could not create the elements, only use what was in their immediate environment.

When they'd mastered fire he'd given them each a small rock, coarse and dark, formed from solidified lava. When they'd mastered water he'd presented them a slim vial of melted snow, harvested from Beinn Fhuar, a mountain so tall that it touched the clouds.

Each kept her collection safe in a leather pouch Tidsear had given them at the start of their training, and with three elements mastered they were the youngest to harbor such control over their powers.

Yet there was still one that eluded them both.

No matter how hard the girls studied and practiced the air element always escaped them. Each failure only reminded them of their inability to fly. Full wing twitching, and the stub of the other wiggling loosely, their fear was reinforced. They would never fly, never master the element of air.

"You are capable," Tidsear reassured them, reading the anxiety of their faces. "It has been predicted, and prophecies are never wrong."

Ond rolled her eyes. "Yes, we know."

Lätt giggled behind her hand. "But, Master Tidsear, what does the prophecy say exactly?"

The old mage twitched his shaggy eyebrows, staring directly at his pupils. He'd argued with himself many times as to whether the girls should know the contents of the prophecy. He was confident they were meant to master all four elements and be the strongest Elementalists ever known, but at the end of his personal debates he always found it best they remain unaware of the details.

There was danger in knowledge.

"That is not the point. The point is it can be done, and you must keep practicing. Now, again."

Many years passed in this way, the girls strengthening their skills and encouraging their magic while always pushing themselves to master the air.

Until the day their training abruptly stopped.

The ritual of death was an intimate affair; more intimate than a mother's kiss on a newborn baby's head, and more intimate than secret caresses by the light of the moon. The royal orchard was located on one of the floating islands that surrounded the castle, stretching long and wide to house many graves. These went back centuries, and were for royalty or those close to the kings who'd ruled over land and sky.

Ond was already in a foul mood; because of their wings she and her sister were forced to ride in the carriage that carried supplies to the floating orchard. It was another reminder of how she and Lätt were flawed, different, their wings not strong enough to carry them to the place where the dead rested. Lätt tried to comfort her by pointing out when the driver picked his nose, or how the roc that pulled the carriage defecated without warning. Still Ond slouched in the seat, arms folded tightly against her chest, and scowled at everything they passed. She couldn't banish the infiltrating thought that she was just baggage in the carriage, a failure who was unable to transport herself.

Encircled in candles, Tidsear's body already tucked up in its open grave, the gathered took turns cutting. The oldest and strongest went first; it was difficult work breaking through the sternum to the softness beneath, as it took a certain finesse and practiced skill. Once the bones were cracked others took their turns widening the wounds, deepening the cavern through layers of tissue. On their turn they'd take up the knife, carefully passed from one crimson hand to one not yet bathed in blood, then they dug the tip into the chest.

It was the first time Lätt and Ond had been part of such a ritual. They watched with wide eyes as their teacher's colleagues and past students took their turns cutting into his body. Blood bubbled on the man's exposed chest, staining his pale skin and coating the thick hairs on his torso.

The blood did not look out of place on the body. The skin had been cleaned to prepare for the ritual, but was still dotted and marred with fresh wounds - a gash to the stomach being the one that had ended his life.

On Ond's turn she grasped the knife and approached the body. As she crept closer she was thankful it was fresh enough that it had not begun to smell. Still, there was a dampness to the air around it, like mud and death. Between strikes the blood on the knife was not wiped away; after all, there was power in spilt blood.

Ond stood over the grave looking down at the stillness of her teacher, at the open wound in his chest. Clenching her eyes shut she threw the knife to the ground before dashing away into the obsidian darkness.

A few elders tried to halt her retreat; this was not the way things were done, but they instantly recoiled as her eyes flared with power. She swept up the flame of a candle in her palm, brandishing it to distance the well-meaning hands. Then she ran from the orchard, silence in her wake.

Lätt stood conflicted, torn between taking part in the ritual and going after her sister. One of the adults had picked up the knife, its bloody surface speckled with dark earth. She glanced at Lätt, the knife extended slightly toward her, waiting for the young princess to make up her mind. The air was still, patient; there was all the time in the world.

Lätt made her decision. The dead could wait, it was the living who needed attention.

She followed the fiery scent of Ond's departure, the death ritual resuming in her absence.

She found Ond sitting in the little courtyard near the entrance of the orchard, staring into the rippling waters of the fountain.

"Ond?"

Silence met her as Ond flicked a clod of dirt into the water.

"It's okay to be sad. You're supposed to be sad when

you lose someone." Lätt tried to sound comforting. She hated seeing Ond so upset.

"I didn't lose him, he was taken," Ond corrected, bitterly. "I'm not sad, I'm angry."

Sensing she had more to say Lätt waited, eyeing her unconventional twin.

"He shouldn't be dead. Why'd he have to open his stupid mouth and provoke them?"

"They said he was standing up for someone they were trying to hurt—"

"A lot of good that did him. Now he's gone forever."

"I know."

"And no one's even doing anything," Ond continued. "They should be out there looking for the cowards who did this to him, not in there cutting him open."

"You know the ritual must be completed. The spirit has to be laid to rest, has to be kept happy."

"And while they do that the people who murdered him run free."

"They don't have any leads, or even information on the culprits."

The tension rose in the night air, the rushing water of the fountain doing nothing to cool the heat that threatened to burst.

Finally Ond snapped. "How could he do this? How could he just leave me like that?"

Stunned, Lätt watched her sister. It was the first time she'd realized how close Ond had been to Master Tidsear. He was one of the few people in the castle who wasn't cold toward her existence.

In the moonlight Ond's eyes flashed menacingly.

"They should be doing something, and if they won't then I will!"

With that, she flung herself from the edge of the fountain and stomped toward the floating island's edge.

Lätt opened her mouth to stop her, to voice her own anger, but a burst of fire erupted from Ond's palm. It snaked and coiled in midair before taking the shape of a large bird. Ond climbed onto the firebird's back, channeling all her rage into flying back to the castle alone, but already she looked fatigued from the effort of conjuring the beast.

At the water's edge Lätt sat alone in the quiet that followed Ond's angry departure. Then she slipped back to the grave, watching the process from the outskirts of the circle.

After layers of skin and muscle had been carefully torn through the heart slowly emerged, connecting all parts of the body. It was usually the spouse that finished the ritual, or a parent if the person was young, but in the mage's case it was his brother.

Tears streaming down his face he climbed into the grave as gracefully as a dancer, as though he had done it a thousand times. Before beginning the old man pressed his lips to the tips of his fingers and laid them softly on his brother's cheek, a postmortem farewell kiss.

The sorrow was written plainly on his face as he mourned the loss of his sibling, and Lätt found it strange that she'd known Master Tidsear for most of her life, had cared for him and loved him, yet no tears fell from her eyes.

With care the man cut through the outer shell of the heart, opening it to the candlelight. Then he took the pouch handed to him and slipped his reddened finger inside.

Within its dark depths there were hundreds of seeds. Lemon seeds and orange seeds, apple seeds and pear seeds, seeds for oaks, maples and elms. They stuck to the blood on his fingers, coating them in bumpy patches. Scooping them in wrinkled hands he packed the seeds into the heart, stuffing it with promises of life.

The seeds had been gathered by those who loved the deceased, and from those who cared for and respected him. The richer and more prominent the person the more seeds they had, allowing the privilege of the dead to choose which would grow. It was best to let the dead have whatever they wanted, as it kept them happy and content enough to stay in their graves.

In the island reserved for commoners grew less extravagant orchards. Poorer families often had only one or two types of seed they could spare, or they accepted donations from others.

The fact that Tidsear had touched many lives made Lätt proud to be his student. She loved to see how many seeds had been gathered, and she marveled at their beautiful diversity.

Once filled the man tucked the heart back inside the chest cavity, wrapping it up in its bed of skin and tissue. He left the bones loose and open, giving room for the promise of a tree to grow, then he climbed back out of the grave.

On top of the bare chest an offering was placed of fruits, vegetables and flowers. They were a sacrifice left to nourish the seeds, to provide any sustenance they could not extract from the body, and they offered more seeds to adorn the base of the tree that would one day grow.

After that the body was draped in thin, cotton sheets, and those gathered took up handfuls of dirt to cover the body in a warm bed for eternal sleep. The grave was dug with shovels, but the body was covered by hand; thick clay collecting under fingernails. It was like tucking in a baby before they went to sleep, bringing a blanket to a spouse or fixing the covers on an aging parent no longer able to take care of themselves. It was love and hard work; the care of the dead was a precious thing.

With the body completely submerged in the earth prayers, songs, wine, and tears followed. Lätt watched it all, always the outsider. She observed and she learned, wishing she could join in with the others. She noted a sensation in her chest, but could not quite say what it was. Like Ond she didn't feel sadness, but there was a dark presence there. Not quite anger, but perhaps a longing for revenge as Ond had said.

Perhaps regret.

As the night wore on those gathered slowly dispersed, returning home to sleep and to wash the dirt from their nails and clothes. Eventually only Lätt and the mage's brother remained. He would stand sentinel all night at the gravesite, making sure the spirit stayed in its grave.

The man felt the young princess' gaze upon him as he stood watching over the last of his family, then he turned his eyes to the starry sky.

He couldn't say when the girl left, but the next time he looked she had disappeared. He was alone with the stars, the moon and the body of his brother.

Ond didn't come to bed that night. As Lätt lay awake in the dark, watching moonlight cast shadows on the ceiling, she felt a burning residing in her chest. Despite not sharing a mother Lätt had felt a connection to Ond since they were children, and knowing Ond was angry kept her awake for hours.

In the morning a pounding on the door woke Lätt from a fitful sleep. She threw off the blankets and rushed to the door, expecting to see Ond, but it was not her sister who stood on the other side. It was Mattius, one of the servants, bowing deeply.

"His Majesty requests an audience with you in his study," Mattius said, glancing at her from under lowered lids. From his solemn expression Lätt knew this was not a joyous summons. She thanked him and set about getting ready, wondering if there was any news of Ond's whereabouts.

When she entered her father's study he was sitting at the long, oak table at which he met with local officials and rulers from time to time.

He smiled briefly as she stepped into the room, but Lätt noted it did not reach his eyes.

Settling into the chair he gestured to she waited in tense silence. The room was still, their breathing barely audible.

It was only when a crash of breakfast plates hit the floor in the hallway that the king shook himself from his stupor.

"You must leave the castle," he announced unceremoniously. There was no emotion in his words, and his face was a mask of blankness.

Lätt looked at him in shock, her eyes wide. "Leave? What do you mean?"

The king dropped his head into his hands, rubbing at the hairline that was trending toward receding.

"It's Ond–"

Just then the door flew open to reveal Mattius' panicked face.

"Excuse me, your Majesty," he said, panting and doing his best to compose himself. "They've found her."

Immediately the king leapt up, moving more quickly than he had in years. He rushed from the room after Mattius, leaving a dumbfounded Lätt padding along behind as she did her best to keep up with her father's frantic wingbeats.

Leading them through the winding halls Mattius opened the heavy wooden door to the courtyard, and even from a distance the party could hear the angry screams just outside the gates.

It wasn't until they were a few feet away that Lätt made out their words.

"Burn her!"

"She's a danger to us all."

"She isn't like us. Get rid of her."

Lätt hid behind her father, clutching the hem of his shirt. The anger in their voices frightened her, even if she did not understand to whom their ill feelings were directed.

As he approached the king lifted his hands outward in an attempt to calm the crowd. "I understand your concerns. I have been informed that Ond has been located."

At the sound of her name the crowd raged, scream-

ing and shrieking as though just hearing that single sylla-
ble caused them pain.

"I assure you, every measure will be taken to—"

"What can you possibly promise us?" an anonymous
voice called from the gathered collective. "You knew how
powerful she was. You should never have allowed her out;
now look what she's done."

The king shifted his eyes, taking in the ferocity of
the group.

"And what of the other one? Are we expected to take
your word about her as well?"

A shiver danced up Lätt's spine with the realization
that they were talking about her.

"You have nothing to fear from–"

The crowd screamed over his words, refusing to let
him finish. It was useless talking to them.

The king nodded toward the three guards who opened
the iron gate, then turned to Lätt. He stilled his wings so he
could float down beside her.

"No matter what," he insisted, "hold onto me."
He gazed firmly into her eyes before taking her by the
hand, guiding her through the gathered villagers with
clumsy steps. As soon as they saw her there were shouts of
disgust. One guard cleared a path for them, the others hovering over them to push away the more robust members of
the crowd.

They were nearly through when Lätt felt something
rain down on her from above, hitting her cheek. A collective laugh boomed from the crowd as saliva dripped thickly from her fingers when she wiped it away. She clenched
her eyes shut, but did not let go of her father's hand.

The guards kept the crowd at a safe distance, preventing them from following as Lätt's father led her to the forest's border.

It was there they found Ond.

She was on her knees at the edge of the forest, head tilted down and matted hair obscuring her face. As they neared Lätt detected seared patches on her sister's dress. Ond's hand were tied in front of her, and there was a chain around her neck. The other end was held by a man with no wings and a swollen eye. Lätt hadn't seen many wingless people, but she knew there were a few who lived in the kingdom such as dwarves and elves.

When he saw the approaching group the man holding the chain took a step forward, but the king raised his hand placatingly.

"Thank you for finding her, Sirus." There was relief in the king's voice.

"Of course, my King. After what she did at the tavern…"

The wingless man's voice trailed off as he handed the chain to the king. They exchanged a look Lätt could not read before the man turned to her. He attempted a smile, but his bruised face gave the gesture a menacing air. Still, Lätt took his offered hand as he led her a few feet away.

The king approached Ond and brushed her hair from her face, but she smacked his hand away.

"Ond, I know you're upset."

Her biting tone cut him off. "You know nothing of how I feel."

"Master Tidsear was a close friend of mine."

She glared at him and pulled away, the chains rattling.

"Let's go home, where we can talk about this."

"I don't want to talk, and I don't want to go with you. Not back to that place where Mast—"

Her words broke off as she tightened her jaw. The king thought she might cry, but instead her fists clenched in anger.

Energy crackled in the air. The king shot a meaningful glance to Sirus, who guided Lätt back toward the palace. She tried to resist, but he held her firmly by the hand with his gaze fixed straight ahead.

"Come on, Ond. Come with me, and—"

"No!" The scream was so loud it sent birds fluttering from the nearby trees with irritated caws.

With intense quickness Ond pressed her palms firmly to the skin at the king's temples.

Instantly the king's mind filled with images. Fire erupted from every corner of the room. There were people screaming, and chaos was everywhere. He looked down and saw Ond's red dress and dark boots. It took him a moment to realize he was seeing through Ond's eyes, living her memories.

All around men stumbled over chairs, coughing and choking on the thickening smoke that filled the room. A few pulled desperately at the doors, but they stuck fast. Others smashed the windows, but when they attempted to jump through a wall of dirt prevented them from escaping. It was as though the earth encased the entire building. They dug at the soil, but were unable to break through.

A new sound filled the room that sent a chill through the king's heart. It was more terrifying than the cries of pain from the men as they burned alive, more sickening than the scent of seared flesh that assaulted his nose.

It was the sound of Ond laughing as she watched the deaths of those around her, the sound of her revenge.

The king was pulled from the vision so forcefully that he almost retched. When he found his feet firmly on the ground he breathed deeply, trying to clear the smell of death from his senses.

He opened his eyes and met Ond's dark expression. There was so much anger blazing inside her, and so much hate.

"I'm not going with you," she declared, jaw set below fierce eyes.

At that moment the king knew he had failed, he and Tidsear both. They'd been unable to keep Ond from the darkness that was always waiting for her, just as the prophecy had promised.

He rose, wings flapping solemnly. In the distance he could see Lätt struggling with Sirus, determined to run back to her sister.

His expression sank into sadness and regret. The king gestured to the guards, handing one the chain. "Lock her in the dungeon," he said. His heart broke with those words, but it was the only way. Destiny is inevitable, a course that cannot be altered.

Behind him Ond shrieked as she wrestled with the chain, the guards forcing her forward.

Suddenly a surprised cry came from one of his men. The king whirled around to find a gaping hole where the guard holding the chain had been, Ond crouched at the edge. The chain around her neck snaked into the hole and she strained to keep from falling in, feet digging into the ground and uneven wings flittering uselessly.

Inside the hole the guard dangled from the other end of the chain, stunned. When he regained his senses he flapped his wings, preparing to fly from the chasm.

When the king looked up Ond met his eyes. Anger flared across them before she spread her hands as far as the ropes would allow, then she clapped them forcefully together. The sides of the hole collided, crushing the man inside.

Ond slipped the chain from the freshly-turned soil, and as the king hovered in shock Ond only grinned.

"Grab her!" he yelled desperately. "Don't let her get away!"

Flames erupted from the shifting earth. Flying with all his force the king dove toward Lätt, who'd managed to escape Sirus' care. Sweeping her up in his arms as the ground cracked beneath them they hovered in the air, looking down at the chaos that had erupted.

The resulting struggle left two more guards buried in the dirt, a third set aflame and a fourth drowned from water forced down his throat.

When the king met Ond's eyes again he could read the anger in them, could decipher how she examined his protective hold on Lätt, could tell she was contrasting his actions with his own declaration to lock her away.

He had failed her once again, and Ond knew it.

With a heave of earth Ond flung herself out of reach, dashing into the forest. Returning to the ground the king sent his remaining guards after her, still cradling his other daughter in his arms.

Those who returned could only report that Ond had gotten away.

Lätt's father supplied her with bags of riches, but could not meet her eye as he sent her away. Now she was little more than a child loaded down with jewels and gold pieces sewn into the lining of her clothing. The guards escorted her out of the palace grounds.

With her wings tucked safely beneath a cloak Lätt could easily pass for a non-flying creature, a witch or maybe even a young elf; she'd always had a slight point to her ears.

When she reached the church, to which her father had given directions, she stared up at its looming exterior. Ond would have wanted to scale its uneven stone walls, always the adventurer, and Lätt's heart twisted in her chest at the thought of her sister lost and alone.

Stepping inside she shook the image away. She couldn't think about her sister now, she needed to focus on her new life.

The couple who ran the church welcomed her warmly, teaching her and caring for her over the years. She helped with cleaning and repairs, working the small garden with her earth magic, lighting candles with her fire magic and mopping and washing with her water magic.

On occasion she tried to call forth the air element, but always met with failure. She learned other ways to get by in the world without flight. She learned to make do, learned to exist. She set up a comfortable life for herself and picked up a few useful skills here and there. That's the way the years passed, time slipping away as smoothly as the distance between the pair of unconventional twins.

Ond had not visited the graveyard since the night she ran from the death ritual as a child. It felt as though centuries had passed since then. Trees at various stages of growth dotted the lush greenery; there was so much life in this place, and so much death.

Weaving through the trees she took her time, her mind briefly pondering from whom each tree grew, and the first glints of moonlight bounced off the spindly pair of metal wings she wore to cover her stunted one. She'd spent years learning, searching and experimenting as she tried to grow out her wing so she could fly. This night's excursion was the latest in a long list of attempts to obtain that which she craved.

She walked toward the largest tree in the graveyard. It was not the oldest, but it was certainly the tallest.

From its branches grew thousands of oranges, each brighter than the sun, like a beacon in the middle of the graveyard. Its canopy stretched out toward the rose-colored sky, obscuring the iris streaks of twilight creeping in. There was great power in this tree; it was exactly what Ond needed.

When she reached its base she brushed aside the dark hair that hung in her face and gazed up into its outstretched limbs. It almost seemed to reach out to her, as though for an embrace. She pushed the thought down, ignoring its implications as she set her eyes on a gleam of ivory in the branches of her teacher's tree.

She wasn't surprised that his body had chosen to

nourish the orange seeds packed into his heart so many years ago. He'd always had a fierceness to him, like a sharp punch to the taste buds; yet there was a specialness to every word he spoke. Every glance, every movement of his hand, was like the prized fruit brimming with juice reserved for special occasions.

Once again Ond found her mind wandering, and she stabbed a wickedly-long fingernail into her palm to drag herself back to the present. She had work to do.

Gaze fixed on the glint of whiteness high up in the branches, Ond clenched her jaw in concentration. A warm flush swept through her mind as it always did when her magic took hold. From the damp soil she collected droplets of water, shaping them to her will. At her side her fingers twirled, spinning the element into a physical mass, gathering bits and weaving them together. When she had enough she brought the sphere up over her shoulder and launched it toward the tree.

It flew with the speed of a bird of prey diving for the kill, then shattered a few feet before reaching its mark. It streaked down the air as though against an invisible force-field before splashing to the ground.

Ond's lips twisted in disappointment. Of course her old teacher would not make it that easy. Her shoulders tensed, clinking her metal wings against one another. The irony was not lost on her that the wings she so desired would make this whole process much easier, this task that would hopefully bring her closer to her goal if all went to plan.

Her eyes searched the surrounding trees. A patch of silky strands, like a giant spider's web rolled up on itself, lay strewn in a nearby mulberry tree. It lit up against the paling sky, the setting sun's orange rays gleaming against its whiteness. Ond strolled over, scrutinizing its branches. Finally, her gaze fell upon what she'd been expecting; the snowy body of a Drury moth, its wings radiant against the darkening sky. It flew around the messy strands that housed the webworms that would one day grow wings and emerge.

Focusing on the moth Ond stepped closer. As she concentrated on it she became aware of its every movement, at first sporadic, then more calculated. Her head swayed with its patterns. Neck outstretched, muscles straining, she pulled a piece of herself from her body and sent it hurtling toward the moth.

It hit like a gust of wind. Instantly the moth grew to three times its size. Ond shook her head, dizzy with the effort of depositing a bit of her soul into the creature. Her dark eyes deepened in hue as the moth spiraled down toward her, hovering an inch from her face as if awaiting orders.

It had taken years to master the process of exerting one's control over small creatures, of creating mindless bodies to bend to her will. It was certainly a useful skill; one she'd wished she'd discovered sooner. Of course Tidsear would not have approved, as opposed to elemental spirit magic as he had been.

She urged the moth toward Tidsear's tree. As it flew it smacked into the same invisible force that the water had, making a soft, hollow *thunk* as though hitting glass. It tried a few more times before Ond released it from her power. It shrank to its normal size and flittered back to the mulberry tree, unaware of its momentary detour.

Realizing her magic would not aid her in this task she twirled her long skirts securely around her hips, keeping them out of her way, then she stepped up to the trunk of the massive tree and placed a hand to the course bark. A jolt of electricity zapped through her skin, making her jump back with a start. She curled her fingers and massaged her palm with her other hand. There was more power in the tree than she'd anticipated, even after all these years.

Worry raced through her mind, questioning the possibility of the task, but instead of giving up she challenged her emotions into the earth. The soil crept up her body, coating her skin like a protective glove that cushioned her from the sparks. Once it encased her entirely she folded down her metal wings and began to climb.

There were no low-hanging branches, which meant she had to wrap her arms around the base of the tree and shimmy her way up in a rather undignified manner. Covered in dirt, and crawling up a tree like a caterpillar, Ond was thankful there was no one around to see her in such a compromising position.

When she'd reached the lowest branch she grasped it and hauled herself into a sitting position. She panted heavily, unused to having to exert so much physical energy. Perhaps she'd been relying on her magic too much of late, a comment Tidsear had always been quick to make. She rolled her eyes and shook her head, annoyed at the lessons her teacher still appeared to instill in her so many years after his death.

She swung herself onto the next branch as the stars began to peek out in the sky. It was more difficult as she rose, her retracted wings catching on the closely-growing branches. During her next rest she plucked a glowing fruit from its branch, letting some of the protective soil slide away from her arms to accumulate at her torso. With talon-like nails she sliced into the fruit, dark-red juice dripping onto her palm and down her wrist. She licked it away, the corner of her mouth curling into an amused grin as she looked upon the merlot hue of the fruit's interior.

A blood orange, how appropriate.

Finishing the treat she climbed the rest of the way, until she finally reached the alabaster object she'd been searching for. Grasping the bone, a femur, triumphantly in her hand, she wedged it securely into the waistband of her clothing. Once she was sure it wouldn't slip she began the long descent to the ground.

By the time she exited the orchard the sky was dark, stars flickering against its immensity. Ond made her way home, victoriously clutching her prize.

⬦━○━⬦━○─────○━⬦━○━⬦

The fire crackled in the corner, heating the tiny room to an almost unbearable temperature.

The man pulled at the collar of his shirt where beads of sweat were pooling, and he watched with wide eyes as the woman before him lit the candles.

"What are those for?"

She looked up at him from lowered lids and cocked an eyebrow. "Ambiance," she answered, then her mouth twitched into a smile.

Her words broke the tension in the room. The man

laughed, and Lätt continued to prepare for the ritual.

"What's your name again?" she asked.

"Samus."

"How long were you married, Samus?" She placed a bowl of water on a small table next to the candles.

"Ten years next month." He smiled when he said it, but his eyes were sad. "She meant the world to me."

Lätt nodded, sensing the truth in his words. Many came to her seeking the same promise as this man, and they always spoke of their love. Though she'd never experienced it herself, she detected the love and the desperation in his eyes when he thought of his late wife. Scooping a handful of dirt recently procured from the floating orchard of the dead, she scattered the brown earth next to the bowl on the table.

When everything was in place she turned her gaze to Samus.

"Are you sure you'd like to proceed? There's no turning back once we start."

"Of course. I'd do anything to bring her back. *Anything.*"

"Then let's begin."

They stood on either side of a long, wooden table to the right of the smaller one on which Lätt had laid out the elemental sources needed for the ceremony. A corpse rested on the table, newly dead, as too far gone and the process wouldn't hold. Above the body they joined hands.

Lätt closed her eyes and began to chant. Samus could not understand the words she spoke, but did his best to keep calm, tightening his grip on her hands. If this worked he'd be the happiest man in the world.

As the intensity of the chant rose Lätt broke away from the man, sifting her hands first through the pile of earth, then the water, then over the dancing flame of the candle. Bringing her fingers to her lips she exhaled a burst of air onto them.

Samus could hardly believe his eyes. Between her hands a sphere of light formed. It was dim at first, but brightened in intensity with every passing second. When it became too bright to look at straight on Lätt opened her mouth wide and jailed the light behind her teeth. Light shone through her skin as she closed her lips around it.

After a moment she opened her eyes. When Samus looked into them all he saw was light, like peering into the face of a pair of stars. Lätt leaned over the woman on the table and, with one hand, parted the dead lips. With a gentle touch she pressed her own against them, pushing the light into the deceased's mouth with a flick of her tongue.

Light exchanged she pulled back, quickly slamming a hand over the woman's mouth to keep the light inside.

Then they waited.

It only took a moment, but Samus held his breath the entire time. A burst of light filled the room, adding to the heat of the fire, the force of which blew out the candles. As the light faded a wisp of it darted through the inky scene, slipping in to Lätt's eyes before she sent a spark from the tip of her finger to the wick of a candle to light the room again.

When his wife opened her eyes Samus burst into tears.

Lätt took her hand from the woman's face, her own eyes glowing a vibrant blue, and stepped back to let the two celebrate their reunion.

Wiping tears from his face Samus pressed the small bag of coins into Lätt's outstretched hands.

"Thank you. Thank you, Sorceress," he kept repeating. "What you have done, I could never repay."

Lätt only nodded, spilling the coins into her palm and counting them. "Payment enough," she said, raising the coins. "And your happiness, of course," she added as an afterthought.

After walking the couple out the door she watched them bounce joyously into the night with retreating whispers of gratitude.

Then Lätt closed the door on the tiptoeing moonlight and prepared for sleep.

◇◦━◦━━◦━◦◇

At that moment Ond was just arriving home. Pulling the bone from her waistband she lay it carefully on the table. Inside were the answers to all her questions, along with the promise of a new future.

She set about the delicate work of scraping slivers of bone, depositing them in the mortar and grinding them down into a fine dust. It was tedious, but it kept her hands busy and let her mind wander.

For so long she had been earthbound, unable to reach the skies, yet now she was so close she could almost taste it.

A puff of powder wisped in the air as she set down the pestle. She examined the white dust, deciding it would do. Then she set about working the spell, combining the ingredients in a large bowl. Last, she sprinkled in the bone fragments and stirred the mixture.

The liquid swirled, a pale shade of emerald. Lowering her face to the mouth of the bowl she inhaled deeply. The smell thrust its way through her nose, burning her from the inside, but Ond did not even flinch. Its vapor seeped into her, infiltrating her mind. Soon images filled her head.

She gazed down at wrinkled hands. They were not her own, but were familiar nonetheless.

"Master Tidsear!" The voice was youthful, carefree and naïve. Ond instantly recognized it.

In her mind she turned and came face-to-face with her younger self. The joyful grin was intoxicating, hinting at the tiniest bit of trouble, but nothing too serious.

"Ah, little one, up to mischief again I see," came Tidsear's voice, ancient and full of wisdom. The hand she'd seen moments before lifted to rest gently on the girl's shoulder. There was such affection in the movement, and Ond pushed down the emotion rising in her throat.

"You run along now, little beast," he continued. "I have a meeting with your father. Go find Lätt."

Obediently the child scampered off, and Tidsear settled in a nearby chair, letting out a heavy sigh as though he held the world on his shoulders.

"What will I do with those girls?" There was a sadness to the words that Ond wondered at, but a knock at the door prevented her from pondering it further.

A messenger appeared and announced the king was ready for their meeting.

When he arrived in the study the king was at the window, wings to the doorway.

At the sound of Tidsear's arrival he turned, and Ond met the eyes of the man she had not seen in many moons, the person she'd spend years seething against. His expression was grave, darkness brooding in his stormy gray eyes.

"Thank you for agreeing to meet with me," he said, gesturing to the chair. "I'm worried about the girls."

Tidsear sat, the body moving Ond along with it. "As am I, Your Majesty."

"A darkness grows in Ond. I fear what may come of it."

Involuntarily Ond jerked at the sound of her name coming from the man's mouth. It was a voice she had not heard in so long, a voice she once wished to speak words of approval to her; a voice she had chosen to ignore all those years ago.

"I agree. The two are so alike, yet also the exact inverse of the other. They've grown quite powerful, but I fear Ond will never be satisfied with the state of her wing."

An ominous cloud filled Ond, a fizzing anger that her deepest desire had been so obvious to those around her. She was ashamed of the weakness, and she chastised her younger self.

"She has great power," Tidsear continued. "During our lessons there is great drive and determination. I'm trying to channel that energy into productive means, but she is dead-set on fixing her perceived weakness. I fear she may go to great lengths to achieve her goal, perhaps reaching a point she could never return from."

"How do we prevent her from going too far?"

There was a still silence before Tidsear finally replied.

He cleared his throat and looked the king full in the face. "I don't know that we can. The girl is teetering at the point between good and evil. The slightest upset could send her over the edge, but she has to make the choice on her own. You know as well as I she cannot be forced to do something she does not want to."

The king did not respond at first. So much time passed that Ond suspected he would continue the silence indefinitely, but at last he stood and took Tidsear's wrinkled hand in his own.

"I trust that you will do your best to guide her in the right direction. I believe you are the only one who can."

Tidsear stood to leave, but the king addressed him once more.

"Is there any way for Ond to fix her wing? Would such a thing be possible? Perhaps if you show her then she will stop all this."

In response the mage slipped his long fingers into his pocket, withdrawing a small object. As he opened his palm Ond caught a glimpse of the ornately decorated, round-edged box cradled in his palm. With his other hand Tidsear lifted the lid, and a voice trickled out like a music box. It spoke words so softly that Ond strained to hear them. They flowed through the air like the faintest of breath, each word precisely uttered, delicate as a butterfly's wingbeat.

*Under blackest moon incomprehensible*
*enter this world, twins unconventional*
*sisters birthed upon the same hour*
*barring unforeseen elemental power*
*adorned with stunted wings yet to fly*

*still, all may not be as meets the eye*
*bound in royal blood spilt on gilded knife*
*the destruction of one to the other yields life*
*within their chests, tension dwells*
*that wages a war within themselves*
*a battle of good and evil is assured*
*a sickness festers if left uncured*
*if darkness should win and one should fall*
*it speaks of an end to destroy us all.*

There was a pause after the last word before Tidsear flicked his wrist, and the lid snapped shut with a click of finality.

Ond sucked in her breath, the potion still filling her senses. It was the first time she'd heard the actual words of the prophecy that had always loomed over her and Lätt's existence.

"The only way for her wing to become whole would be to find a perfect match from another."

"Another?"

"Another so like herself they could be one and the same, a twin so identical one could not tell them apart."

The weight of the old mage's words sank into the king's chest, and tears sprang to his eyes as he realized what Tidsear meant. *"The destruction of one to the other yields life."*

"Only then could she be whole, yet extracting the wing would inevitably kill the original host."

The tension in the room was thick.

"So, you see," Tidsear continued, his voice heavy now, like a weight pressing all the air from the room. "Ond could never fix her wing. Doing so would kill any good-ness left inside her. Doing so would end us all."

"I understand." Resolutely the two men shook hands, though the conversation they'd hoped would ease some of their worry had only increased it.

As Tidsear left the room the image faded in Ond's mind. She opened her eyes and was met with the swirling green of the potion.

She lifted her face, straining to stand straight against the weight of her prosthetic wings. A curling smile formed at the corners of her mouth.

"So, it's a twin I need." She turned from the table to retrieve a mirrored dish. Pouring water into it she blew across its surface.

"*Show me the one that I seek, the one I once knew - young, mild, meek, show me as clear as the dawning of day, show me my twin, my sister, Lätt.*"

Ripples marred the surface of the liquid. When they settled Lätt's peaceful face appeared, sleeping comfortably and unaware of her observer.

Ond dipped her finger into the reflective surface and took in Lätt's surroundings.

"There you are, sweet sister. I'll come for you soon."

◇━◇━━━◇━◇

When Lätt opened her eyes the sky was still pocked with stars. Raising her head she wondered what had disturbed her. It was when she reached a hand to brush the hair from her face that she realized her limbs were bound.

Sticky, white threads wrapped around her torso, securing her arms tightly to her sides. The casing reflected palely in the moonlight.

Lätt's eyes darted to the nightstand, hoping to reach the stone from which she could call forth fire, but it was not there. Instead she came face-to-face with the largest spider she'd ever seen.

The creature was enormous, its hairy body covering the entire surface of the table, legs slipping off the sides. A pair of large pinchers protruded from its face, opening and closing slowly as it watched Lätt through eight kaleidoscopic eyes.

Panic welled up in her chest, and she opened her mouth to scream, but before she could emanate a sound the spider lunged forward to plunge its fangs into the side of her neck. The scream died in her throat, crumpling into a desperate whimper as everything went black.

When she opened her eyes again she was no longer in her room. Instead she appeared to be inside a stone structure, laying on some sort of table. The air was cool and the room dark, her nose filling with a musty scent like being deep underground.

Shelves lined one wall, filled with books, jars, bottles and other assorted items.

When she tried wriggling she found the spider silk still wrapped around her. The material was fine and delicate, yet surprisingly strong.

Her eyes fell on a candle in the wall sconce near the door. Wax dripped down its side as the flame flickered, hope rising in Lätt's throat.

Gently she forced air through her lips, concentrating all her thoughts and energy. She pooled her anger inside of her, her response to being taken, tied up and trapped. She gathered all her raging fury and coaxed it toward the flame.

With a sudden burst the light intensified, then snaked a line directly toward her. The webbing encasing her quickly dissolved in its heat, deteriorating into ash as she shook away the remaining bindings.

Once freed Lätt swung her legs off the table and headed for the door, but a chanced peek at a book on the table gave her pause as she stopped to examine it more closely.

On the open page were neatly-scrawled columns of numbers. There were notes and figures, likely measurements of some kind.

Curious, Lätt flipped through the book. There were countless drawings, along with hastily-written notes, as though the author were fearful of losing the idea before it was committed to paper. She stopped on a rear-view image of a person, which caught her attention because of its strangeness. The person's wings had been removed, a gaping hole in the spine. There were notes about the spinal column and how fairy wings attached to the vertebrate, tendons wrapped around the bone for stability. It had an odd medical feel to it; the notes were detailed and clinical.

She flipped another page to find longitudinal and latitudinal coordinates written, circled, then crossed out in an angry slash. Something about a falling star and absorbing its power through consumption, but much of it had been scribbled out with the same ferocity.

Next came a page that detailed how to prepare an elixir. Lätt wondered what kind of mage would be interested in such a diverse range of studies as astrology, anatomy and potions. She read down the ingredients of herbs and plants, then her eyes locked on one line. *Freshly-ground fairy wings.*

Her wing stump twitched behind her as horror crossed her face.

She was just closing the book when the door to the room opened, and Lätt spun around to meet the newcomer.

It was like looking into a mirror.

The woman glanced up as she entered, one corner of her lips forming a grim smile. Her eyes flicked to the burnt remains of the spider silk. "I see you managed to wiggle your way out."

Lätt watched the woman carefully as she set a pile of books on the table.

"Why am I here, Ond?"

The woman's back straightened. She was still for a moment, candlelight shimmering off her metallic wings. "Oh, Lätt, isn't it enough to want to see my dear sister again?"

Lätt's hand shot out, a stream of water from the basin encircling her protectively. "What do you want, Ond?"

Her sister took a step toward her, but the water snapped out like a whip. It made contact with Ond's wrist and she clutched her other hand over it, glaring at Lätt through dark eyes.

"I need something from you, Lätt. I need your wing."

⟡━◦━━━◦━⟡

Lätt's jaw hung open as she took in her sister's words.

As children Ond had always been resentful of her stunted wing, convinced she'd easily master the air element if only she had the experience of flying with her wing, but this was insane. It had been years since they'd last seen each other, but Lätt would never have guessed how desperate Ond had become.

Deep down guilt thrashed. Perhaps if she'd been there for her sister, if she'd searched for her or if she hadn't run away, then maybe Ond wouldn't have reached this point.

"You can't be serious," Lätt whispered.

"Oh, I am more serious than I've even been. I've tried everything, as that volume can attest." She gestured toward the book Lätt had been paging through moments before. "Elixirs and transplants, shooting stars and powdered wings. All failures." Her eyes fixed on the fluttering motion behind her sister's head. "But that, that is how I can reach the heights I desire. That is the answer to everything."

Bile churned in Lätt's stomach. Thinking back on the diagrams in the book they were grotesque enough in theory, but realizing her sister had actually carried them out made her squirm.

"There has to be another way..."

Before she could finish Ond turned on her, her face a snarl of disgust. "Don't you think if there were an easier way I'd have done it? I heard it from Tidsear's own mouth. This is the only way." Instead of responding to Lätt's confused expression she leaned in close, an inch of tense air between them.

"I will be complete, no matter the cost."

Ond flung herself backward and reached behind her.

With a sickening tearing sound she ripped away the pair of metal wings that sprung from her back, blood dripping from their base where tiny screws had connected to the vertebra of her spine.

A shudder ran along Lätt's limbs. Ond hadn't even winced when she'd removed the wings, and for the first time Lätt wondered how much of the girl she once knew was left in the woman standing before her.

"You can't do this," Lätt pleaded. "There's no going back from this."

"Oh, come off it," Ond snapped, upper lip raised in disgust. "Don't pretend you're so perfect. You've done your fair share of sinister deeds; you've dabbled in soul taps just as much as I have. I've heard about your acts to raise the dead. You pretend like you're so kind to help those poor, unfortunate people, but you take more than their thanks, more than their money." She watched Lätt carefully, savoring her discomfort. "Don't you?"

Lätt refused to meet her sister's eyes.

"Yes, my eyes are dark from controlling others, from transplanting a little sliver of my soul into all those under my power, but tell me, dear sister, why are your eyes so bright? I don't recall them being such a remarkable shade of blue when we were children."

Lätt only scowled in response.

"Is it perhaps that, each time you wake the dead and shake their souls back to life, you take a little something extra? A little of their soul as payment for your kindness? Your eyes would not be quite so bright on one soul alone, but you have raised dozens, haven't you? Collecting bits of many souls is how you've managed to get by all these years, enhancing your magic with the souls of others. At least I make no attempt to hide my desires, to slink around in the darkness while pretending what I'm doing is okay. I know it's horrible, deplorable and disgusting, but I'm beyond caring. I'm sick of waiting for what I want. I've learned to only take."

With those final words Ond pounced.

⸻◈⸻◈⸻

Lätt ran.

It was the only thing she could think to do. She pushed past her sister and threw herself through the door. In the hallway she spun in each direction, trying to decide where to flee; she sensed Ond right behind her.

From a sconce on the wall she collected a handful of fire, then used its force to burst through the stone ceiling. Pebbles showered down as the air filled with a fine powder. Channeling her worry into the blocks that made up the walls she yanked a few toward her, creating a wobbly patch of footholds to climb.

The room above held less of the damp, earthy smell. She was getting closer to the surface.

Pushing her way through to the next level she was relieved to see windows adorning the walls. Rushing toward one she shot blasts of fire at its panes and leapt through the resulting opening. Behind her she heard Ond raging, and could almost feel the heat of her anger.

What she hadn't counted on was just how close the building was to the edge of the island on which it was perched.

Lätt's heart sprang into her throat as she felt herself falling. The wind rushed past her ears, whistling wildly, and not for the first time did she think how much easier it would be if she could fly.

With a painful jolt her elbow smashed into a protruding root, and she flung her hands out to catch hold of it.

With fingers securely wrapped around the mass of roots sticking out from the side of the floating island she held on desperately.

When she looked up Ond's face stared down at her, dark eyes fierce against the star-studded sky.

Lätt held her breath, unsure if her sister would help or not.

Relief flooded her system when Ond crouched down, hooked her legs around a thick root near the surface and swung down with an outstretched hand toward Lätt. She moved with such grace, such control over her body, even with useless wings hanging from her back that were no longer masked by their metal coverings.

Just as Lätt reached for the hand offering salvation her body lurched, the root slipping through the soil with her weight. There was a crack, like a rope snapping, as the root broke away from its source. Her body dropped down, and suddenly there was a sharp pain radiating up and down her spine.

Regaining her senses she realized that Ond had grabbed her full wing, and she now hung suspended by it over the gaping vastness below.

There was tension in Ond's expression, her brow furrowed in concentration. For a fleeting moment Lätt wondered if her sister were trying to save her, or only her wing.

Before she could contemplate further the pain in her back intensified, accompanied by a sound like paper tearing.

With the discomfort of realization Lätt knew her wing was ripping, unable to bear the load of her full body weight.

When she looked back up Ond's face revealed fear, and desperation. With a swell of power Ond pulled Lätt upward by her wing, close enough for Lätt to grab onto a root higher on the rockface. From there Lätt ascended, tugging at roots while Ond assisted her up the side of the floating island.

At the top Lätt collapsed, breathless and relieved. She felt Ond's eyes watching her, but allowed herself a moment to catch her breath.

◆━◇━━━◇━◆

When Lätt stood she saw the golden hilt of the knife in Ond's hand. She dove away as Ond slashed out, and she ducked through the slim trees that dotted the island. As she ran a root snaked out, twisting around her ankle and sending her sprawling to the ground.

Her back ached from the tear in her wing, now intensified by the branches that snagged at it.

Concern filled Ond's eyes as another tear opened in Lätt's wing. She approached to detangle the sticks that poked through its bright colors, and she was so preoccupied with keeping Lätt's wing from danger that she didn't pay attention to her footing. The earth shifted and her ankle buckled under her, sending her crashing to the ground, knife spinning from her grasp.

In a moment Lätt was on top of her, knees pressing into Ond's chest. She gripped the knife in her hands, preparing to plunge it through her sister's heart.

Looking down at Ond, Lätt hesitated a second; it was all the time Ond needed.

With ease Ond flipped Lätt onto her back, straddling her and squeezing her forcefully between her knees.

Lätt still held the knife, but Ond clamped her hands over Lätt's to break her grip. One of Lätt's wrists snapped with the force. She cried out in pain, but refused to let go. Slowly Ond turned the knife toward Lätt, overpowering her.

Clearly Ond was stronger.

There was only one thing she could do; Lätt let go of the knife. Not expecting the sudden lack of resistance, Ond's momentum sent her tumbling onto Lätt, in turn releasing the knife. Quickly Lätt snatched it up, pointing it threateningly.

Ond's clumsy attempt to rise sent her falling back down once again, and Lätt felt resistance against her arm.

Above her Ond stilled, looking down at her sister in shock. Then she glanced at the hilt sticking out of her chest, blood dripping down Lätt's arm. Rasping breaths of surprise and pain emanated from Ond's throat before she rolled onto her back.

Panicked, Lätt crouched above her while putting pressure on the wound.

"Oh, Ond! I'm sorry, I'm sorry. I didn't mean to. I just…I'm sorry!"

Tears spilled from Lätt's eyes. She hadn't meant to hurt her, not really, and she kept apologizing like a small child guilty of some minor misdemeanor.

Ond's breathing quickened, muscles going rigid.

From Ond's pouch Lätt grabbed the bottles and rock she knew would be inside and arranged them around Ond.

"Don't worry, I can fix this. I'll fix this. I will."

Water sloshed as she retrieved the vial of soil to the sound of Ond's pained moans.

Ond roiled on the ground, hand to her chest. "It burns," she wept. Lätt worked as quickly as she could, making the necessary preparations for the soul transfer.

As she did Ond pulled the iron blade from her chest, blood pouring onto the dirt.

"Don't worry, Ond. Almost ready. I'll bring you back, I can help. It's okay."

As she reached toward her Ond grabbed Lätt's hand weakly to stop her. From her expression she was in great pain, but there was a softness in her eyes that Lätt had not seen in a very long time.

Ond shook her head. "No, Lätt," she said so quietly it was only half a whisper. "I'm tired. Let me sleep, please."

Looking deep into her sister's eyes Lätt saw the pain that still rippled through her, pain that had been building for years. Ond threw back her head as another wave of agony hit.

Her chest ached with the thought of Ond suffering, and she wished she could stop the pain. Gently, Lätt brushed Ond's cheek, then leaned down and planted a kiss on her forehead. She hovered inches from Ond, then something pulled in Lätt's chest like a string as though tying her to Ond. Lätt took in a sharp breath, lips tingling. Suddenly Ond's eyes went wide, mouth agape. Her breath came out in a single, soft gasp. For a moment her eyes bulged, as though she couldn't breathe, then softness returned to her features.

She was still.

The muscles in Ond's arm slackened, her hand falling to her side as dark eyes stared sightlessly past Lätt.

Pain radiated through Lätt's body as she brought a hand to her numb lips. A complex medley of emotions swirled inside her. Guilt and fear, anger and loss. Raising her face to the sky she screamed out her anger, fire shooting from her limbs and her stomach wrenching.

She screamed loud enough to crack the crust of the earth, to tunnel down to its very core and unleash the pent-up fire inside.

When she'd exhausted her voice she lay next to Ond. The anger had dissipated, but there was something still lingering inside her. Something hard, yet smooth like a stone worn down by the waves of the sea. Something calm and dark, which felt like the color blue. She didn't know quite what it was, but she could feel something rolling around inside her and tumbling on currents of air.

Ond's last words echoed in her mind. *I'm tired. Let me sleep, please.*

Lätt closed her eyes and let herself sink into the infinity of space.

◇━◇━━◇━◇

When she came to she gaped at Ond's lifeless body. An overwhelming pain heaved in her chest to a level she had never experienced before. She felt like she was choking, drowning, unable to breathe; it was like there was not enough air left in the world. Lätt collapsed, overcome with emotion and exhaustion. She lay there for what felt like an eternity.

By the time she finally stirred the sky was dark. She looked up at the moon, a shining orb decorating the cloudy sky. It was a perfect moon by which to complete the death ritual.

Since Tidsear's ritual Lätt had never attended another ceremony. She'd never gotten close to another living soul to be included in one. Even when her mother died, and her father died, she did not attend the public ceremonies where thousands gathered. She'd gotten used to the safety of anonymity, of blending into the background and ignoring her past and the connections to it.

Worry swept over her as to whether she'd remember all the necessary steps, or if she'd be able to complete the ritual alone. The sight of the still body of her sister told her she'd have to do her best.

Using the worry in her mind she lifted the earth around the body, convincing it to carry the woman she'd shared such an intimate connection with, yet had never truly known.

Ond's body hovered beside her, carried by a wave of soil as Lätt made her way to the orchard.

After using a fire elemental to carry her and her sister's body up to the floating island to find an empty plot, she collapsed, utterly exhausted from the effort. She did her best to keep Ond's body from crashing to the ground.

With a swipe of her hand the soil settled, creating a soft bed for the corpse to lie in while she dug the grave.

Dirt clung to every inch of her skin, forcing its way under her nails as she dug the hole. The earth was slightly damp, caking her in muddy streaks as tears dripped onto her work. She couldn't recall the last time she'd cried; even when Tidsear was murdered she hadn't cried. She'd been confused and angry, but the feeling that rolled around in her soul now was like nothing she'd ever experienced. It was as though a piece of herself was gone.

As she rested, stretching her aching hands, she gazed at the soon-to-be-occupant of the grave. Perhaps she *had* lost part of herself along with the sister she had longed for. After Ond had left the castle she always felt a piece of her was missing, and now that piece was gone for good.

Lätt smudged the tears on her cheeks with the shoulder of her dress, one of the few unsoiled parts left, and resumed her work. The physical task allowed her an excuse to push away the difficult thoughts threatening to infiltrate her brain. She took advantage of the intimate distraction, refusing to utilize earth magic.

When the hole was finished, the earth open like a wide mouth ready to swallow its prey, Lätt carefully scooped Ond up in her arms. She was mindful not to wrinkle the single wing on her back, the twin of her own.

Placed in the grave Ond looked so small, like a child in a crib sleeping peacefully despite the blood and wounds that suggested otherwise. Lätt's heart lurched and she stifled a sob.

She pulled out her dagger and began cutting through the soft skin of Ond's chest, widening the hole already there. Blood pooled beneath the blade, so vibrant and red, so full of life even after its host had gone still. Lätt pushed the blade deeper, pain resonating in her own chest as though it were her skin beneath the knife.

It was torture to perform this death ritual, to cut open this body so like her own. It pained her to know that she was the cause of it, that it was she who had ended this life. Yet she could not take it back, and didn't know if she would even if she could. The options had been few, and this was the one she'd settled on. She'd have to live with that.

Bone cracked as she put her full weight against the dagger, digging further into Ond's chest like opening a second grave. Lätt bit back the bile and revulsion that threatened to spew from her, and continued her work.

Finally, after pushing her way through layers of tissue and muscle, she reached the organ she sought. The heart was so fiercely red that it was almost a bruised purple in the moonlight. Blood clung to it, tiny marks from Lätt's clumsy blade marring its otherwise perfect surface.

Stopping a moment to stare at the heart, Lätt thought of how it must match her own, how easily it could have been her heart exposed to the stars this night; how close she had come to her own demise.

Tears forced themselves from her eyes, and a sob erupted in her throat. She screamed at the night, at the uncaring sky and at the moon bearing witness to her pain. Her voice rang as she bellowed out her frustration, her disgust and her fear. There was something else too, something she had not felt before.

Sadness. Sorrow. Grief.

They overwhelmed her.

When Lätt opened her eyes she was no longer

crouched over the body of her dead sister. She was no longer on the ground at all. She was levitating a few inches above the grave, little currents of air swirling around her. With a surprised gasp she crashed back to earth, banging her knee on the hilt of the abandoned dagger.

She had flown. Lätt had flown. She closed her eyes and tried to grasp onto how she'd felt the moment she'd lifted from the ground.

Sadness.

It was her sadness that had allowed her to control the air. It was her sorrow that had given her the strength to fly, despite her broken wing.

Lätt rested her hand on her sister's chest, wondering if this knowledge could have saved her, or if it could have changed the course of history.

It was no use dreaming about what was not. Perhaps Ond had gone too far already. Perhaps by the end she'd been incapable of feeling that sadness, so removed was she from feelings for others. Perhaps that's where sadness comes from; loving, losing and suffering. Not just anger at having someone taken from you, and not just frustration. Sadness was what one felt at the loss of another for their own sake, not for the selfishness of being left behind.

Lätt picked up her knife once more and gently caressed the heart, preparing to slice it open. It was then she realized her oversight in preparations.

She had no seeds for Ond's heart.

Panic rose, and Lätt cried out at having failed her sister in this one last, desperate act to show she cared. She laid her forehead on Ond's chest and cried, tears seeping into the disheveled clothing and bloody heart.

Above her the wind picked up, howling through the branches of the surrounding trees as if matching her own pain.

Lätt sat up. The wind. The wind was the answer.

She stood in the grave, Ond's body at her feet.

Then she called upon all the sorrow that weighed down her chest. She pushed at the air with all her might, calling it to her and tasking it to do her bidding.

Eyes clenched firmly, the wind swirling around her, Lätt caught the distinct scent of different currents originating from all directions.

When she chanced a peek she saw pockets of wind whispering around her, dropping little offerings at her feet. A quickly-growing pile sprinkled her shoes, countless bits scattering around her.

Seeds. Seeds blown by the wind. Dandelion seeds with their fluffy, white hats. Clumps of cottonwood as thick as wool. Swan plant seeds, having burst forth from their pods with their dark, black bodies and ivory tops. Winged seeds of maple trees swirling like tiny propellers. Jacaranda tree seeds fluttering in the air along with seeds Lätt had never seen before. They swooped and soared, dancing on the wind as though in recognition of the sacred event.

She collected the seeds from all over the world, her sadness reaching all its dark corners.

Then she set about depositing them into the slit in the heart. With the organ packed full she continued sprinkling them into the chest cavity, filling it with the diversity of seeds. She hoped to please her sister in this one thing after failing her in so many others.

When it could hold no more Lätt closed up the wound

and arranged the tattered garments over the bloody gash. She did not have the cotton sheets usually draped over the body, so she cast her eyes about for something to cover the hole in Ond's chest.

A twinge at her back forced her eyes closed as a muscle twitched her torn wing. She glanced over her shoulder at the wing that hung wilted, barely attached to her body.

Gritting her teeth she reached around and jerked the wing the rest of the way. It came off in her hand, light as air, and after a moment her shoulders relaxed. Holding the wing in her hands she fingered the delicate design, then gently placed it over Ond. The thing Ond had wanted all along, a twin to her own.

Lätt took a moment to compose herself, to smooth Ond's hair and straighten the collar of her ripped dress.

Climbing from the grave she dropped handfuls of dirt one by one. It pained her that she was the sole attendant of Ond's death ritual, the moon the only witness to the sacred events. It hurt that Ond had been missing for so much of her life, and that perhaps some of this had been preventable. If only things were different. If only she could go back.

Handful after handful Lätt covered the body, the earth sliding through her fingers and sprinkling down onto the sister she'd loved once.

The grave full, a fresh mound of dirt in the spongy ground, Lätt sat and watched over it. She surveyed the skies, following the tails of shooting stars, and mourned the loss of her twin.

❖━◆━ ◇ ━━ ◇ ━◆━❖

It had been one year since she'd buried her sister. Lätt walked slowly through the town, others flitting around her as they carried out their business.

When she reached the edge of the market she looked up at the floating isle through dull, gray eyes. She no longer had her wings; the skin on her back had grown over where they once protruded, leaving a trail of scars. They would not get her to the island.

She hadn't used air magic since the night her sister died, and she did not use it now.

Instead Lätt reached out and stroked the feathers of the hippogriff who stood beside her.

She leaned over and momentarily rested her forehead on its neck. When she pulled away she looked deep into the creature's dark-brown eyes, which seemed to hold the world.

"Will you take me there, Balans?" she asked.

The hippogriff nuzzled her lovingly with its snout. It felt good to form connections, and to love another being.

Lätt swung her leg over Balans' back and the creature kicked off, flying for the floating orchard. For the first time since Lätt could remember she was happy. No longer content to live in solitude, Lätt had found a way to fly.

# McKenzie Richardson

## About the Author

McKenzie Richardson lives in Milwaukee, WI. A lifelong explorer of imagined worlds on the written page, over the last few years she has been finding homes for her own creations. Most recently, her work will be published in Eerie River Publishing's It Calls From the Sea and Dark Magic. Her stories and poetry are also featured in anthologies from Black Hare Press, Iron Faerie Publishing, and Dragon Soul Press. In addition, she has published a poetry collaboration with Casey Renee Kiser, 433 Lighted Way, and her middle-grade fantasy novel, Heartstrings, is available on Amazon.

McKenzie loves all things books and is currently working towards a master's degree in Library and Information Sciences. When not writing, she can usually be found in her book hoard, reading or just looking at her shelves longingly.

For more on her writing, follow her on:

Facebook: http://www.facebook.com/mckenzielrichardson/

Instagram: http://www.instagram.com/mckenzielrichardson/

Blog: http://www.craft-cycle.com

# The Hound Of Oakenhall

## Austin Shirey

### I.

Had it been any other tavern, in any other town, every eye in the place would have marked the wilderknight's heavy steps as he approached the bar. As it was, the Ill-At-Ease was mostly empty, and the handful of customers spread about did not care about one lonesome, dark-skinned stranger. Nothing interesting ever happened here, not anymore.

Straw covered the dirt floor, and a great, blazing hearth in the center of the tavern painted everything in warm, golden hues. The smell of roast pig and venison stew wafted out from the kitchen behind the bar. A gaunt serving girl with sad eyes and a fake smile made the rounds, giggling when a drunkard pawed at her. A group of farmhands around another table chuckled at something only they could hear.

The wilderknight was a big man, and tall, his face obscured by the hood of a thick cloak. Beneath the cloak he wore an old, leather cuirass pulled over a light hauberk, a bastard sword at his left hip. A pair of daggers hung at his right hip from the belt crossing his leather trousers.

He laid a pair of copper pieces on the bar.

"Ale," he said to the innkeeper, voice full of gravel.

The innkeeper — a round, red-haired man named Brunnar — nodded. He poured the ale, slid the tankard across the bar and collected the coins.

The wilderknight took a long, deep drink, then tossed four more coppers onto the bar.

Brunnar eyed them. "You wanting food, then?"

"Looking for someone."

"Who's that?"

"Varg Valgrim."

Brunnar swallowed. He pointed quickly across the room to a man sitting alone at a corner table, then swiped the coins from the bar and wobbled into the kitchen.

The man Brunnar had pointed to was bald, his face wedge-shaped, nose sharp and crooked. He wore a loose tunic and a seal-skin coat.

He motioned the wilderknight over.

When the wilderknight had taken his seat and pulled back his hood, the bald man cleared his throat. "Varg Valgrim. Who're you?"

"Gedric."

"I've heard that accent before. Where you from?"

"Yranor.

"Ah. You here about the bounty?"

Gedric nodded.

Varg sighed. "If you value your life, turn around."

"Bit overdramatic."

"You're not the first bounty hunter the Shipping Guild's hired for this," Varg said. "Not even the first from Yranor. Won't be the last, neither. They've practically been feeding men like you to whatever's been haunting Oakenhall these past few months. Damn thing can't be killed."

"I've heard the rumors."

"Not rumors. Truth. It can't be killed."

"There's nothing in this world that can't be killed."

"Tell that to those who've died trying to kill it."

"The Guild's not willing to give up their best ship-wrights, not yet."

"The Guild's in denial," Varg said through clenched teeth. "I've told them, but they won't listen. They're too greedy to listen. Ears stuffed full of gold."

"It's bad form to speak ill of your employer."

"It's bad form for my employer to knowingly send men to their deaths — even if those folks are just boun-ty hunters. I don't want no more blood on my hands. I'm done. I'm telling everyone the Guild sends this way the truth. So, I'll tell you again: turn around."

"The Guild knows."

"Knows what?"

"They know what you've been up to, and they're not happy." Gedric brought a dagger up from under the table. "They offered me extra for your head."

Varg's eyes widened, his lips quivering as the blood drained from his face.

Gedric brought the knife down.

Naked steel lodged into the table between Varg's fin-gers. He stared in silence, fingers trembling.

"Listen," Gedric said. "Tell me how to get to Oakenhall, then disappear. When I go back to collect I'll tell them I never found you. Heard you'd been eaten by a troll or something. Consider it a reward, for having a conscience."

Varg looked up.

"If," he said.

"What?"

"If you make it back."

The wilderknight grunted.

## II.

Dusk fell as Gedric nudged his horse, Shadow, to a stop at the crest of a hill.

He had left the Ill-At-Ease a little after dawn, as Varg had suggested, following an old road that trailed northeast through rolling hills and dense forests of alder, spruce and pine. Everything was dusted in a thin blanket of snow. There had been no sound of birdsong, or any other wildlife, as he travelled, and he found the unnatural silence unsettling. Passing through the small town of Illingrod had been even more so. Abandoned homesteads, and the smaller shops that made up the town's central market, stared lifelessly at him from either side of the road — cold, quiet, and unwelcoming.

And if Illingrod was a ghost town, then Oakenhall was a graveyard.

From the top of the hill, several hundred yards distant, the blackened remains of the manor loomed like the broken rib cage of some long-dead leviathan. A ghostly wind howled through its gaping corpse, sending wisps of snow dancing down empty halls. A semi-circle of ruined longhouses surrounded it, along with an empty stable and an abandoned forge. To Gedric's surprise he noticed smoke puffing from the roof of the westernmost house, a faint light glowing in one of its windows.

Great. The land was supposed to be abandoned — the Guild had said as much.

He didn't need people getting in his way.

He sighed and urged Shadow closer. Nearing the

manor, he caught a flash of movement in the corner of his eye and pulled Shadow to a halt.

A massive, black wolf-like creature sat watching him from the edge of the forest east of the ruins. Its eyes blazed with an emerald fire like distant, angry stars.

Gedric's throat went dry. He'd never seen a bargast that big. From this distance, even while sitting on its haunches, it looked to be at least two- or three-heads taller than himself. On all fours it would be bigger still.

Something howled behind him.

He turned in his saddle.

Nothing.

He glanced back at the edge of the forest, but the bargast was gone.

Gedric dismounted, taking Shadow's reins and directing the horse to the manor. They'd camp there tonight.

He tied Shadow to a broken railing attached to the main entryway. He stooped to enter the ruined doorway, kicking aside shards of wood that reached for him like dead hands. Rubble crunched beneath his boots.

The eviscerated structure was nothing more than a mausoleum of ashes and mildewed wood; a ghost of a great hall, unfit even for ghosts. Walls and roofing had been torn asunder, with monstrous gouges and scratches scarring everything. Beneath splintered tables and chairs, shattered glass gathered dust. A great fire had burned through here, covering everything in a patina of black ash. Charred skeletons stared up at him, half-buried by the remnants of rampant destruction: some bore the armor of bounty hunters and mercenaries, while others bore no armor at all.

Gedric pushed aside a dangling beam, stepping deeper into the blackened heart of Oakenhall. No crunch sounded beneath his boots, though he felt something soft give under his weight. He looked down, finding a homemade doll. The white fabric was now a dark, blackish-gray, and straw sprouted through a hole in its side. It was missing an arm and one of its button-eyes. The remaining eye held his gaze, and he felt a chill creep across his flesh.

His thoughts returned to the longhouse, to the smoke billowing from its roof and the light shining in its window.

Wood creaked.

A monstrous, living shadow hit Gedric with the force of a stampede. He burst through the manor's broken frame, plummeting to the ground several yards away, air ripping from his lungs on impact.

The bargast roared.

Dazed and wracked with pain, Gedric picked himself up, trying to find —

Claws slashed through the night. He rolled under them, quickly returning to his feet. He pulled his sword free from its scabbard, the blade singing a cold chorus of promised violence.

He swung.

The sword *shattered*.

The bargast was on him in a flurry of fur and teeth. Long, iron-like claws slashed through his leather cuirass, piercing through the small, interlinked rings of his hauberk and pinning him to the earth. Green-orb eyes blazed at him like hungry suns, and a ferocious growl showered him in hot, stinking saliva; its breath reeked of sulfur.

Gedric roared, bringing the pommel of his broken sword down again and again on the monster's head. His arms reverberated with pain, as if he were beating a boulder.

The bargast snapped at the shattered sword, wrenching it from his hand. It landed somewhere out of sight with a sharp *clang*.

He groaned beneath the beast's weight, struggling to pull his daggers from their sheathes. He screamed and stabbed them into either side of the monster's snout, the knives splintering into glittering shards.

The bargast snapped at his neck. Gedric brought his right hand up in a fist and connected with its snout just as it was about to rip open his throat, feeling cartilage give beneath the force of his blow.

The bargast snarled, shaking its monstrous head, eyes surprised. It lunged forward. He knocked the great head back and forth with both fists, blood and spittle covering him.

It roared, claws raking across his chest. He screamed. It tried again for his throat, but he brought up both hands and grasped either side of its open maw.

He kneed the bargast in the stomach, wrenching the lower jaw back with his left hand while grabbing one of its great fangs with his right.

The bargast whipped its head back and forth, but Gedric held on. It snarled, trying to snap its jaws shut; he barely kept its mouth open, arms shaking with the effort. The fang sliced his hand to the bone.

In a desperate effort Gedric pulled with all his remaining strength. The giant tooth ripped free, trailing shreds of bloody flesh.

The bargast whined, releasing him, and pulling back.

It shrieked, shaking its head back and forth. With a final, bewildered cry, it disappeared into the forest.

Gedric held the bargast's fang in his tattered hand. He felt his strength trickle away like wine leaking from a wineskin, and as pain bloomed in his body, darkness enveloped him.

III.

*Tir-Na-Vale looms before you. The earth is burnt black from years of battle, blood, and sorcery.*

*Victory here is an impossibility; blood cannot buy victory in Tir-Na-Vale, no matter how much is shed for it, but you keep such thoughts to yourself. Your duty is to your lord, as his duty is to his king.*

*Honor is everything.*

*The enemy is vast, like an unconquerable sea. Their pale, slender bodies seem to glow in the murk of the battlefield. The antlers crowning their heads appear as sharp, creeping shadows in the fog. Elves are wicked warriors, and even more wicked sorcerers.*

*Bodies rush forward from every direction brandishing thirsty blades, some wearing armor, others wearing nothing; a surging, cascading wave of antlered elves against a wave of fathers and brothers and mothers and sisters and sons and daughters. Teeth bared, mouths snarling, collectively charging toward doom.*

*And you are caught up with them.*

*You hack and tear and stab and cut for what seems like a hundred years. Screams become a buzzing drone in your ears, amorphous and undefined. Your muscles feel like water; your arms, legs and head grow numb, appendages in name only, phantoms in truth. Your world is black, except for bright, spurting splashes of crimson. Hovering over everything is the smell of blood, sweat and shit mixing with the sickly-sweet scent of discharged sorcery.*

*You don't know why you look back, but you do. You*

*watch in disbelief as your lord, and the lords of your comrades-in-arms, turn their horses from the battlefield, fleeing to safety.*

*Leaving all of you to die.*

*To shed your blood for nothing.*

*Something burns to life inside of your broken body at the sight of the retreating nobles — the men and women who demand you fulfill your duty to them, even as they forsake their duty to you.*

*You throw down your sword and shield, rip off the colors of your master's house, and discard your armor as battle rages around you.*

*Victory here is an impossibility.*

*Honor is nothing.*

*Your blood is worthless.*

*You almost make it to the edge of the valley — almost make it to freedom — when darkness takes you.*

## IV.

Gedric woke.

A pale, blonde-haired woman yelped and stepped back from him, wringing a bloody cloth in her hands.

He'd been laid atop an old table in a drafty longhouse, his cloak and armor piled on the floor. He glanced at his chest where the woman had sewn shut the many gouges he'd received from the bargast; a foul-smelling balm was smeared over them. Several layers of torn cloth were bandaged around his midsection, with more wrapped around his shredded hand.

"You should be dead," the woman said. Her face was gaunt, her high cheekbones sharp under skin lined and stretched by time and tribulation.

Gedric grimaced as he sat up.

"I thought everyone had forgotten us," she said.

He grunted, tried standing. His vision went hazy and he grasped for the table, missing. The woman caught him under an arm.

"Who are you?" she asked.

Gedric wrenched his arm from her grip and steadied himself. "I can take care of myself."

The woman huffed. "Hardly."

"What are you doing here?"

The woman placed her hands on her hips. "I'm Lady Hredda Oakenbrok."

Just what he needed — a damned noble. Gedric cursed the Guild. If the Oakenbroks were so damned important, why hadn't they moved the woman somewhere else?

"It's customary to share your name with someone who has shared theirs," she said.

"Gedric," he said, if only to shut her up.

Hredda smiled. "Thank you for coming to aid my family, Gedric."

"I'm not here for your family. I didn't even know anyone still lived here."

Hredda's countenance soured. "What are you here for, then?"

"Gold," Gedric said. He didn't tell her the Guild also wanted a report, an idea of how long it would take them to rebuild, to have the shipworks back up and running. But, based on what he'd already seen, Oakenhall was too-far gone. It'd be quicker for the Guild to just employ one of the many other shipwright clans that dotted Skellangard's coast.

Hredda made a sound he'd heard many nobles make before — a sound intended to indicate indignation. To his ears it sounded like a small animal being trampled to death.

He ignored her and looked out the window behind Hredda. The afternoon was as bright as it could be under such a gray sky. "How long was I out?"

"A night and a day."

Gedric's brows rose. He didn't think it'd been that bad.

"You were gravely injured," Hredda said. Her tone insinuated that he was lucky she'd been around to save his life.

Gedric bent to pick up his hauberk and cuirass from the floor, wincing as pain throbbed throughout his body. He pulled the chainmail shirt over his head, then the leather armor. When he finished, Hredda placed something hard and sharp into his bandaged hand.

The bargast's jagged fang dwarfed his palm. Clumps of dried blood darkened it, and strips of flesh still hung from the edge where he had ripped it from the jaw.

"How did you do it?" she asked. "No-one has ever so much as given the creature a scratch."

He grunted. The truth was he didn't know. His sword and daggers had shattered upon the creature, yet he'd been able to rip out a fang bare-handed. None of it made sense.

"Mama?"

Gedric startled, looking up to see a pair of painfully thin children — two girls not more than six or seven winters old — peering out from behind Hredda as they clutched her skirts. Wet eyes looked up at him from behind curtains of red hair.

His chest grew tight, and he felt lightheaded. One thought — a worry that had dug its way into his mind like a splinter — one he'd tried time and again to ignore, to pretend it didn't terrify him to his very bones, overwhelmed him now. Was there a family somewhere out in the world still waiting for him to come home from Tir-Na-Vale? So much of his memory had been lost —

"Mama, did he kill the monster?"

"Hush, Frenya," Hredda said to the tallest girl. "Didn't I tell you and Astrith to remain in your rooms?"

"Did he kill it?"

Gedric remained silent as Hredda herded the girls back toward their quarters.

"Is it possible?" she asked when she returned. "To kill it?"

"Anything that bleeds can die." He hoped so, at least. He wrapped his cloak around his shoulders. "You and your girls should leave this place."

Hredda glared at him. "You think we choose to stay here?"

"Why else would you be here?"

"It won't let us leave."

His brow furrowed.

"It watches," Hredda said. "It knows. If we try to run, it attacks. Corrals us. Tears apart another shelter as a warning."

"The other longhouses — "

"We've tried to leave many times."

"This thing has killed everyone here, except you and your girls?"

Hredda looked away and put a hand to her mouth, a tear rolling down her cheek.

Gedric sat down on the bench at the table. The kitchen was bare, yet there were signs of at least occasional meals: a dirty dish here, a half-filled goblet there.

"How are you staying fed?" he asked.

"It...brings us food."

"The bargast brings you food?"

She nodded. "It...waits. It's like it knows when we can't go one more day without food, and then it'll leave dead things at the door in the morning."

"Dead things?"

"Half-eaten deer. Rabbits, sometimes. Squirrels. Rats, even, or a crow here and there."

"How do you get water?"

"The well, behind the houses."

Something was off, here. The fact that the bargast watched Hredda — that it could intuit when she and the children needed food — suggested a high intelligence. It wasn't just an animal; it could think, plan. It punished the Oakenbroks when they went against its wishes. Its actions were spiteful, as if it wanted Hredda and her family to suffer—a trait he had only ever encountered in races like his own.

"My horse?" he asked, remembering he'd left her at the manor. "Is she — "

"She's fine," Hredda said. "Still right where you left her. I gave her some feed I found in your saddlebags."

"Good." Gedric stood up, ignoring both his pain and Hredda's unspoken request for his thanks. He placed the bargast's fang in one of his trouser pockets.

"What are you doing? You're in no condition — "

"The blood's not fresh, but I should still be able to track it."

"Track it? I can promise you the beast will return here, and soon. Why not just wait for it? Give yourself time to heal?"

"Waiting gives it more time to heal, too."

## V.

The eastern woods were dark, cold, and silent. The foliage was so thick it blocked out what little sun was able to pierce the cloudy, gray sky, and the forest wallowed in a kind of blue twilight. The still air smelled of earth and pine.

Shadow had stopped at the edge of a wide clearing where the bargast's blood — just barely visible enough to track, as he'd figured — had led them. At its center a gnarled stump jutted up like a broken fang. A large, snow-covered mound rose from the ground next to it.

Gedric felt a tremble course through Shadow, then he felt it, too. There was something oppressive smothering the clearing; a cold, suffocating weight hung invisibly in the air.

Something terrible had happened here, something that had left its mark upon the spirit of the land like an angry wound.

He pushed his uneasiness aside, dismounted, made his way to the stump.

It was several hand-spans wide and came to a sharp, pointy end around his chest. He ran his fingers over the jagged ridges, noting the irregular edge. A hasty cut; sloppy. Angry.

Gedric circled the stump, noticing strange carvings at its base partially obscured by snow. He knelt, uncovering the marks with a few swipes. If it was a language, then it wasn't one he'd ever come across.

He turned, checked his surroundings, stepping closer

to the mound living in the stump's shadow. It was as wide as he was long, and only rose up to the top of his boots. He thought it might be a barrow, or a midden heap.

He caught himself as he tripped on something sticking out of the mound. He kicked at it, disturbing snow and soil, but it didn't give. He knelt and dug around the object, clearing away dirt, snow, and clumps of something like rotted leather until he revealed a rusted, curved scimitar.

Gedric ripped it free from the mound and stood. A fractured arm bone hung limply from the scimitar's hilt, charred black. He shook the bone free and appraised the scimitar; it wasn't a thing of great craftsmanship or beauty, but once upon a time it'd been a sturdy blade.

He slipped the scimitar into his belt and made his way back toward Shadow. He hadn't moved more than a few paces when something else caught his eye — something round and off-white.

He returned to the mound and pulled at the object. It broke apart, the rounded piece remaining in his grip while whatever had been attached dropped to the ground. He turned the round piece over in his hands.

The skull was large — bigger than his own — with a thick, protruding brow shadowing wide eye sockets. A charred piece of leathered flesh or tendon hung from its side.

Gedric bent and picked up the piece that had fallen off, held it in place beneath the skull. The jawbone pushed outward, two long tusks rising up from either side of the bottom teeth.

Spriggans....

But spriggans hadn't been seen in these lands for a long time.

Gedric knelt at the mound and dug, grasping and pulling at whatever he could beneath the ash and snow. It felt like he was digging for hours.

When he'd finished, his lungs were on fire and his breath came in gasps. Sweat glistened on his brow where it mingled with ash and grime.

Then the gaping mouth of the mass grave devoured him whole.

## VI.

You awake in darkness, under a great weight. When you try to push the weight off yourself, your hands come away slick and stinking of blood.

*You are buried beneath the corpses of your fallen brothers and sisters.*

*You can't breathe, can't think, can't move. You push and shove while someone is screaming, but nothing moves, nothing gives, and all around you is blood, blood, blood, trickling into your mouth, your eyes, your ears, your nose. Dirt and blood and dirt and blood and dirt and blood.*

*You kick, push, claw, and kick again until the weight is lifted. Then you're shoving bodies and parts of bodies and armor and weapons aside, crawling, crawling, crawling through layer after layer of flesh and bone. Familiar faces stare sightlessly at you as you push them down and use them as stepping stones to make your frenzied ascent back to the land of the living.*

*Now you're free, only to find you're still in Tir-Na-Vale, the sky dark and rumbling with thunder as rain stabs your skin.*

*Then comes the moment you'll never forget as long as you live, the moment you'll never be convinced actually happened.*

*The moment, you realize much later, when you lost everything.*

*She is standing several hundred yards away from you, naked and radiant, in a field of corpses. Her antlers are withered hands grasping toward the sky, and her long, black hair dances hauntingly in the breeze. Two gigantic crows perch upon her shoulders.*

*You've heard the stories of the elves' matron of war, the devourer of the souls of the warrior dead.*

*The Mabbigan.*

*A chill courses through you as she turns. Now blood is falling from the clouds, painting her alabaster skin in brilliant streaks of red. Her crows begin to caw, their voices so loud you fall to your knees clutching your ears.*

*The Mabbigan strides toward you, seeming to float. Her bare feet are black with blood. Her eyes burn brightly gold, and your vision grows dark as you stare into them, until those golden eyes are the suns your entire being revolves around.*

*She brings you to your feet, wraps herself around you, forces your mouth to hers and drinks deep of you. You feel something leave you, something you can't name, and emptiness and darkness take its place.*

*The Mabbigan pulls back, a wicked smile on her beatific face, and she licks her lips.*

*"A deserter," she says, but her lips have stopped moving. "A wanderer."*

*She lets you crumple to the dirt as she strides away, back across the valley.*

*"Scavenger of darkness," her voice sings. The crows on her shoulders flap their wings, the sound like thunder. "Harvester of sorrows."*

*She disappears, and you are left with nothing but your name and this nightmare.*

VII.

Hredda's longhouse was burning when Gedric and Shadow exited the forest.

Thick, black smoke and wild, orange flames billowed from the house, igniting the half-light of dusk with garish color. Hredda was screaming.

Gedric snapped Shadow's reins, sending the horse into a gallop. They neared the burning house and he saw the bargast sprint off toward the western woods with something limp hanging from its mouth.

Hredda knelt in the snow, one of her daughters cowering beside her. She screamed again as the beast disappeared, lurching forward as if to go after it, but her daughter held her back by her skirts, wailing for her to stay.

Gedric brought Shadow to a stop in front of Hredda and the girl — Frenya, the oldest — and jumped down, kneeling quickly to grasp the woman's shoulders.

"Astrith!" Hredda shrieked. "It has Astrith!"

He shot to his feet, turning in the direction the bargast had fled —

And stopped.

He looked down at Hredda and Frenya, huddled together in the snow in the shadow of the blazing ruin of what had been their last shelter. He watched as the longhouse was smothered in a bright, orange-black shroud of fire.

There was nothing he could do. Astrith was gone. Dead. It was pointless to chase after the monster; retrieving the child's body wouldn't ease Hredda and Frenya's grief. It would only cost him time, time he'd desperately need.

Gedric moved as close as he dared to the longhouse and grabbed a splintered plank of wood laying partially out of the flames.

He walked back to Hredda with his makeshift torch and pulled her to her feet, placing the torch in her hands. She accepted it without a word.

He bent again and pulled Frenya up from the ground, then hefted himself back into Shadow's saddle. He motioned for Frenya to climb up behind him.

"Hold on to me," he said. She wrapped her arms around him, sniffling into his cloak.

Hredda cried. "What are you — "

"Just get on," Gedric said, reaching down to take the torch from Hredda with one hand and then offering to pull her up with the other.

"But Astrith — "

"She's dead."

Hredda recoiled. He expected her to begin screaming anew. Instead, she let out a deep, defeated breath and grasped his outstretched hand. He pulled her up into the saddle behind Frenya.

Gedric snapped Shadow's reins and the horse trotted into the eastern woods, back along the trail they'd made earlier.

The woods were now night-black, the only light that of the burning plank Gedric held aloft to light their way. Frenya sputtered and burst into tears several times as they rode deeper into the forest. Hredda softly hushed her, as only a mother could.

"I — I don't understand," Hredda said after quieting Frenya again. "Where are you taking us?"

"There's something you need to see," Gedric said.

"What?"

Proof of her family's crimes, most likely. But he said nothing, and they rode on in silence in a lone sphere of light surrounded by darkness.

## VIII.

When they reached the clearing, Shadow stopped again at the edge. Gedric had to click his tongue several times to get her to approach the gnarled tree stump and the mass grave.

Gedric hopped down with the torch, leaving Hredda and Frenya atop Shadow. He stepped over to the stump, illuminating it.

"Do you know what this is?"

Fear flickered across Hredda's eyes, but she quickly regained control. "It's a tree stump. Why — "

Gedric held up a hand to stop her. "Did you know about this clearing?"

"No," Hredda said, avoiding his eyes. "I've never come out here. I took care of the manor and the finances. Lord Torgrom was the one who oversaw the lumbering and the ship-making."

"Lord Torgrom?"

"My husband."

"How did he die?"

"The beast…It tore him in two the day it first attacked Oakenhall. Killed him along with all…all our workers."

A terrible understanding burned in Gedric's chest. The vengeful intent the bargast displayed, the spite with which it preyed upon — and played with — Hredda and her girls. Reciprocation, perhaps?

Gedric stepped past the trunk and brought the torch over the mass grave he'd uncovered. Hredda cried out and quickly covered her mouth.

"Do you know what these are?" he asked.

"Tusker bones," Hredda whispered.

"Spriggans," Gedric corrected, gritting his teeth at the slur that had flowed so easily from her tongue. "An entire tribe, from the looks of it."

"Tribe?"

"Did your husband ever say anything about spriggans living in these woods?"

Hredda shrugged. "Once, maybe. A long time ago."

Gedric stepped toward her. "What did he say, Hredda?"

She swallowed. "Just that tusk — spriggans — had made their home far out here, but he'd said they were no trouble."

Gedric glared at her in the torchlight. She lied with such practiced ease. "He said that? That they were no trouble?"

Hredda nodded slowly.

Gedric sighed, nodding as he placed his free hand in his trouser pocket to keep it from the cold. His fingers felt along the jagged edges of the bargast's fang.

Time to end this, then.

He took his hand out of his pocket, withdrew the rusted scimitar from his belt.

"You're not going to like what comes next," he said, "but you don't have a choice."

Hredda began to weep.

## IX.

The longhouse was a burning eye on the horizon a league behind them. Hredda and Frenya sat clutching each other atop Shadow, Gedric following behind with the torch in one hand, scimitar in the other.

"Why are you doing this?" Hredda asked again. "You know it'll just run us down!"

"I'm counting on it," Gedric said.

"You're a monster!"

He couldn't help but laugh at that, ignoring her tear-filled glare. The thing about monsters, he knew, was that it often took one to recognize another.

Behind them, he heard the crunching of snow as another monster gained on them.

The bargast was coming.

Gedric clicked once to stop Shadow in her tracks. He'd need to do this next part quickly, before the beast overtook them.

"Get down," he said, motioning Hredda and Frenya out of the saddle with a flick of the spriggan blade.

Hredda dismounted first, turning and grasping Frenya under her arms to help her down.

"Walk forward."

"What are — "

"Hush, woman! Just do as I say!"

The bargast's footfalls grew louder.

Hredda shut her mouth and grasped Frenya close to her, her eyes stabbing Gedric hatefully.

"There. Stop."

Gedric bent, dragging the scimitar in the snow behind him to carve a wide circle around himself, Shadow, Hredda, and Frenya. He moved swiftly through the inside of the circle, cutting down, up, and side-to-side several times, making the seven-pointed star of Yrises — just like he'd seen the League of Light do back in Elba several years ago, when he'd taken a job hunting a cabal of necromancers.

He connected the last line just as the bargast bounded into the torchlight.

Hredda screamed, wrapping herself protectively around Frenya. Gedric stood unmoving, his breath catching in his throat and his heart thundering in his chest.

The moment of truth....

The bargast roared, jumping for Hredda and the girl. It seemed to hit an invisible wall in mid-air, yelping as it was thrown backwards into the snow beyond the light.

The circle had worked. But that meant —

Gedric stepped forward. Hredda gave him a panicked look as he moved in front of her, putting himself between the Oakenbroks and the edge of the circle.

The bargast moved cautiously from out of the darkness and back into the torchlight. A growl rumbled deep in its throat, its head down, its remaining fangs bared, emerald eyes burning like hateful, unblinking furnaces at the wilderknight. It moved along the edge of the circle, growling and sniffing, confirming there was no way through the invisible boundary.

It roared one last time, then slumped back on its haunches.

And spoke with a woman's voice.

"The star of the Scarred God," it said, motioning with its snout to the sigil carved into the snow.

Gedric nodded, slid the scimitar back under his belt. "It's said it protects against vengeful spirits."

The bargast cocked its head. "How did you know?"

"I didn't," Gedric admitted, "but the more I pondered your actions, the more it seemed...possible."

"A daring gamble."

"Ran out of options. You forced my hand."

"True. Your presence disrupted things."

"Thought as much."

"They deserve everything I've done to them," the bargast said, indicating Hredda and Frenya. "The lady especially."

"Probably," Gedric said.

The bargast snarled. "And what do you care?"

"Maybe I agree with you, with your course of action."

"What?" Hredda cried.

"I know your people were slaughtered," Gedric said, eyes on the bargast. "I know the what, but not the how, or the why."

"What are you doing?" Hredda asked.

The bargast laughed, its smile mirthless and wicked. "You are a cunning man, to have figured out so much already. But why should I trust you?"

"Honor demands that I allow justice to run its course."

"This is not justice!" Hredda screamed. "Justice is restoring my family's name! Our honor!"

"You would truly step aside?" the bargast asked Gedric. "Wipe out the sigil and give me justice?"

"You can't," Hredda said. "Please, Gedric. You can't. Don't listen to it."

Gedric put a hand over his heart and bowed to the bargast. "I, Gedric, wilderknight of Yranor, give you my word."

The bargast bowed its head in turn. "I, Sorin Rhoag, shaman of Orgru Tribe, thank you, wilderknight."

Hredda burst into incomprehensible pleadings.

"How did your people perish?" Gedric asked. "Why were they killed?"

"I can tell you how," Sorin Rhoag said, "but for the why, you must ask the woman."

## X.

Hredda shook with an uncontrollable rage.

"I did what my husband lacked the courage to do!" she screamed. "You tusker filth were taking up acres of our land, impeding our business!"

"But it is not your land," Sorin Rhoag said. "The northlands have belonged to spriggafolk since time immemorial. You are the invaders here, not us."

"The grave I found was recent," Gedric said. "Six, seven years old at the most."

The bargast nodded. "Several winters ago, under cover of night, Lady Oakenbrok came with a band of mercenaries. The tribe was slaughtered, including my two life-mates, and our two beautiful daughters. My own life was taken from me, by her command. Our sacred tree was hacked down, desecrated."

"You got what you deserved," Hredda said.

"Shut up," Gedric said, pointing at her. "Or I'll cut out your tongue."

Sorin Rhoag glared at Hredda, the malevolent green stars of the bargast's eyes seeming to burn brighter.

"But how are you in this form?" Gedric asked. "And if this happened so many years ago, why attack Oakenhall only recently?"

"Because I swore an oath," Sorin Rhoag said. "A powerful oath, woven of blood and magic. I swore my spirit would not rest until my people and my family were avenged. That no weapon should harm the vessel I inhabited, nor any other magic. When my spirit fled my body, it found this beast wandering the wastes, and took it. Then I waited. I watched from shadows, until the Oakenbrok's daughters were the same age as my own."

"You didn't kill them, though," Gedric said. "Until Astrith, tonight. Why?"

"I want the bitch to suffer," Sorin Rhoag said, and the bargast smiled.

## XI.

Gedric stood silent for a long while, eyes downcast, avoiding the green blaze of the bargast's eyes.

Hredda paced behind him while Frenya mumbled incoherently, shaken and frightened beyond the point of understanding.

He was shaken as well. Shaken by the anger and pain in Sorin Rhoag's voice, by Hredda's prejudice and the violence of her hate. He was angered on Sorin Rhoag's behalf, but he was also angry at her for what she'd done to two innocent children. He could feel the anger taking root in the soil of his soul, joining with his own and budding to the surface, threatening to blossom.

He toyed with the bargast's tooth in his pocket, thinking.

"Hredda is yours," Gedric said, finally. "But leave the girl alive, with me. Killing Frenya won't heal your heart or bring your family back, but sparing her might save what little soul you have left."

The beast shook its head. "I am bound by my curse — just as you are bound by your own."

Gedric stiffened.

"Yes," Sorin Rhoag said, "I can see the aura of the elf-curse roiling about you like blackened chains. We are much alike, you and I."

He knew they were, and yet he hoped they weren't.

The bargast growled. "I've spoken true. It is time for you to give me justice. Or will you break your word to me?"

Gedric swallowed and shook his head. "No. You'll have your justice."

A strange look came over the bargast's face, one Gedric could not quite decipher.

"You are an honorable man," Sorin Rhoag said, approaching the edge of the circle and licking her lips. "A rare thing indeed."

He shook his head. He'd made his peace with what he really was a long time ago.

Gedric moved to the edge of the circle across from Hredda and Frenya.

"Mama!" Frenya cried, pulling on her mother's skirts. Hredda bundled her daughter up in her arms, clutching her to her breasts.

"It's alright," Hredda whispered. "It'll be alright. Just close your eyes, love. Close your eyes. We're going to see Papa and Astrith again, very soon. Hush, now."

"Now, wilderknight," Sorin Rhoag demanded. "Justice."

Holding the torch aloft, Gedric broke the Yrisian circle in the snow, rubbing out part of the outer line with the heel of his boot. He pulled the scimitar from his belt and flung it beyond the circle, into the darkness.

"It's done," he said.

The bargast pawed at the invisible barrier. Nothing happened.

"It is done," Sorin Rhoag agreed. "At long last."

The beast made a roaring leap.

Hredda's throat was gone in a surge of blood. Her lifeless body slumped over Frenya, pinning the girl to the ground.

Sorin Rhoag snarled over Frenya, and the bargast opened its gory jaws.

Gedric spun, pulling the fang from his pocket, and leaping upon the creature's back.

He stabbed the fang through one of the bargast's eyes, gouging through the viscous orb and deep into the monster's brain.

The monster's claws flashed. With a whimper and a spasm, Sorin Rhoag died one last time, the bargast's body slumping over both Hredda and Frenya in the snow.

An icy wind moaned in the night, the only sound in a world of sudden, violent silence.

"Frenya?" Gedric said breathlessly. "Frenya?"

No answer.

He rolled off the bargast, dragged it from Hredda's body.

Frenya lay pinned beneath her lifeless mother, eyes staring sightlessly at the sky. Blood flowed from the mess the bargast's claws had made of her.

Gedric's shoulders fell. He knelt, cold and numb. The faces of Frenya and Astrith, very much alive — the day he'd first seen them — flashed before his eyes.

Children. They were just children.

It wasn't...None of it had been their fault. It was so... pointless.

Needless.

He shivered as cold enshrouded him. The wind whispered about him, and he thought he heard a voice echoing from across time, from another life:

*"Scavenger of darkness...Harvester of sorrows..."*

Something broke inside of him then, something he'd

fashioned within himself to barricade against the pain. All of it, everything, came pouring forth in a bitter torrent, flooding his defenses and drowning him in darkness.

The wilderknight wept bitterly.

## XII.

Gedric shoveled the last bit of dirt over Sorin Rhoag's grave. He'd buried her at the foot of the hewn trunk of the sacred tree, hoping she might rest with the spirits of her tribe; hoping she'd find the peace she'd been denied in life.

A light snow was falling from the sky, sprinkling through the open canopy of the clearing. It was a little colder than it had been the day before, but he'd worked up a sweat. Early that morning he'd built a funeral pyre for Hredda and Frenya, as was the custom in Skellangard, before he'd set about seeing Sorin buried with her people.

He picked up the sack he'd set next to the stump and walked back to where Shadow was waiting at the edge of the clearing. The horse nuzzled him as he tied the sack containing the bargast's head to the saddle-horn. When he finished, he stroked Shadow's broad nose affectionately.

Gedric pulled himself up into the saddle, looking at the jagged stump and the new mound that rose from the ground next to it one last time.

"Forgive me," he whispered.

He clicked his tongue, and Shadow began trotting back through the woods. He'd make his way past Illingrod and spend another night at the Ill-At-Ease — just to startle Brunnar again and make sure that Varg Valgrim had heeded his advice — then continue on to the Guildhouse in Fringvast to collect payment. Then, eventually, south.

Back home.

"Somewhere warmer," he said to Shadow, patting her side. She neighed in agreement.

The wilderknight rode on in silence, leaving the ruins of Oakenhall behind him.

# Austin Shirey

## About the Author

Austin Shirey has been telling stories ever since he first read THE HOBBIT as a kid. If he's not writing, he's probably reading or enjoying time with his wife, their two daughters, and their two cats in Northern Virginia. His fiction has appeared in Orca, All Worlds Wayfarer, Stonecoast Review, Blind Corner, and the MIDNIGHT SHADOWS anthology from Eerie River Publishing, with stories forthcoming in the WEIRD FICTION anthology from Black Hare Press and the FROM THE YONDER 2 anthology from War Monkey Publications. You can find him and his work online at www.austinshirey.com.

Follow him on:
https://www.austinshirey.com
https://www.amazon.com/Austin-Shirey/e/B08VDN3DPZ/
https://twitter.com/tashirey87 https://www.instagram.com/shirey_writes

# Dith the Fire Witch: A Night Order Story

## Rachael Boucker

I dance my fingers on the water, watching the ripples spread and distort the moonlight. I've been strumming this lake for a while, trying to tease out what lies beneath. Like plucking a web string and waiting for the spider's pounce, only I'm ready for this monster.

The night air speeds through my hair, whipping up a blur of black against my face. As it stills a few reeds continue to wave above the surface. The monster thinks itself sly, crawling on its belly through the silt of the shallows. If I stare through the reflection of the stars and clouds I'll see it, but I keep my face turned away. It must believe I'm prey to come within striking distance. Water sloshes against my hand, displaced by the monster creeping ever closer. You'd think it would know better; no villager would sit so calmly on the shore by the lake they've all learned to fear.

The drowner pierces the lake in an explosion of water, but I'm quicker. I throw down the man-sized beast and mount it. It wriggles beneath me, a slimy mass covered in fish skin. Crossing my dual daggers on either side of its throat I slice in deep. Blood sprays onto my face, and I wipe my eyes and mouth on my sleeve. There's nothing sweeter than demon blood, though I could do without the aftertaste.

I've nigh decapitated the thing with the first strike, but I need to finish the job. I wield my daggers once again. Heads are paid for in coin, and while I can scavenge many things from the land I'm craving a decent ale.

Like all demons the drowner was once human, before its soul was destroyed and replaced with something ungodly. I wipe some blood off the severed head to admire the fish scales covering its flattened features, even in death they shimmer with dancing colors. The skin almost looks alive. I turn it 'round and lay my hand on its gills. Its large, unblinking eyes are dark pools, and its mouth is filled with needle-like teeth. I sigh. Sometimes these hunts are just too eas —

I headbutt the ground as my legs are pulled from under me. Something is dragging me into the lake. Slipping along the shore I dig one hand into the sandy ground, and, foolishly, reach for the rolling head I dropped with the other. The sandy grit slips under my fingers and I take a huge breath as the cold water hits my breasts — a beat later I'm below the water. Bubbles spill from my lips in the struggle; nothing I do, not the flailing, kicking or even the dagger jabs to the scaly hands around my ankles, stop the monster from dragging me to drowning depths.

I take one last glance at the shrinking moon. *Damn it!* The head, my prize, bobs on the surface above, lazily sailing further into the lake. It fades from sight and I turn away. The head is worth a few coins, but the prize in this fight is my life. Chanting is out of the question, and there's nothing I can easily carve runes into, so there's only one magic that is mine to wield without the need to conjure; blood gifted to my family every generation or so. I call to the fire within, and the warmth of budding flames builds through my body.

We reach the bottom of the lake, and the drowner ties my foot to a weed; the demon means to watch me drown. It floats in front of me, smiling garishly with pointed teeth. I smile right back, grab its arm, and pull it to me. Closing my hands around its throat I channel all the heat into them, gazing into the monster's filmy, black eyes until that tender fish skin sizzles. Flames will not bloom underwater, but I can still draw out blistering heat.

All life leaves the demon; I release the body to focus on the weed. I need to surface, to take a breath, but the weed doesn't come untied. I bring out a dagger and saw through it.

The drowner corpse has risen beyond my view, though there is a shadow on the water to aim for. I follow its path to the surface, my lungs burning, and take huge, spluttering gasps the second my lips meet air. I see now that the shadow was a small rowboat, not the body — one of its oars smacks me in the head.

"Hey," I yell, but the boatman ignores me and rows on. Weighed down by my leather armor and heavy boots I struggle to stay afloat. "A little help?"

I slowly swim toward the shore, where the man has already landed. He hauls his boat up from the water's edge. I watch him drag a drowner body from his boat, then hack off its head with an axe. "Hey, that's my kill!" The last word is gargled as I sink. It takes great energy to break the surface again, and when I do I find the cloaked man is bundling the head into a sack, then he picks up a second from his boat. "They're both mine!" The lakebed is finally beneath my feet. I wade through the shallows and chase after him, but he mounts a waiting horse and speeds off into the night.

"Bastard," I hiss. My pack is untouched at least, not that a bandit would have much use for a worn change of clothes and witch's herbs. "Utter bastard." I wipe water from my face and shoulder my sack, taking the trail away from the lake.

The path winds through the dark woods. A large oak, the victim of a recent lightning strike, has toppled a neighboring tree onto the path. I climb over the trunk blocking my way, then groan at the horseshoe prints on the other side. The blockade didn't even slow the thief. Owls hoot, and in the distance a lone wolf howls. The woods around the path have become overgrown without the taming from man's axe. I could avoid the brittle twigs and leaves crunching beneath my soggy boots, but I'm not afraid of the creatures in the night. In fact, after my run-in with the head stealer, I'm daring something to fight me.

Many trails lead off from the main path, though only one leads to a village with a tavern. Most of the settlements around here are deserted, populated by corpses and ruins. I look down one such trail and shiver, like I'm being blasted with cold. 'Good instincts' is what the witch who raised me called it, when it first started a few years back. I think it's something more, like the icy grip of a lost soul beckoning me from their grave.

I trudge the lengthy walk with my arms wrapped around me. The freezing wind bites and whips up leaves, dirt and tree needles that stick to my wet clothes. I'm a mess, but I'm too angry to change. My rightfully-earned drink will have to be bartered for, or begged for.

*Wait, is that...?* The bastard thief is selling my heads right outside the tavern. I stomp over with a brewing rage large enough to topple the thief, the four men he stands with and the company of soldiers. "Where'd you get the drowner heads?" I yell.

"From a drowner, of course. If you're looking to buy, I'm 'fraid I already sold them to these fellas," says the thief. There's nothing redeemable in that grinning mug, with his bulbous nose and balding head, nor in the lazy way he leans on the crates stacked against the tavern wall.

"I'm looking to add your head to the pile if you don't give back what you stole," I shout. I could burn him, just a little, to teach him a lesson. He doesn't have the look of a rogue, but the men he stands with do. One, a son of a drowner, has vestigial gills peeking out from his collar. All rogues are first generation descendants of demons mated with humans, though some inherit more than strength and speed from their demon fathers. This thief doesn't look like he even inherited that.

"Didn't steal anything, and you can't prove I did." He stands up straight and folds his arms.

"Those are my kills!" The flames build again, this time manifesting as a ball of fire in my hand. "You can see the scorch marks on that head there. I killed it, the other one too."

"Sorry, miss," says one of the three soldiers packing

up their haul, "The duke pays for heads, not kills."

My heads are wheeled away on the horse-drawn cart, with others collected from around the woodland settlements. The payment isn't gone though. I scowl at the bulbous nosed rogue. "My kills, my coins. Hand them over."

"Blood is on my axe," says the smug rogue thief. "Who's to say I didn't kill it after you burned it?"

I can barely contain my rage, and it shows in the growing fireball.

A slimmer rogue with long, brown hair and bright-green eyes moves between us. "Don't be a fool, Corman. That witch will fry you where you stand, and *I'm* to say you didn't kill them. You've got a sixth sense for thievery, but you're hopeless with that axe."

"You wanna see what I can do with this axe?" Corman snarls, squaring up to the smaller rogue.

"Tell me, Corman," says the green-eyed rogue, pinching and opening his fingers and thumb like a moving mouth, "Who killed the drowners?"

Corman's eyes widen. "The witch drew one in and beheaded it, then got taken under by another. I took a small boat and rowed out to collect the head she lost, and grabbed the second body when it came up." Corman frowns as the other man's hand lowers. "That ain't fair, Greg, you ain't supposed to use your truth-thing on us. I watched her for ages, bored as Hell I was, and that boat wasn't in good shape. Risked my life getting those heads, and I deserve to be paid."

"Give her the coin," says the one he called Greg.

Corman digs inside his pocket and slaps some coins

into Greg's hand. "She gets half, and don't say I ain't being generous." He skulks off into the tavern, and all of his men but Greg follow.

Greg hands me the coins. "I'm sorry about him, and I hope you won't judge all rogues by his actions. If you wait here I can get the rest off him for you."

I look at the bronze in my palm; it seems the duke's soldiers are more generous to rogues than witches. "No, half will do." I can afford a whole pitcher with this.

"You must be the one they call Dith the Fire Witch." Greg smiles and holds out his hand.

I don't take it. "Edith, Dith to some, and you're the Ventriloquist." It's rare for rogues to inherit any usable traits from their demon fathers, but this one has. "You're a puppet-master spawn."

"Guilty, but all I can do is make people talk truth. I don't pull strings like the demons do."

I've seen what a puppet-master can do, making people take up arms against each other or making them commit suicide in the most horrific ways. This rogue seems harmless, and is certainly pleasing to the eye. I turn away before I'm bewitched by his sparkling smile. "Goodbye, rogue." I walk past him and push through the creaky door into the tavern.

It's busy tonight. The musty smell of unwashed fighters and spilled ale creates a noxious stench. Typical - all the tables are occupied, and I'd hoped to sit alone. That lake holds bad memories for me, and this isn't the first time I was caught off guard by its drowners.

"Dith, over 'ere!" I recognize the croak of Iris's aged voice. A group of witches have taken over the middle bench. The last time I saw a gathering this large was when we were warned of an advancing demon army, so I hope there's no such news tonight.

"Dith, is it?" Corman smirks and leans back in a chair with his legs spread. "More like Ditch, as that's where you'll end up." His table of cronies erupts in forced laughter. "Come find me, Ditch," Corman shouts after me, "when you're ready to feel the heat of a real man."

I roll my eyes and sit at the end of the bench with my fellow witches. They're too deep in conversation to offer more than a grunted greeting.

"Excuse me," I call to the serving girl as she moves from table to table with a pitcher. I call her a second time but she ignores me, so I grab her arm as she passes. "An ale, when you're ready." She leers at me, snatching her arm away before walking on with a deepened scowl.

They've taken to calling it the dark ages. These last remnants of humanity stay huddled in the hovels they share with their livestock, tilling the earth no further than their fenced boundaries. They used to have candles to ward off the dark, and fires to keep them warm, but now they hide in the night. Any fool could tell them they're as likely to fall prey to demons in the daylight.

"What say you, Edith?" Beatrice says, elbowing me in the ribs.

"About what?" I ask. A tankard of ale is slammed down in front of me, splashing droplets onto my already sodden clothes. I give the serving girl a glare, then place a coin into her waiting palm. She's safer among us than she would be in her own home, yet she still treats us with contempt.

"About the alliance," Beatrice says. "Iris wants to forge a truce with the clergy, make the demons our enemies too."

"They're already our enemies." Before they surged in numbers you could get a decent drink. I swirl the swill in the tankard, sniff it, then gulp some down with a grimace. "My daggers have tasted demon blood this very night, and shall do so tomorrow as well."

"Keep your voice down!" Iris chalks some runes on the bench and whispers to them, the noise from the bar silencing. The drunken patrons still laugh and talk, but in sight only. Iris has locked us in a sound bubble. "I'm talking about organization, girl." Iris's eyes shift to Beatrice. "Something you wouldn't be capable of even if you did know the meaning."

The need for secrecy only grows my unease. "The humans forced us to live in the shadows once, cursed for being born, so what do we get out of an alliance?"

"We would be organized, connected. The second a demon is spotted word can be got to our closest hunters, and with the humans on side we'll never be persecuted again — equals among men. We're not just doing this for us, but for future generations of witches."

Of the ten of us seated around the bench Iris is the oldest, and no doubt the wisest. I suspect her gift lies in foresight, an ability even rarer than my own. "Whose ear do you have?" I ask. I give one last disgusted look to my ale before pouring it on the floor.

"A cardinal up north, and two to the east. The dukes may sign the decrees, but you better believe it's the cardinals that write them," says Iris. The old woman's steely stare is framed with wrinkles. She's bent more ears than that, no doubt.

"You'd think the cardinals would have been the first people the demons slaughtered," says Beatrice. Her disappointment is shared; it was a cardinal that wrote the decree demonizing magic and all who wield it.

"Petulant child, so blinded by the past you can't see the bridge to the future." Frail as she may look, Iris still had a mean backhand. "You, Beatrice, may one day mother a child, and think differently about the world."

I snigger. Beatrice is an uncomely woman; I doubt any man will mate with her.

"Something funny, Dith?" Iris's graying eyes bore into me.

I compose myself. "No, Iris. Please continue."

"The next half moon we'll meet in Arle. I'll present the duke with a proposition, all you need do is bring some demon heads, as a..." She waves her hands and grins a toothless smile, "...visual demonstration."

"I'll be there, Iris." As a rule I avoid the larger cities, such as Arle, but Iris has earned my respect and support.

I feel a breeze as the door opens, and I turn as another patron wanders in. A ghostly chill comes with him and beckons me outside. I lean back, outside of the sound bubble. The tavern may be full of roaring laughter and conversation, but something is off about this night.

Beatrice grabs my arm as I stand. "Don't leave yet," I watch her mime.

I lean into the bubble and pat her shoulder. "I'll see you in Arle."

When I reach the door there's a smell in the air of

primal fear. *The village!* I sprint along the puddle-pocked lane until I have the mud huts in view. I know these people; I've bartered with them and taken shelter with them on stormy nights. It's quiet, and all looks as it should, but the strengthening smell draws me nearer. I slow my pace, listening and scouring. A snapping stick causes me to jerk round. "Are you following me?"

"No," the green-eyed rogue whispers. "I'm following the scent of fear. Something dreadful is happening down there."

I don't remember seeing Greg in the tavern, but perhaps he was tasked with looking after Corman's horse. I creep along the path to the first house where the pulling chill feels the strongest, and gesture for Greg to check the next. Wind blows the door woven from twigs, peeling forward the top corner until the only thing keeping it closed is the mud wedging the bottom rim. I hear a whimper over the breeze and pull the door open, stepping into the small, windowless hut.

"Please, stop me...please." Blood soaks everything from the ground to the beds made from sacks. It surrounds a kneeling woman, and two dead sheep lay on either side of her.

"Germaine?"

"Please, Dith, please, I beg of you." Germaine holds a baby in the crook of one arm, a knife raised high with the other. There's something about the way her wrist hangs limply, as though held up by a string. "I can't stop," she breathes.

Germaine plunges the knife toward her baby with a wounded squeal. I leap forward, grabbing her wrist before the blade reaches the child. "Why are you doing this?"

"I'm not," she whimpers. "I love all my children."

Tiny, butchered figures lay among the sacks and blood, curled up in deathly slumber. She had three children the last time I met her; the baby made four. The only survivor stirs in her grasp and begins to cry. Germaine renews her efforts to stab the infant while still begging me to stop her. I snatch the child away, releasing her wrist, and draw one of my daggers. "I warn you, if you come at me with that knife I will kill you."

She stands up in the most peculiar way, as though she's being dragged up by her hands — a marionette on invisible strings. The knife speeds down, bloodying her abdomen in a flurry of stabs. It's not a quick death, nor a painless one. I grab the knife, tossing it away, and kneel at Germaine's side. Her eyes are wide and slick with tears; she means to speak, but only rasps and groans form in her dying moments.

This is the work of a puppet-master, a demon that looks human. It must be close to have pulled the invisible strings. *Windowless hut!* It's in here with me. Germaine lets out one last breath, and I close her eyes. "Come on, little one," I say to the baby, hoping the lightness of my tone will make the demon feel unseen. "Let's see if we can find anyone else."

I walk out of the hut and wedge the door shut without turning around.

"Dith?" Greg calls as he runs over to me.

"What did you find?"

"A baby. Can you hold it for a moment?"

Greg looks perplexed, but takes the child from me.

"That hut is drenched in blood. I've never seen anything like it," he says, pointing at the hut he ran from.

The fire builds up inside me. I know I should bury my feet in the earth to ground a magic of this magnitude, but the demon will not stay hidden for long. A torrent of fire streams out of my hands, engulfing the hut. I hold it steady, not letting up for a second. The toll is taken from my energy stores, and if I spend too much now I'll leave nothing to fuel the beat of my heart and the heaves of my lungs. Memories are triggered of Germaine shearing her sheep, her children chasing one another around the hut, and I pour even more rage into the flames.

"Dith, stop!" Greg yells, "That's enou — "

One wall of the hut splinters open and the demon crashes through it. It glances back, and I catch a glimpse of its moonlit face. A woman — this puppet-master is female. I start after her, but on the third step I crash to the ground, my body awash with fatigue. Breaths and heartbeats are all I can manage on my current reserves.

"Dith, Dith!" The ringing in my ears drowns out Greg's voice. I keep my eyes on the fleeing demon for as long as they stay open.

◇━◈━◇━━◇━◈◇

"How long was I out?"

Greg helps me sit up. The hut burns with tall flames, and the infant screams in Greg's arms. "Not long. I gave you a potion to aid your recovery."

"We should go after her." I stare at the empty space where I last saw the demon and begin to rise.

Greg puts his hand on my chest. "You can't overexert yourself. The potion hasn't fully returned your strength."

I lower back down with a sigh and push his hand away. "Were there any other survivors?"

"The three far huts were untouched, and other than that it looks like they're all dead."

"Looks like? You didn't check them?"

Greg puts his hand on me again when I try to stand. "I looked through every door, after I gave you the potion. Couldn't do much more than that with you unconscious and a baby in tow." The hand at his side balls into a fist.

"You're angry."

"Of course I'm angry! The more the flames poured out of you the paler you became. I told you to stop, and you didn't listen."

"I wanted to kill the demon."

"Kill yourself, more like. The hut was ablaze long before you stopped. If you'd told me what you were doing I could have gone after the demon the second the fire drew it out, but instead I'm stuck here looking after you." We stay locked in a silent glare until Greg lowers his eyes and shushes the crying child. "I'm going to the tavern to get help. You stay here, and don't move."

I watch him leave. Hopefully someone in the tavern will raise Germaine's baby, or know of kin nearby.

Greg might have been right about me overspending on fire, but he doesn't know all of my tricks. I stand before the hut and suck all the flames back into my hands; the power is mine to give and mine to take back. With Greg's potion bolstering my energy I feel better than I did before, invincible even.

Kicking through the charred remains I find a deep hole dug into the hut's mud floor. This must be where she hid and watched, pulling her strings from under one of the sacks. I'm careful to step over the blackened remains of Germaine and her three children.

It's such a waste. There must have been over two hundred souls crammed into this village, and after a single attack only a handful remain. I want to bury the burned family, but soon all the witches, rogues and a few of the braver humans will descend on this place. There's enough hands to dig, and mine still thirst for blood.

The chill of death calls me into the forest and I heed it, leaving behind the destruction. I follow the path of the demon that wrought it into the darkened trees.

I hear my name called over the wind rustled leaves. Having traveled far from the slaughtered village it only takes a short walk for the calls to fade completely. I'm alone, and that's just how I like it. The chill tugs me on as I wind through trees, step over logs and stomp through bushes.

A howl makes me pause. It sounds like a wolf, but with a trained witch's ear I discern it for what it is. Creeping closer I crouch down and watch through the leaves of a berry bush. For all my wayward walking I've stumbled onto a path, faintly worn and rarely used, and on that path is a cart filled with demon heads. Two men and a woman sit next to the duke's murdered soldiers, slicing the skin from their bodies. The killers are naked, save for the wolf-skins they wear. *Skin-wearers, demon juveniles.* Their souls have taken over adult humans, but the demons are immature. Unguided in an unfamiliar world, they kill and wear the skins of others to role play how to live as each creature. After wearing prey animals they move on to wolves, and finally they wear the skins of men before reaching maturity and developing into monsters. Drowners and puppet-masters are most common in these parts. Females typically become drowners or plagues, unrecognizable from their human forms, and the one I hunt now is the first female puppet-master I've encountered.

One of the men gives off an elated howl as he tears the skin from a soldier. He discards his wolf-skin and slips the human head skin over his own, wearing the rest of the soldier like a cape.

That's enough watching for me. I etch runes into the ground with a stick: runes for position, runes for scale, and runes to shrink the grains of dirt and rocks that sit beneath my quarry. Then I wiggle the tips of my fingers into the ground and chant. The ground shifts underneath them, but they're too preoccupied to notice. I have them all now, thousands of grains at my command. My whispered chant ends with a trill, and all the grains shrink in unison. The skin-wearers shriek and flail, but there's no escape from the hole that's opened below them. Their heads and arms are all that remain above ground. They paw at the dirt, trying to drag themselves out, and with a smile I reverse the chant and listen to their crushing screams. The reversal causes the dirt to spill out, burying the beasts. I remove my fingers from the ground and stroll over to uncover my prize.

The cart is full of heads that are already marked with the duke's stamp to deter thieves. I've no doubt rogues like Corman inspired that precaution. The skin-wearers aren't marked, though. When it comes to the beheadings I sometimes wish I carried an axe, but once I've cleared the mounds I find the crushing dirt has partially done the job for me. I slice through the remaining flesh and tendons with my daggers and line up the three heads; there's something familiar about their faces.

The chill pricks me with a sudden rush of goosebumps. I stay crouched next to the heads, listening intently. A low growl comes from the trees behind the cart, slow steps pushing through the overgrowth from the left. The cart creaks, a single head rolling off the pile.

They come at me in unison, both wearing wolfskins, their human eyes staring through the holes that used to surround animal ones. The first leaps from the cart as the second one barrels into me head first; I lose my balance and falter back, tripping over one of the neck-stump mounds. The one from the left has my wrist in his mouth, shaking it back and forth like a rabid dog. He can't pierce my vambrace with his human teeth, and even if that wolf head was real the teeth would have a rough job getting through the hardened leather cuff. The other lands on top of me and mashes the wolf's teeth against my face; I can smell the fetid skin still attached to the fur.

I stab the one on top of me as his hands curl round my throat. The one to the left loses my hand and jumps on his friend, the weight of them pushing the air from my lungs. I can't say where the stabs are landing, but I keep thrusting the dagger into them.

An arrow speeds into the strangler's eye, and his hands fall away from my neck. His weight remains though, and the second one is trying to pry my fingers from the dagger with his teeth. Another arrow whizzes above my head, and the biter grows still.

"We sent a search party looking for you, wiped blood off every dead face in case it was yours," Greg says. He heaves the bodies off me so I can better see his scowl.

I set to the task, cutting the wolf-wearers from their heads.

"Those villagers need burying. You could have been helping."

"So could you, but here we are." I bundle the five skin-wearer heads into a sack. The next half moon is still four days away. They'll be rancid by then, and I don't fancy carrying them around with me. "Help me dig a hole under this birch."

Greg glares at me. "If you wanted to dig a hole you should have stayed in the village." The only response I give is to point at the dirt below the birch tree; he sighs, then begins to dig.

I move to inspect the cart. The horse is missing, but there's no evidence that it died here.

"What are you looking at?" Greg is standing over the hole I was supposed to help him dig.

"Hoofprints trailing off down the road." It troubles me. A scared horse would take off at speed, but the spacing and depth of the prints suggest a slow pace. I can see small boot prints too, most likely from a woman, ending where the horse's begin. The chill returns, and is at its strongest when I'm facing the horse's trail. I throw the sack into the hole, cover it over, then follow the tracks down the path.

"Where are you going?" Greg shouts after me.

Ignoring him I go after the horse, or rather the thing

that rides it. It's easy to think of demons as mindless thugs, and some — like the skin-wearers — are, but the ones you need to watch out for are devious and cunning. This puppet-master is surely that. Energy tingles through me at the thought of a lengthy hunt and worthy opponent.

"Dith, don't leave me behind!" Greg races to catch me up.

"This is where we part ways, rogue. Always been a lone hunter, and I'm not changing that for you."

"I can help. Back when you tried to burn it we would have defeated it as a team. Your flames to drive the thing out, and me waiting to pounce. This one's smart; a second hunter can't hurt." He catches up and grabs my arm. "My arrows felled those last two, not you."

I consider cracking his knee and leaving him on the path to squeal. A second hunter? No, I don't need that. Bait and distraction couldn't hurt though. "If you come with me, you need to do as I say."

Greg nods in the dark, with an earnest look. "I saw what it did. I want it dead too."

He only saw the aftermath, not a mother forced to butcher three of her children, begging for the life of the fourth.

◇━○━─○───○━○━◇

We've walked all night. The horse's tracks left the path, and we followed them into the woods. "They're gone," I say. The hoofprints stop at a stream, and there's no sign of them on the other side. "It could have walked the stream in any direction, alighting either side at any point." The chill of deathly intent surrounds me, growing no stronger no matter which way I turn.

"We have fresh water, plenty of firewood and…" Greg pulls out his bow and looses an arrow, "…squirrel for breakfast. I say we rest."

I'm not physically tired, with that potion of his still bolstering my strength, but the mental drain sways me. I can't think clearly. "We'll rest, but just for a bit." If the chill is anything to go by then I must be surrounded by threats; may as well sit down and let them come to me.

Greg builds a fire, skinning the squirrel and then cooking it over the flames. I try not to look into the fire for too long, or the thing I control will control me. Flame madness, they call it, a curse put upon all those who wield fire magic.

"Here," Greg says, handing me the skewered squirrel.

"You've given me all the meat."

"Not all, I kept the brain for myself. Best part."

I look at him sliding the tiny brain into his mouth and grimace. "Then you have something in common with my wolf. Silver likes the brains, acts like they're a treat."

"You have a wolf?"

"Had, I rescued her as a pup. Skin-wearers killed her pack, and she followed me for years. She was the perfect companion." I know the question he'll ask next, so I move to one of my most painful memories. "That lake near the tavern is a drowner hotspot. I kill one and another moves in the very next week. One day me and Silver were clearing it again, an easy few coins every time we're out this way, only there wasn't just one or two. A whole nest had set up there. Nine drowners, and I'm sitting there with a fishing rod goading them to come out. They took me by surprise, and in saving me Silver lost her life." Her wounded yelps still echoes in my nightmares. I've seen much death in my life, but with so few attachments Silver is the only true loss I've known.

"How many of the drowners did you kill?"

"Every last one of them, and to this day I still go back."

"I'm sorry," Greg says. "It sounds like she was a valued companion."

I'll never kill enough drowners to avenge Silver. The strange thing is, the night after she died was the first time the chill came to me. I've talked about it with a few trusted witches — they call it nonsense, but I swear either a sixth sense was triggered when I no longer had her guiding nose, or part of her is still with me. I hope the latter is true. Silver is the chill, warning me of danger.

I've been lost in thought for a while, and when I look up I find Greg staring at me. He quickly looks away.

"Some of the survivors took the baby in," he says, breaking the silence. "Turns out most of the village was related." I stay quiet, still absorbed in my memories of Silver. "They're rebuilding their huts right next to the tavern. It seems the noise of our lot is an acceptable price to pay for greater security."

How ironic that the humans who once banished us now seek us out for protection. Iris has read the mood of the people right; now is the time to forge a union. "Do you think we can ever defeat them all? Witches and rogues culling them the way we do?"

"It's possible. Unlikely, but possible." Greg kicks some dirt over the fire to extinguish it. "We'd need to be organized, working together with the people and each other. This nomadic hack and slash we do can never be as effective as a united force."

I sling my pack over my shoulder. "We should get going."

"Slow down! When did you last sleep?"

It's been a few days, but I can do without the rest. "I'm fine, let's go."

"What if we rest for a few hours? You might feel great now, but that puppet-master was powerful."

I groan and put down my pack. He has a point. I could walk all day, but the fight will be draining. "One hour." I mark the sun's position in the treetops. "No longer."

My mind is slowing, thoughts becoming splintered and unfinished. As soon as I close my eyes I drift into a light slumber, only vaguely aware of what's going on around me. I keep my eyes closed and listen to Greg sneaking over. He lays his cloak over me, then returns to his sleeping spot.

❖━◇━━◇━━◇━❖

When I awake I find the sun has traveled much further in its arc than the passage of an hour. "Wake up, rogue, the light is waning." I ball Greg's cloak and throw it at him. The chill has returned to guide me, strengthening my belief that Silver still walks by my side. She would often refuse to move when she sensed I was fatigued, just like the chill this morning. "The horse went this way."

"What makes you so sure?" Greg says, rubbing the sleep from his eyes.

"Call it an intuition." Or the silver-furred wolf I sometimes see from the corner of my eye.

We find the tracks where the horse left the stream just as the sun sets. No matter, the chill will pull me through the night with greater speed and clarity than hoof-prints brightened by daylight.

"For you," Greg says, holding a flower out for me. I don't claim it. "I just thought, you know, because it's pretty, and you're — "

"When you find a gift that's as fierce as me, let me know." I turn my head from his wounded look to hide the smile creeping onto my lips. I can't allow friendship to sway me. Greg will be the distraction I need to end this beast, not the distraction that helps the beast end me.

The thick, leafy eaves bar the moonlight in this part of the forest, and even in the day they must cast it in shadow.

"Do you hear that?" Greg whispers.

"Silence." No bats, no wolves, no owls; nothing but the wind and our footfalls.

A branch rakes across my arm, and a stinging, moist cut opens in my skin. I reach for the branch, but find nothing except air.

"Ah, damn it," moans Greg.

I hear him stumble and strain to find his silhouette in the darkness. "What's wrong?"

"Nothing, just a branch or thorn or something."

A quiet noise drifts past me, like the swish of fabric,

and I receive another cut. "You think you own the night?" I call out, funneling fire into my hands until I hold two pillars of flames. The forest is illuminated by firelight, the most beautiful of lights, and figures leap almost silently from tree to tree seeking out the shadows. *Goddamn breeders.* Demons start out as skin-wearers, then mature into any number of unsightly or human-formed beasts, but the final evolution in the demon life cycle is a breeder.

They're human-like monsters oozing charm and beauty who drink blood and trick humans into becoming vessels for demon souls. They can't tolerate daylight, and only holy weapons can kill them. Holy my daggers are not. I extinguish one fire tower, swinging my bag round to rummage in it one-handedly. Greg yelps in pain again and stumbles toward me. "You got any holy weapons, rogue?"

Greg takes a glove from his pocket, and with it on he pulls a large, metal spike wrapped in leather from his boot. Great, he had the foresight to bring a glove. I hiss and wince as I bring out my stake. I cut it from a decommissioned church altar, making it about as holy as wood gets. Without a glove or wrappings it stings and burns to touch, but I'm only part demon — for the breeders this will be deadly.

Greg calls out as another breeder glides past and inflicts a wound, and he spins around with his spike raised. His assailant has disappeared, but that doesn't stop him stalking toward the trees.

I'm watching Greg with such focus that I don't hear the swish of fabric until the moment my leg is slashed. "Heathen bloodsucker!" I scream, spinning round. Six of them crouch on the ground before me, their pale faces grinning as the black rags they wear billow up like an ethereal smoke. I shoot a line of fire at them, setting their rags alight, then my fire burns out. The damn stake I'm holding is zapping my magic. All I have to defend myself with now, in complete darkness, is a pointy stick. I wrap my sleeve around the stake, hoping to lessen the drain.

The chill spreads, and I can feel six cold spots pointed at my skin. One is moving closer, causing the chill to prick me, and where sight and sound fail me the chill keeps getting sharper. As the breeder makes its move I stab out, catching it in the throat. The wound hisses and spits blood that turns to ash; nothing is more potent than a holy weapon. I twist the stake, burning through its neck until the head hangs by a single thread. Before I can complete the decapitation all the cold spots grow and freeze my skin. I wrench the stake back and lash out at the moving shadows, but five is too many. I fall down under them, their sharp nails ripping fresh cuts in my skin.

My sleeve slips, and the bare wood of the stake sears my scratched hand. I flinch at the shrill scream involuntarily leaving my lungs, and with renewed rage I stab wildly. Some hits land, though the breeder's razor-like nails are doing more damage to me.

Greg shrieks. He must be inj — no, not injured. He's barreling toward me with a battle cry. I feel the weight of the breeder bodies lifted, along with the breeze of movement. I lie still for a moment, looking up through the leaves for the moon, and find the faintest glow behind thick clouds. Then the rain starts. The eaves are thick enough to stop it falling heavily, but cool droplets seep through the leaves and patter on my face.

My magic returns when I drop the stake, and I bring back the flames. Greg is fighting with his holy spike. Two dance around him, their gracefulness and flowing rags giving them the illusion of floating phantoms. Greg is solid, using swift, jerky movements that are stabbing more than slashing. His metal spike enters the stomach of one, and he rips it sideways through hissing flesh until the body falls down in two halves.

To say I'm impressed is an understatement. I get up, not expecting him to need my help, but a cold spot rushes from behind. The beast grabs one of my daggers from my belt and continues on. "Behind you, rogue!" My shout comes too late. The breeder embeds my dagger in his side, and Greg drops to his knees.

I run forward while screaming, my rage pouring into my flames. The breeders are set alight, and this time I'm not giving them a chance to escape. By the time I reach them and pull back the flames fabric is burned into their blistered, bubbling skin. I grab the spike from Greg's limp hand and end every one of them.

"Look at me, rogue. Can you hear me?" Greg's green eyes roll without focus. "What are you saying?" Incoherent mumbles pass his lips. "Greg?"

"I'm fine," he croaks. "Just a scratch."

More of the rain leaks through, pouring in spurts from filled leaves. I drag Greg to the base of a large tree. "Here, hold this on your wound."

"It's just a scratch," Greg protests, batting away the folded cloth. He holds up his ungloved hand, which is a throbbing red. "I fell because I switched hands with the spike and it drained me, not because of the dagger, which you can have back by the way."

I take the dagger from him and find only a smear of blood on its blade. I could have sworn I saw the blade go in almost to the hilt. "Okay, if you're sure you're — "

The chill has gone, but a faint warmth strikes me from the right. I leave the sentence unfinished, rising to follow the warmth. As I move through the trees I hear whimpers over the dripping rain and wind, and I follow them. The growing warmth leads me over mud mounds and thick roots.

My front foot finds air, and I snatch it back. Before me is a large pit. I light a ball of fire to peer in, and cowering at the bottom is a group of humans.

With the death of the breeders their entrancement is wearing off, as the ritual to make new demons takes five nights. For four nights the breeders feed from pliant prey, and on the fifth the prey feeds from the breeders, killing the human soul and opening a gateway for a demon to take their place.

"I found people, and I recognize them!" I yell back to Greg. They're from the slaughtered village, people I've bartered with and people I've seen in the tavern. "You said all at the village were killed."

"It looked like they had been. I didn't know how many people there were supposed to be." Greg has staggered after me, but is now slumped against a nearby tree.

There were badly drawn missing person posters pasted over older posters in the tavern. Nothing unusual about that, since humankind is an endangered species, but more familiarity leaks through my recent days. "The skin-wearers, I think they were from the village too." Demon souls can't exist in children — both host and soul die — so what if the puppet-master has been leading these people to the breeders? What if her slaughter at the village was of children and livestock alone? "You say the dead were being buried when you left. Wouldn't it have been easier to burn down the huts with the dead inside?" If the remains were burnt and covered over, would they ever have realized that people were missing from the slaughter?

Greg sits up with a groan. "I left to find you before the burial began. With so many they may have burned them."

"Did you see any adults when you looked in the huts?"

Sweat pools on his brow and upper lip, and even in the warming firelight from my hand, he looks pale. "It was dark and there was a lot of blood. God, Dith, I can't say for sure."

The puppet-master must be working with the breeders. A small army could have amassed here with the missing villagers presumed dead.

"Give me your hand." I reach in and pull the first victim from the pit. These people won't join the demon ranks, but who knows how many already have. "Walk in this direction until you hit the stream," I tell a dazed man. "Then follow it west. Eventually you'll reach the road between the lake and the tavern. I trust at least one of you'll know your way from there."

A young man keeps hold of my hand after I've pulled him up. "Come with us, miss, to protect us from the evil of the night."

I face the way I mean them to go, and all the chill

sits on my back. "That way is safe, for now. I must journey further to kill the evil that stalks you."

Reluctantly the youth lets go of my hand. I light some torches for the survivors and watch the fire disappear through the trees.

"Do you think they'll make it back?" Greg doesn't answer. "Speak to me, rogue." I rush over to the slumped figure. "Greg?" His pulse is weak, and his hands are cold and clammy. Blood is seeping through his clothes. "You said it was a scratch!"

I empty out my pack, building a fire and working close to it. I measure out pinches of herbs into a mortar, then add a splash of sesame oil and two drops of gray moth's blood. I have to temper my hand, or I would ruin the mix by grinding the pestle with too much urgency.

When the consistency is just right I peel Greg's shirt away from his wound. The cut is deep, slicing through two of his abs into the softer flesh underneath. I mop up the pooling blood and press the remedy inside the gash. Placing my hands over the wound I chant out loud and pray in my head; this will aid his healing, but it may not be enough to save him.

The lashes lining his closed eyes are thick and dark. I trace the curve of his brow with my finger and follow his cheek down to his stubbled jaw.

"That was a stupid thing you did," I say. "I would have defeated those breeders without you." No one should die for me, not a wolf and not a rogue. He's in deepened sleep and can't hear my words, nor should he. It's unfair to blame him for his injuries. Brushing away some sodden hair that clings to him, I dampen a cloth and wipe his face.

He's not going to make it, and that's on me. He wanted to go back, to help those at the village, and it's his concern for me that kept him on this journey — his concern for me that made him rush the breeders. I had just laid there, looking for the moon and feeling the raindrops. He had a better weapon for dealing with the breeders, and I thought…I thought wrong. I open up his pack and rummage inside. The potion he gave me must be in here somewhere.

"What're you doing?" Greg says weakly.

"I'm looking for that potion you used to aid healing."

"It doesn't aid healing, it replenishes energy, and I used the last on you." He groans as he reaches out for his bag.

I pass it to him, but keep hold of a chain I found. "This is an interesting talisman. I've never seen another like it."

Greg holds out his hand and I pass it back to him. "My mother gave it to me. The place where I grew up is wary of strangers, and wearing the talisman marks me as a friend." He clasps the chain around his neck and tucks it into his shirt. "Can you pass my waterskin?"

I hand it to him, but take it back when he starts to drown in it. "This place where you grew up, do you still have family there?" If I can keep him talking, keep him awake, he might just survive his wound.

"I never met my father." Not surprising, as demons aren't known for seeking out their offspring. "My mother, though, she raised me. She taught me how to be the man I am today."

"Is she still with us?"

"Yes, I go home often." The color is returning to his face, and his eyes sparkle when he says the word *home*. I've never had one, never cared about one either, but he makes the word sound like more than a place to rest your head.

"Why do you need the talisman if you're a frequent visitor?"

"I don't always go home alone," he says with a grin.

I feel a twinge of jealousy and bury it deep. "You're lucky she kept you. Your mother, I mean. Most humans would abandon their half-demon babies. I've even heard of rogues strangled at birth."

"I am lucky. She has vision where others would only have hate." Greg pushes some of his hair behind his ear. As far as rogues go, he's not bad looking. "How about your parents?" he asks.

"My mother was a witch, and my father was a rogue." The only way to ensure a witch has enough demon blood in her veins to conjure magic is a union between the two. Rogues are first-generation demon spawn, always born male, and every generation after that is born female until the demon blood is so watered down they may as well be human. "I inherited my family name from my mother, nothing else. She left me at a haven to be raised with other abandoned witch children. And, like you, I never knew my father."

Greg pulls a pair of carved cups from his pack and a corked bottle. He pours two drinks, passes me one, and raises his. "To the hunt."

It's remarkable how well he looks. One drink might

take the edge off his pain, but I shouldn't encourage him further. "To the hunt." I bump my cup on his, then take a large gulp. "Wow, this is potent mead."

"You don't like it? I picked it up in Arle a few weeks back." He turns the bottle around in his hands. "Cost three demon heads, if you can believe it."

"I love it. If they served this in the tavern I'd be there every night."

"Having secret meetings with fellow witches," he says with a smile.

I shake my head and swallow the second glorious swig. "I seldom meet other witches. The other night was pure chance."

Greg tops my cup up to the brim. "What drew you all together?"

"Iris most likely called the others. I just wanted a decent drink, not that I got it. What about you and those rogues? Corman is a real charmer."

"Like you it was a chance meeting, although I think there's a good chance of meeting Corman in that tavern every night."

"Noted," I say, then finish the cup. Before I place it down Greg is leaning over to refill it. "Are you trying to get me drunk, rogue?"

"Not at all, but if we finish the bottle tonight my pack will be lighter."

I raise my full cup once more. "To lighter loads."

Our fingers meet as his cup touches mine. I take my hand away and glare at him; this moment of merriment doesn't change the fact he is badly wounded. "Do you think you should be drinking with a mortal wound?"

He lifts his shirt, revealing the gash that now looks no deeper than a graze. "It's not so bad."

I reach out, running my fingers over his side. This makes no sense. The tips of my fingers were just in that wound packing in slimy paste. I'm good at mixing, but still...

"I'm a quick healer," Greg says, lowering his shirt.

"No rogue can heal that fast." I scowl at him.

"C'mon, Dith, don't look so sour. I'm not like other rogues. I inherited more than most in my demon half, but that doesn't make *me* a demon, does it?" He scoots over until his shoulder presses against mine. "Demon blood runs through your veins too, giving you the rare gift of flames. You and I are alike."

We are alike, more so than I am to other witches and he is to other rogues. I'm ashamed of my reaction; I must have worn the same look others do when they see my pyromancy. He reaches over for his cup, and when he sits back, I place my hand on his cheek and lean in for a kiss. He meets me halfway, pressing his lips on mine and cupping the back of my head, his fingers lacing through my hair. I can smell his interest in his strengthening scent, hear it in his racing heart, feel it in his touch. All my senses are heightened, the same way as when I'm mid-hunt. We undress each other next to the fire, and, encircled by breeder bodies, we mate under the dashes of moonlight streaking through the eaves.

◇━◇———◇━◇

"Dith, it's time to wake up."

"Greg?" I rub my eyes. I hadn't felt that drunk when I fell asleep, but my head screams in pain now. The chill punches me in waves, telling me I'm in the gravest of dangers, but Greg seems calm. His fuzzy face comes into view and I smile. I've never been one for company, but I fear I may spend all my days seeking his. I reach for his dangling talisman. There are runes on it I hadn't noticed in the dark, but it's not dark now. Sunlight streams from my right, and when I look up I see a curved ceiling of stone. "Where are we?" There's stone beneath me too.

"Dith, I'd like you to meet my mother."

The chill is so strong that it steals my breath. A white mist in the shape of a wolf stands between me and Greg's mother, though she doesn't seem to see it. I know that face. It was a single glimpse, but I burned it into my memory. "Puppet-master." Her image is bound to Germaine and her crying baby, a family bathed in blood. A demon didn't father Greg — his mother is one. I try to move from the cave floor, to run into the light, but I find my wrists are not only shackled — they're burning.

"The shackles are forged from holy metal." The puppet-master smiles, leaning in even closer.

I turn my glare to Greg. "Why would you bring me here? You know I mean to kill her." I can read the runes now; the talisman marks him as a friend to demons.

"Oh, Dith," Greg chuckles. "You were never going to kill her. I brought you here because you sat in on the witch meeting. You have information I need." He taps his fingers on his thumb like a moving mouth. "Tell me, Dith, what are you witches up to?"

The only words I can speak now are truths, but

there's more than one way to be honest. "We're to collect many demon heads, like the skin-wearers we buried under the birch."

"Where are you going to take the heads?"

"From their necks." I can sense his hold on my mouth fading with his frustration.

"When will you meet the witches again?" he growls through gritted teeth.

"When we're all in the same place, providing none of us die in the meantime."

"What do you need the heads for?"

"Proof of kill, isn't that why any of us take the heads?" That face of his doesn't look so pretty when it's reddened and furrowed.

I scan the cave, looking for anything that might aid my escape. The shadows are dark enough to obscure the far wall, so I can't tell its true depth. There's a small sleeping area tucked in one alcove, and the only light comes from the mouth of the cave. A handsome man sits to the side of the opening, he's more muscular and rugged looking than Greg. "Freeze once for rogue, and twice for demon," I mumble to Silver's misty ghost. She paws at my knee twice. Each touch has no pressure, just the familiar cold sensation. As far as I can tell it's just the three of them, and one of them must hold the key for my shackles.

The puppet-master grabs my face and jerks it toward her. "You witches are children of our children," she says. "Why side with the humans?"

"We're not siding with them, but we have sided against you, and I promise that if I live through this day I'll add your head to my haul."

Greg slaps my face with rage in his eyes. "You insolent — !"

That smarts. I want to rub the sting away, but can't raise my chained hands high enough. Silver brushes her face on mine, cooling my skin and soothing the pain.

The puppet-master grabs Greg's hand before he can strike me again. "Leave her to think through her options. She can tell us her secret, or she can die. There are other witches who sat in that meeting."

The puppet-master guides Greg away from me, and whispers to the rugged demon on her way out. I don't like the way he smiles at me when she leaves. He sits in the light so he can't be a breeder, nor is he disfigured like a drowner or a plague. "Puppet-master?" I whisper to Silver. She doesn't respond.

The rugged demon moves closer.

"A morph?" Silver stays still. "Surely not a lover demon?" Silver paws my leg. I haven't seen one since the last demon army battle. A lover demon has two faces, one of which is of a man that shifts to fit your desires and tempt you to your death with true love. I've seen women smile as they were beaten, stabbed, and defiled, entranced with love in their hearts. The other lover demon form is a monstrous beast, standing taller than any hut on all fours, with a thick, scaly hide and horns. These were what we fought before the demon armies disbanded and scattered.

My stomach churns as he moves closer. At least in his monstrous form my end would be swift; this handsome creature will torture me for pleasure.

Silver's misty ghost nuzzles my face. I can see every strand of her beautiful fur, but I feel only cold. She nudges each hand and looks at me. "I can't undo the shackles," I whisper. Images appear in the reflections of her eyes: one shows chains, the other shows fire. I scoot back until I'm flush against the cave wall. That gives me enough slack to take hold of the chains.

It takes several attempts to forge a spark with the cuffs working against me. I call to the flames with more volume and urgency than I ever have done before. My hands bear fire while the holy metal tries to steal it back, but I manage to keep it alight. The heat I channel melts the chains. Molten metal pools in my hands and I draw it into the flames, molding it into balls. I'm no longer tethered to the rock, but the stinging shackles remain leaching my strength and dulling my magic. I throw the liquid metal at the lover demon just before my fire dies.

He lets out a howl of pain and anger. Before my eyes he transforms, bones shifting and lengthening under his thickening skin, his mouth becoming a muzzle as horns sprout from his scalp. The towering beast fills the cave entrance, blocking much of the light.

I call to the flames, but this time they don't respond. "Daggers it is then, eh girl?" Silver's misty form slips out of view, but I can still sense her presence.

The lover demon lets out a mighty roar. "DIE!"

I leap over its swiping claws and scale its other arm, digging my daggers between the scales to pull myself up. The behemoth shakes like a wet dog while trying to throw me off, but I keep going and make it to its head.

The beast bellows again, calling for the puppet-master to return.

Holding on to one of its horns I slice through the

back of its neck. The cut starts to heal the second I remove the blade. I slice it open again, and this time thrust my hand inside the wound. The demon's warm, moist flesh makes me gag, but I keep pushing in further, until that holy metal around my wrist, sizzles his insides. I reach up under his skull, boiling his brain with the blessed metal.

The heavy corpse crashes down and rolls. I wrench my hand free and leap out the way. With the body settled I bring my cuffed wrists to either side of his neck, pushing through with the heat of God's wrath until my hands meet in the middle. It's only now that his head is severed that he retakes human form. I pick up the head and smile. *One more to add to the collection.*

I slip out of the cave, this time walking away from the chill instead of towards it. Silver appears at my side once more. Seeing her almost brings me to tears, and my hand slipping through her misty fur does. I want nothing more than to hold her close and feel the warmth of a loyal friend. "I messed up," I say to Silver, wiping the tears from my cheeks. "I liked Greg, even dared to think I could love him." Such foolish trust almost cost me my life. I know what I plan to do next is unwise, but I'll need all my magic to take on the puppet-master and her bastard son.

I dig one hand into the ground and chant. The bones in my thumb splinter and I almost lose the chant's momentum, but I can't focus on the pain. My thumb, as pliable as jelly, squashes as I pull the shackle off. The one on my other wrist still drains me. I wriggle the fingers of my damaged hand into the dirt, using the last of my strength to shatter the other thumb too. Free from the holy cuffs I pause to let my magic replenish, keeping the order of each break in my mind so I can reverse the chant.

Once my hands are healed I lay my daggers in the mud, pushing them in until there are two dagger-shaped holes. Again I pause, not just to regain my strength but to follow the cold spot making its way back to the cave. Then I place the shackles over the holes and blast them with heat; when I'm done I have two rough daggers made from holy metal. I let them cool, then rip off my sleeves and wrap the hilts.

The chill is close to the cave by the time I've finished sharpening my new daggers. I sneak up and watch from the tree-lined embankment. The puppet-master has her hands raised high, her moving fingers controlling many strings as she forces the people in front of her to walk. They step over the lover demon's headless body and enter the cave. I sneak up to the entrance and wait for my moment to strike.

"We couldn't stop her," says a raspy voice from deep within the cave. "She fought in the light and never ventured close enough for us to take her."

"No matter, she will die soon enough," says the puppet-master. "I've retrieved your lost lambs." The puppet-master lowers her hands, and the people fall into a heap on the floor. To my horror I recognize them as the pit survivors I'd sent away last night. Greg knew which way they went, though I don't see the wretched rogue among them now.

"How many of our kin did she kill?" the voice rasps once more from the darkness.

"Eight breeders, one of our smallest sects. You understand my son had to participate in the kills to gain her trust?" The thing in the shadows hisses. "Good. We can still make many demons with those remaining."

That was a small sect? I dread to think how many breeders are lurking in the forest. Iris is right — it'll take an army of witches to take down an uprising like this. The puppet-master and breeder in the shadows are mine though. I wait a little longer to see if Greg will return, but the chill only comes from the cave.

As I step over the threshold the puppet-master raises her hands, the villagers rising to stand with arms raised and heads lolling. She walks her fingers forward, her puppets forming a wall between us. The cave is as tall as it is wide, and no doubt deeper than it appears, but I know any gap I try to slip through will be quickly filled by a human shield.

A memory surfaces of three girls at the home picking on me. It's not the helpless feeling of being bullied that sparked the memory, but a spell I used on them. I close my eyes and chant. I can hear the advancing steps of human marionettes. Pulling the spell out of my memories I weave and knot the invisible strings together, just like I did to the bootlaces of my bullies. The humans fall to the ground in a tangled heap and the puppet-master shrieks, desperately trying to pull her fingers free from the knotted spell.

I leap over the crumpled puppets with my new holy daggers ready. The puppet-master draws a blade, but without her servants on strings she's nothing. My dagger edges are so toxic to demon blood that they burn as well as cut, and the blades slice through her neck as easily as cutting through wet dough. I grin and pick up her severed head. I'll never complain about wanting an axe again.

The villagers stir, the strings of control dying with their master. The chill hasn't left me though, rather it pulls me to the back of the cave where I find a tunnel in the shadows. There's an animalistic smell back here. My boot sinks into a squishy mound, and I summon a ball of fire into my hand. I continue down the curving tunnel until it opens up into a second cavern, and in the middle of the stone floor, covered in tiny slices, is the missing horse. Its massive chest falls and rises with labored breaths. As I step further into the cavern the shadows come alive, climbing silently on the walls. *Good grief, how many?* I count at least five breeders, but there could be more.

I run back down the tunnel. They may think I'm scared, but in truth I need the narrow space to thwart them. I stand little chance of surviving if they surround me, and as predicted the shrieking monsters follow me. I back up, facing the oncoming foes with walls of rock either side of me. With my hands running along the walls, I chant quietly. One breeder lashes out at me, tearing my arm with his nails, but I keep chanting and backing up. I have to be careful to keep them close, after all. The left-hand wall ended, now just an illusion chanted to match the stone that already passed under my fingers. We're now far into the first cave when another one comes at me and digs its nails in.

*Slowly, slowly, that should just about do it.* I call out and the illusion vanishes. Sunlight spills onto the breeders, and it undoes their eternal youth. Four of them age out past death, their skin growing wrinkled and saggy until it hangs off their bones. The desiccated waifs fall down, leaving only two elderly breeders. They're not beautiful anymore, and though they may still be charming prey will never surrender to them so readily again. The old woman screams and launches at me, but her aged nails are brittle and crack under the pressure without breaking my skin. I draw my daggers and remove her head.

The old man, as hunched as a crescent moon, tries to walk past me. A stout woman, one of the recently freed puppets, grabs me. "None of us gonna sit 'ere and let you hurt a little old man." She moves away and puts her shawl over the breeder.

"Does this hurt?" I ask, placing my blade on her arm.

"Why, should it?"

"No, because you're human and this is made from a holy relic. If you were a demon, however…" I place the same blade on the old man, who screams out in pain, "…well, now that's going to hurt a lot."

The woman shrieks and takes back her shawl, so without further protest I remove the demon's head.

I follow the tunnel back to the cavern. I can't be sure I got all of them, but with six fewer to fight I've improved my chances at least. With a fireball in hand I search all the dark corners and find nothing lurking. "It's okay," I whisper, kneeling at the horse's head and stroking his mane. "You're safe now." I have some healing paste left over, which I push into the deeper wounds. It's hard to say how effective it will be on a horse, but life has returned to his eyes. With a whinny he gets up, and I lead him through the tunnel out into the cave.

"Why are you still here? Go, all of you, be free!" The crowd of villagers gawk at me. I collect all the heads and place them in a sack I find near what must have been the puppet-master's bed. I take another sack for good measure and mount the horse.

"Please don't leave us, miss. They'll get us again if you do."

I look down at the frightened young man, and this time I can't refuse his pleas. "Fine, but I'm going the long way back." There are demon heads I need to pick up on the way.

⟡⎯⎯⎯⟡

I tie the horse up to the rail outside the tavern and follow the cold inside, shouldering three heavy sacks. I left the survivors to rebuild the slaughtered village, and it was there that the chill came back.

"Well, if it isn't Ditch." Corman saunters over to me. "I knew you couldn't stay away."

"Do me a favor, Corman, hold on to these for me?" I pass him the sacks of heads and his eyes bulge.

"Never been given a gift like this before."

"You'll give them back, of that I've no doubt." The chill leads me to the back of the tavern where I find Beatrice standing against the wall, chuckling as a rogue whispers sweet nothings into her ear.

"We're going to Arle, two moons from now, to forge an alliance with the clergy," she says.

Greg grins broadly and runs his fingers down her neck. "Arle, you say? And who are you having this meeting with?"

"The cardinal and duke will be there, and other clergy that Iris has invited."

Dear, sweet Beatrice; he didn't even need to use his gift to get the information from her. I come up behind Greg and draw my daggers.

"Dith, so good to — "

Beatrice's greeting isn't warning enough. I cross my blades on his throat and take Greg's head off in one move. There's no blood since my holy blades have seared his flesh, and I take both his head and his talisman. Marking myself as a friend to demons may come in handy when hunting them.

"Your heads, I mean sacks, sir, miss, Dith, sir." Corman bows holding out my sacks with trembling hands.

I open one and roll Greg's head in next to his mother's. "Thank you, Corman." That's one rogue that won't steal from me again.

Beatrice follows me outside. "What's wrong with you? He was a rogue, not a demon!"

"He worked with the demons, Beatrice." I show her my blistered wrists. "He and his demon mother tortured me for information on Iris's meeting, and here I find you giving away all the details for free."

"He said I was pretty," she mumbles.

I hold her face in my hands and stare into her watery eyes. "And you are pretty, Beatrice, brilliant in your own way. Come with me to Arle. The horse is big enough to seat two."

"I haven't any heads to bring."

"You can have one of my sacks." I don't need all three to make a point. Beatrice and I mount the horse, and for the first time in a long while there's no chill to chase. I feel its absence, no, her absence, as a loss, and hope that I will see Silver again.

⬦—⬦——⬦—⬦

I leave the horse just outside of Arle the next day, figuring walking the length of the city is better than someone recognizing the horse and asking about the soldiers that used to own it. Arle was once a bustling city with buildings made of stone, and many even had upper floors. Now the only things to line this cracked road are mud huts, not dissimilar from the ones in the village.

"Not much of a city, is it?" says Beatrice.

"I saw it once as a child. It was impressive, a prosperous place with sellers calling out their wares in the streets. They sold jewelry, trinkets, things no one makes any more."

"Too busy tryin' to stay alive."

I think that's why we adapted so well; we witches have been outcasts and survivalists through the ages.

The further we walk into the city the better-built the dwellings become. They're now made of solid wood, and some are even made of stone, but the jewel of Arle is still the duke's castle. Though crumbling in places most of its walls stood strong against the demon army that tore through the city a few years back, and it'll be a long time before it resembles the place in my fading memories.

Beatrice sighs and adjusts her grip on her sack. "I'm going on ahead to find Iris before the meeting starts."

There's still resentment in her eyes from Greg's death, and thirst on the lips she keeps moistening with her tongue. "Enjoy your ale, Beatrice. I'll see you at the meeting." She doesn't deny it or take the long route, turning on to the next path that heads into a tavern.

I find a place to bed down for the night, where I dream of gathering armies. Not just one made up of demons, but also one composed of powerful witches.

✧━◇━━◇━◇◇━◇━✧

I wake with piercing hunger and decide to spend my last few coins on a hot meal. Cooked tomatoes, mushrooms, and eggs fill my plate. The woman who serves it to me does her best to be courteous, but her hands shake and her smile is far too broad to be natural. Warm tomato juice dribbles down my chin. I'm enjoying the meal far too much to care, although I should make myself somewhat presentable before the meeting. I use the knob of bread to mop up the rich, orange yolk, and leave an extra coin of thanks next to my empty plate.

The older heads in the sacks are starting to smell, and I'm getting strange looks from the few people I meet. There seems to be a hierarchy to this place. The outer city is full of the poor and the expendable who live in the greatest fear, while the further you get to the center the more at ease and important the people feel.

I step over a shin-high wall and walk through a ruin which was once a house. The well I spotted to the rear of the ruin looks to be in good order, and to my relief the pump still works. I fill a pail and wash. My change of clothes isn't the nicest, but it has far fewer holes and bloodstains than the set I leave behind.

I waste some time meandering down the streets, marveling at the recovery Arle has made so far. It may well be a bustling city again one day — though not as good as Merle, of course. Arle's sister city, Merle, was built atop a mountain. They haul all goods up to it from the river that passes it, and since Merle is so remote it has had very few demon attacks. I think I shall go there after I leave here. Take in the sights of what once was, and with the culling of demons may well be again.

"Edith, Edith!" Beatrice runs toward me. She trips, drops her sack, and offers apologies to the dumbfounded couple who watch her roll heads back into it. "Edith, it's starting early. Iris called the cardinal a sabotaging toad! I mean, not to his face, but we need to go now if we're to make a show out of these heads."

"Fine by me, I'm sick of the stink." Beatrice runs on ahead, and with a sigh I walk toward the castle. Never been too welcome around dukes and clergy, and moving the meeting serves to muddy any alliance we could make. We need this though, since only by working together can we bring the numbers down, and places like Merle will become the norm.

Soldiers man the steps up to the duke's castle. "State your business."

"I'm with Iris, I've come for the meeting."

"Then you're going the wrong way. The meeting is in the chapel, at the back of the castle."

I want to groan, but instead flash a smile. The chapel backs onto, but is technically not part of, the castle. It's not that I expected them to throw a banquet in our honor, but this just seems like we're not wanted at all.

The cardinal is mid-speech when I walk through the large, oak doors. I listen for a while. He's talking about the great human army he has, and the fantastic job they've done killing demons. "Each week our soldiers come back with a cart filled with heads. Do you really think mere witches can do that?"

"I've never seen a human kill a demon," I call, "Sold plenty of heads to them soldiers though, when they come my way."

If the cardinal's scowl could take corporeal form, I would no doubt face a worthy foe. Iris waves me forward. I step onto the mud floor and wince; the bastard cardinal has lifted all the flagstones. He'll no doubt say it's warding off demons, but he knew we were coming and he knows what it does to us. I suffer the sting of the consecrated ground until I reach one of the lonely flags positioned around the table.

"Show them what you brought, Dith," says Iris.

I untie the sacks and roll the demon heads onto the floor. Immediately they sizzle and hiss.

"That one isn't smoking as much as the rest," says the over-fed duke.

I chuck a handful of salt on Greg's head and it hisses with vigor. "That one is a demon, I'm certain of that." If anyone present recognizes Greg they're not letting it show. "Fourteen heads in four days, and that's just my haul. A good mix too — puppet-master, breeder, lover demon, skin-wearer. I had drowners too, but they've already been sold to your mighty soldiers."

The cardinal walks up to the heads and turns them over, looking for a stamp. I'm assuming they haven't found their missing cart yet. Not that I'll tell them where to look, wouldn't want the blame for the soldier deaths. "And you did this alone?"

I nod; dead rogues and ghost wolves don't count. The rest of the witches turn out their sacks and add to the pile. They've been busy, as not a single witch has come with fewer than five. Soon the floor is all but covered with hissing, putrid heads, and my full count is there as Beatrice rushes in huffing and wheezing to empty my other sack. "I looked all around," she tells Iris, "Couldn't find any more witches."

"Hmm, I suppose that's because the meeting was due tonight," Iris says. The cardinal dodges her glare.

The duke looks impressed at least, which makes the cardinal scowl even deeper.

"You may leave now, while we speak with Iris." The cardinal might think her a frail, hunched woman, but that toothless mouth still has bite. I trust her to get us a good deal.

It seems like we've spent an eternity pacing this small hall waiting for news. When the large door finally swings open Iris walks out of it with a blank expression. "We've got our alliance. From now on all witches will be part of the Night Order, an army of fighters working with the clergy for good. We've done it, ladies. The witches of the Night Order will be a force indeed." The rabble of witches take their celebrations outside, and I'm left alone with Iris. "There were some stipulations," she says, "that I'm afraid pertain to you, my dear."

I knew it. When I rolled out those heads they weren't impressed, they were scared. It's a good job I gave away the third sack. "I can't be part of the order thing, can I?"

"You can, and most certainly will, but they've outlawed certain magic. Necromancy for example, and, well, pyromancy." She lowers her voice and comes in close. "I'm not saying don't burn things, Dith, just do it where no one's watching. Try to keep demon heads burn-free." She links arms with me and walks us out of the duke's chapel. "There's something else, which I'm suspecting you haven't guessed yet. But, as that branch of future has settled and the Ventriloquist is no more, I think it's safe to say you're with child."

I touch my stomach, then jerk my hand away in revulsion. I can't allow Greg's line to continue. "There's herbs to remedy that."

"I caution you, Aramay Dith, that the fate of that bloodline runs deeper than a single child. In a few centuries the descendants of that girl will hold the very fate of witches in their hands."

"I would ask no witch to hold that much burden."

"You might think differently if you knew them. A pair of sisters, in particular — Shade and Dellena — have a big role to play, and I think you would get along."

"I won't live through the centuries to meet them."

"No, but I know of a place where you could see them."

The old woman has me intrigued; perhaps I should see what this bloodline has to offer before snuffing it out.

# RACHAEL BOUCKER

## ABOUT THE AUTHOR

Rachael Boucker lives in the Forest of Dean UK with her partner, three children, and two attack cockatiels. When she isn't slaying household chores that magically reappear, or moulding her younglings into respectable humans, you'll likely find her at her laptop, tapping out all kinds of creative, weird and sometimes gruesome fiction. Before turning her hand to writing, she got a degree in fine art (because those are always useful in the job market), and won some awards for her paintings. She has short stories featured in a number of anthologies, and published a zombie trilogy called Decaying Days in 2020. You can expect to see more inventive horror stories from her in the future, and much more from the Night Order witches in an upcoming dark fantasy series.

Check out her website for more on her books and art www.rachaelboucker.com
Or find her on Facebook www.facebook.com/RachaelBouckerAuthorArtist

# Don't Miss Out!

**Looking for a FREE BOOK?**
Sign up for Eerie River Publishing's monthly newsletter
and get **Darkness Reclaimed** as our thank you gift!

Sign up for our newsletter
https://mailchi.mp/71e45b6d5880/welcomebook
**Here at Eerie River Publishing,** we are focused on
providing paid writing opportunities for all indie authors.
Outside of our limited drabble collections we put out each
year, every single written piece that we publish -including
short stories featured in this collection have been paid for.

Becoming an exclusive Patreon member gives you
a chance to be a part of the action as well as giving you
creative content every single month, no matter the tier.
Free eBooks, monthly short stories and even paperbacks
before they are released.
https://www.patreon.com/EerieRiverPub

# MORE FROM EERIE RIVER PUBLISHING

# WITH BLOOD AND ASH

COMING SOON

IT CALLS FROM THE SEA